Christine.

VAYENNE

BY

PERCY BREBNER

Author of "Princess Maritza"

ILLUSTRATIONS BY E. FUHR

New York
GROSSET & DUNLAP
Publishers

CONTENTS

VAYENNE

A LONG, straight road, no hedge or ditch separating it
from the fields on either side, but at intervals of fifty
yards or so trees in pairs; tall, thin trees, but heavy-
headed and with foliage spread out fussily near the
ground, all bent forward in one direction, and looking
for all the world like ancient dames with their petticoats
held out of the mud as they struggled wearily homeward against a strong wind. In its season this road
could be muddy, as many a traveller knew, the fierce
storms which raged across the low country making it
almost impassable for days together in winter-time.
To-day the ancient diligence which traversed it at an
even, jog-trot pace only left a long cloud of dust in its
wake; and the driver, an old man who had driven along
this road at regular intervals for more years than he
could count, who possibly knew the exact number of
trees which lined it, sat hunched upon his seat and had
nothing to do. Perhaps he slept, for the horses knew
the way well enough to have performed the journey
without him. Earlier in the day there had been half a
dozen passengers, but of these only one remained, and
he had found the driver so taciturn, and his patois so
difficult to understand when he did speak, that he had

given up all attempt at conversation. He was weary
of the long journey, and dozed whenever the jolting of
the somewhat crazy vehicle would allow him to do so.

For two days he had waited in the little frontier town,
for the diligence only performed this journey twice in the
week, and he had been travelling since early morning.
At the last moment, indeed, he had hesitated whether
he should take the journey at all. It was an absurd
fancy that had brought him to this Duchy of Montvilliers, a wonder and speculation which had lain latent
in him since childhood. As a boy a few chance words,
and an elderly woman's earnest looking into his face, had
stirred his imagination. Since then the work of life had
come to fire him with other ambitions, some partially
realized, perhaps, some found to be unworthy of pursuit;
and then, suddenly as it were, almost as though some
compelling voice had spoken to his inner consciousness,
the old wonder and speculation had sprung again into
life, and at last he was nearing the end of a journey which
as a lad he had promised himself one day to take.

The sun was fast sinking westward when the jolting
of the vehicle again woke the traveller, and he saw that
the aspect of the land had changed. The monotonous
pairs of trees had gone, and the diligence was ascending
a stiff incline between two swelling downs, part of a long
line of hills which had risen mistily in the distance before
them all day. It was a long climb and the horses stopped
at intervals to rest without any suggestion from the
driver; on their own initiative they went on again, and
finally paused on the summit before beginning the long
descent on the other side.

"Vayenne?" asked the traveller, suddenly leaning
toward the driver and pointing down into the valley.
The man looked at him with sleepy eyes and nodded.

It seemed a foolish question to him. What place could it be but Vayenne?

It lay in the gathering twilight like the city of a dream, indefinite, unreal, mystical. The hills overshadowed it, keeping silent watch; and spanned by a stone bridge, a river, dotted with green islands like emeralds upon its bosom, swept around its southern and western sides, holding it in its arms. Over all was the diaphanous haze of evening and silence, save for the thin music of bell and chime from belfry or clock tower, joyous little cadences which rose and fell at short intervals. Indistinctly the eye could trace the direction of some of the wider streets, and toward the northern side, dominating the city from rising ground, five gaunt, weather-beaten towers, with massive walls and battlements between, frowned over all below. There was menace in this castle, power, and perchance cruelty. It spoke of despotic government, of might as right, of stern repression, of feudal laws and the crushing of all liberty; and yet close to it, the crowning glory of a glorious church, a great spire pierced upward through the haze, telling of other things and a time to come.

They were complex thoughts which filled the mind of the traveller as the diligence swung rapidly down toward the town. To him, indeed, Vayenne was a dream city, an unknown city; yet somehow it had always seemed a part of himself. In an indefinite way he had always known that some day he would come to it, would have a part in its life, be of it; and now, as every moment brought him nearer to it, he forgot that he was a casual traveller merely, that only a few hours ago he had hesitated whether he should come at all. He was obliged to come. He was only fulfilling his destiny.

Lights began to blink in the houses as they crossed
the old stone bridge and passed under a massive gateway on the city side of it. Lights swung at street
corners as the lumbering vehicle passed over the cobble-
stones with much rattle and noise upward toward the
castle. Even the driver roused a little from his leth-
argy, and cracked his whip. They had proceeded some
distance when he suddenly drew to the side of the
street, and the horses came to a standstill. They were
evidently used to such pauses; for in these narrow
thoroughfares traffic was difficult, and the diligence
made no pretence of keeping time. There was the
sound of horses' hoofs behind, and in a few moments a
woman, followed by half a dozen horsemen, rode by.
She checked her pace as she passed, and turned to look
at the traveller, while the driver slowly raised his whip
in salute. The light from a lamp swinging from a
bracket on the wall fell upon her, and the traveller saw
that she was young, two or three and twenty, her figure
slight and supple. Her dark gray habit may have
made her look smaller than she really was, and the
mare, which she sat like an accomplished horsewoman,
was a big and powerful animal, almost too much, it
seemed, for those little gloved hands which held the
reins to manage. Yet there was strength in those little
hands. There was a suggestion of strength about her
altogether, strength of will and purpose. It shone out
of a pair of dark gray eyes set under gracefully curved
brows and veiled with long lashes. The firm little
mouth showed it, and there was just enough suspicion
of squareness about the chin to emphasize it. She had
nut-brown hair, a curl of which fell upon her forehead
from underneath a gray astrakhan cap, and the little
head was poised proudly on her shoulders. No ordinary

woman this, not one to be easily swayed by love or any
other passion, a woman to rule rather than be ruled.

"Who is that?" asked the traveller, leaning toward
the driver as the cavalcade passed on.

"A beautiful woman," was the slow answer.

"But her name?"

The driver cracked his whip and the diligence began
to rattle over the cobbles again.

"Some day she may be Duchess," he said, as though
he was following his own train of thought rather than
answering his companion's question.

There was no time to tempt him into being more
explicit, for the horses turned a corner sharply, and
with a shake of their harness stopped before a long, low
building, on which the traveller could just decipher the
words, Hôtel de la Croix Verte. It was an old house,
redolent of the past, the lights within shining but faintly
through the small windows. Its upper story projected
over the narrow footway, and its lower walls bulged
outward, as though they had grown tired of the load
they had had to bear so long. Its age seemed to have
infected its inhabitants, too, for some moments elapsed
before the door opened, and a man came out leisurely
to receive the parcels which the diligence had brought.
That it had brought a traveller also did not excite him,
nor was he in any hurry to welcome him. Perhaps the
traveller was half dreaming, for he almost started when
the man turned and spoke to him.

"Yes; it's a long journey," he answered, "and I am
ready to do justice to the best you have."

He followed the landlord along a narrow passage
and up a twisting staircase.

"The best room," said the landlord as he opened a
door and lit a candle. "There's no one else staying

in the house. Strangers do not come much to Vayenne."

"No?" said the traveller interrogatively.

"No," returned the landlord. "It's not an easy journey, and, besides, what can strangers want in Vayenne? By your accent you'll be——"

"Well, to what extent does my accent betray me?" asked the traveller, with a smile.

"English or German," was the answer.

"Englishman," said the traveller—"Roger Herrick by name, a casual visitor who may be interested enough to stay in Vayenne some time."

The landlord nodded, as though he were not surprised at anything an Englishman might do, and went out promising an excellent dinner forthwith.

"So I am in Vayenne at last!" Herrick exclaimed as he glanced around the old room, pleased with its panelled walls and low, beamed ceiling. "In Vayenne! I hardly thought when the time came that the fact would impress me so much."

He went to the window, opened it, and looked out. Like shadows in the darkness he could dimly discern the towers of the castle above the roofs opposite, and the slender spire with its top lost in the night. The chimes made little bursts of ecstatic music like the voices and laughter of spirits in the air. Somewhere there was the low rumble of a cart over the cobbles, but the street below him was empty. The diligence had gone; no pedestrian was on the narrow footway. It almost seemed as though he were deserted, left here for all time; that, however anxious he might be to leave Vayenne, he would not be able to do so. The city of his dreams had him fast, and already the first of her surprises was preparing for him. Could he have looked but for an instant into the near future, he might possibly have gone to dinner with less appetite than he did.

The long, low room had its windows toward the street, and was broken up by partitions. A waiter pointed to one of these separate retreats as Herrick entered, and he saw that his table was laid there. On the other side of the partition four men were sitting, a bottle of wine and glasses on the table between them. Herrick casually noticed that one was in uniform and that another wore the cassock of a priest, but took no further interest in them, and he had come into the room so quietly that they did not look up at his entrance, and were perhaps unconscious that any one was dining on the other side of the partition.

The landlord had been true to his word, and had provided an excellent dinner. It was good wine, too, that was set upon the table, and Herrick began to discover how hungry he really was. For a long time his attention was confined to the business in hand, and then he suddenly became conscious of the conversation on the other side of the partition. It seemed to have taken a more serious turn, the voices were dropped a little, and it was this fact, no doubt, which made Herrick listen unconsciously.

"Such men as he is die hard," said one man. "The old Duke may hold death at arm's length for years yet."

"Not so, my son. I know something of his disease, and naught but a miracle can help him. A few weeks perhaps, and then——"

It was evidently the priest who spoke. His voice was soft and persuasive, and Herrick thought that some suggestive gesture, explaining what must ensue, had probably finished the sentence.

There was silence for a few moments, and then the ring of a glass as it was placed on the table.

"When the reins fall from a strong hand there is always trouble," said another man.

"And opportunity, don't forget that," said the priest.

"You have your ambitions; have we not talked of them before this? They are within a few short weeks of realization, if you will be guided by me."

"Ay, or I am within measurable distance of losing my head, if things go awry," was the answer. "There are always two sides to such a scheme as this."

"I hadn't thought to find a coward in Gaspard Lemasle," said the priest.

There was a sudden movement and quick shuffle of feet, then a laugh, the laugh of a strong man, deep-chested and resonant.

"Bah! I forgot. One cannot fight with a cassock. See here, Father Bertrand, granted I have ambitions, were it not better to stand by the stronger side? Count Felix is strong, even as his uncle. The old Duke looks upon him as his successor. Strong hands are ready to catch the reins as they fall. In the face of such a man will Vayenne shout for a pale-faced scholar it has little knowledge of, think you?"

"And what reward is Gaspard Lemasle to win from Count Felix?" asked the priest. "Is Gaspard Lemasle's support necessary to him? Rewards come only to those who struggle for them. For you they lie in the hands of that pale scholar at Passey. There will be many to shout for him, and, with a determined leader to fight for him, I can see enthusiastic crowds in the streets of Vayenne."

"Father Bertrand speaks nothing but the truth," said another man, and it seemed certain that only Lemasle's consent was wanting to complete a scheme which had long occupied the priest's attention.

"Maybe," Lemasle returned, "I care not overmuch which way it goes."

"And you have forgotten Mademoiselle de Liancourt," said the priest.

"A second time your cassock protects you, father," laughed the other. "It were a sin, indeed, to forget her. Pass the bottle, and let us have brimming glasses to drink her health. Christine de Liancourt, the most beautiful woman in Montvilliers."

"In the world," corrected the priest quietly. "She is heart and soul for this pale scholar, and she has mentioned Gaspard Lemasle to me."

"By the faith, you shall tell me what she said," the other cried, striking the table until the glasses rattled.

"Nay, nay, it was for no ears but mine; yet, mark you, she knows a brave man when she sees him, and——"

The priest stopped suddenly. The silent street had suddenly awoke. There were hurrying feet and men shouting to each other as they ran, then the sound of a gun which boomed in deep vibration and died slowly away in the distance.

With inarticulate and fragmentary exclamations the four men sprang up and hurried to the door. Herrick followed them more leisurely.

"The Duke is dead!" a man cried to them as they stood in the doorway, and as he ran he shouted the news to others who had been brought from their houses by the sound of the gun. "The Duke is dead!"

"Dead!" said the priest slowly, crossing himself, more by habit than intention it seemed, for other thoughts than of death were reflected in his face. He looked at his companions one after the other, deep meaning in his look, and last of all his eyes rested on Roger Herrick, standing a little in the rear, his face lit up by the light of a lamp hanging in the passage. For a moment the priest did not appear to realize that Herrick was a stranger, and then his eyes opened wider and remained fixed upon him.

"A sudden death," said Herrick. "I heard you say just now that he might live for weeks."

Father Bertrand glanced back into the room they had left, to the place where he and his companions had been sitting.

"Very sudden," he answered, and then after a pause he added, "Very strange."

CHAPTER II

"Does the death of a man prevent the living from finishing the bottle? It's a sin to waste good wine," said Lemasle, striding back into the room.

He spoke rather as a man who was perplexed than as one who was callous. Whatever scheme Father Bertrand was persuading him to, had been in the future a few moments ago; there was plenty of time to weigh it and digest it, to play with it and calculate the chances; that cannon booming out into the night had made a quick decision imperative, and Gaspard Lemasle was troubled.

"Leave him to me," said the priest to the other two men, and then as Herrick turned and went down the passage toward the stairs, Father Bertrand drew his companions closer to him, and talked eagerly to them for a few moments.

When Herrick descended the stairs a few minutes later the passage was empty, and only a waiter was in the long room. The conversation he had chanced to overhear had made little impression upon him. Was there ever a state yet in which every citizen was contented with his rulers? Here in Montvilliers there were contentions, and the coming demise of the Duke prompted men to talk. How dangerous such talk might be, Herrick had no means of judging. He had heard a few names which had little meaning for him— a count, a beautiful woman, and a scholar. Evidently they were of import in the Duchy, but of what interest could they be to him? Nor had he particularly noticed the priest's close scrutiny of his face. Father Bertrand had been astonished to see a stranger there, one who had certainly overheard something of what had been said, and, being a politician as well as a churchman, more loyal as the latter possibly than as the former, he had naturally sought to understand what manner of man this stranger might be. That was all.

So Herrick sought to dismiss the occurrence from his mind as he passed out of the inn, and, after standing on the narrow footway for a moment looking up and down the street, turned in the direction of the castle, bent on a short walk before bed.

There is ever a sense of mystery in an unknown city when it is traversed for the first time after nightfall. Seen over the intervening roofs, some tower or battle-mented edifice, rising gray and ghost-like in the dim light of the moon as it did to-night, seems full of mystery; there is a secret in every street turning to right and left, leading we know not whither; in every narrow alley, looking dangerous betwixt frowning walls; in every dark window, from whence evil might peep out unseen. In Vayenne this sense of mystery was intensified since for long centuries history had been busy with it. Its interest lay in the folded mantle of the past rather than in the open lap of the present. Its foundations were in the days of Charlemagne, and in war and peace it had played a foremost part since then. Hate and ambition had fought out their deadly feuds around it and in its streets. Thrice it had closed its gates against the invader and stood a siege. Chivalry had held sway in it, and in cruel ages deeds unspeakable had been perpetrated within its walls. It had had its periods of great glory and of even greater neglect, of victory and defeat, yet it stood to-day as it ever had stood, the capital of the Duchy of Montvilliers, the centre of an independent state, the dukes of which could still link themselves with those Frankish pirates who had conquered and made their home here.

But to-day Vayenne had fallen behind in the march of modern civilization. For the most part its streets were old and ill-lighted. Men still inhabited houses which had stood for centuries, the castle still frowned over the city as it had done in the Middle Ages, and the ruling hand had still an iron grip in it. Perhaps nowhere in Europe had the ways of the foreigner made less progress. Travellers had not yet marked Vayenne as a place to visit. It was not easy of access, and no one had written eulogies concerning it. That it had fallen behind the times in this manner may have been a potent factor in keeping it inviolate and independent. What wonder then if its rulers, and its people, too, were satisfied with things as they were?

Well might a traveller feel strangely alone and out of the world in this city, whose monuments of chiselled stone and sturdy oak had defied the ravages of the conqueror and of time. Yet no such strangeness took possession of Roger Herrick. Vayenne had been to him a dream city. He had known of it from earliest childhood, why and how he hardly understood; as a boy he had vowed one day to see and know it in reality; and to-night the sudden rushes of bell and chime music, the very cadences of the carillon, which came from the belfry of the great church whose spire rose high toward heaven, seemed familiar. They were not new, he had only forgotten them for a while. He

2

seemed to have known these dark streets with their overhanging houses in some other life, and in this present existence the death of the Duke to-night seemed to hold some meaning for him.

This sense of familiarity with his surroundings was particularly strong as he stopped at a corner with the intention of turning and retracing his steps to the inn. Some distance down, the street was spanned by a deep archway, in the upper part of which was a great clock. By the light of a lamp swinging at the corner, Herrick saw that it was called the Rue de la Grosse Horloge. Its upper end, at least, was better lighted than most of the streets he had passed through, and he walked toward the archway, which was old and weather-worn, and must have been a familiar object in Vayenne long before any clock was placed there. There were small shops, part of the structure on either side of the road, and in the deep arch itself, above and on the sides, were bold reliefs, some past history of the city carved into permanence in stone. Herrick paused to look up at them, his action marking him for a foreigner, for who amongst those who passed daily through that familiar archway would give them a thought? Two men walking a dozen yards behind him stopped to watch him, and when he went on, they went on, too, quickening their pace a little and drawing closer to him. The street beyond the arch was darker, most of the shops there being closed for the night, and the fact reminded Herrick that it was time to return to the Croix Verte. He turned so suddenly that he almost collided with the two men who followed him, and had walked so lightly that he was quite unconscious of their presence. One stepped aside and passed on, the other stepped back and began a voluble apology.

"Pardon, monsieur, I did not see. I was walking with my eyes on the ground. It is a bad habit."

Raising his hat and bowing even as the other did, Herrick was explaining that if there were any fault it was his, and that no apology was necessary, when an arm was thrown suddenly across his throat from behind, and he was dragged violently backward. Immediately the man in front closed with him, endeavoring to prevent his using his hands; and the attack was so unexpected that for some moments it was all Herrick could do to keep his feet. He was, however, a strong man, a wrestler and a fighter of no mean skill. With the hand that he had succeeded in keeping free he gripped the arm about his throat, and with one great heave of his body threw the man over his head on to the roadway, where he lay motionless, as though all life were beaten out of him. In another moment it would have gone hard with his other assailant had the man not slipped to the ground, keeping his arms tightly clasped round Herrick's legs, however.

"A spy! Help! A spy!" he shouted. The effect of that cry was wonderful. Before Herrick could kick himself free, a score of men were upon him. He attempted to shout an explanation, but to no purpose. This way and that was he thrown, his arms were seized and twisted behind him, and then a noose was slipped over his wrists, rendering him helpless.

Hatless and with torn clothes he was hustled down the street, the crowd about him becoming larger every moment, those on the outer fringe of it loudly questioning who he was and what he had done.

"A spy!" some one shouted.

"A quick death to all spies," came the ready answer.

Herrick had been severely handled, and for a few

moments was hardly conscious of what was happening about him. The reiterated cry of "Spy" served to rouse him. For these people the word appeared to have a special interpretation. They expected and feared spies, and were inclined to be merciless. Revenge was in their minds rather than justice. That the two men who had attacked him took him for a spy, Herrick did not believe; the man clasping his legs had only raised the cry to save himself, knowing full well how promptly assistance would come to such a shout. A quick death seemed likely to follow capture, and, one man as he was against a multitude, Herrick nerved himself for a last struggle. The cord that bound his wrists was not fastened in too workman-like a fashion, he could work his hands free, and it should go hard with some before they succeeded in stringing him to some lamp at a corner, which he imagined was their intention.

The cry, however, had gone farther than the street of the great clock. There was a spirit of excitement abroad in Vayenne to-night consequent on the death of the Duke, and the closing of the shops had only sent more men into the taverns and streets to talk and perchance to plot. The cry of "Spy" had leaped from lip to lip far beyond the man who had been the cause of it, and now as the excited crowd poured out of the street into a wide, open square, and Herrick was about to make a last struggle for his life, there came a sharp word of command, a ring of steel drawn from the scabbard, and the crowd halted in confusion before a body of soldiers.

"What have we here?" said a voice which sounded familiar to Herrick.

"A spy, captain," shouted a dozen voices.

"You may easily call a man that, but the proof?"

There was silence, each man expecting his neighbor to speak.

"You may well ask for the proof, since there is none," said Herrick. "Some scoundrels——"

"Ay, and the accusation is as easily denied," interrupted the soldier, turning toward Herrick. "There was never a spy yet but had plenty of lies ready to his tongue."

"I am a stranger in Vayenne—shall I seek justice in it in vain, Captain Lamasle?" For Herrick recognized him as the soldier who had been with the priest at the Croix Verte that evening.

An expression of astonishment crossed the captain's face at being known by this stranger. It was evident that he did not recognize Herrick, but perhaps he remembered what company he had been in not long since and what had been said over the wine.

"Being so ready with my name is not much in your favor," he said; "you'll get justice, I warrant." And then in obedience to a quick command, Herrick found himself a prisoner amongst soldiers instead of in the midst of a crowd. It would be useless now to attempt to escape, and at the word of command he marched forward.

Until this moment Herrick had taken little note of his surroundings. Now a sudden rush of music in the air above made him look around him. The square was of great size, misty and ghost-like in the pale, uncertain moonlight, but in front of him there loomed a great gateway flanked by towers, and behind and on higher ground, there were other towers and frowning walls. It was the castle, and near it rose the stately pile of a great church, its spire piercing far into the night.

As they approached the castle the great gates were flung open, and Herrick saw that the court-yard within was full of men hurrying to and fro. Horses' hoofs impatiently beat the stones, which were rough and uneven. There was much jingling of harness and ring of spur and steel. Lights shone in narrow doorways, and there was the flame of a torch here and there. All was hurry and excitement; and in some silent chamber near, the Duke lay dead. Herrick remembered this, found himself speculating upon it, yet even as he passed through the gate he hardly felt strange in playing a part in this drama.

The word "Spy" seemed to have run before him even here. That grim gateway had not kept it out. Men paused a moment to look at him: some were silent, some uttered a sound of hatred and contempt, but all seemed convinced that the accusation was a just one.

The soldiers halted by the wall some twenty feet in height. Herrick concluded that there was a terrace or garden above, because several persons, women and pages among them, were leaning over the wall looking into the court-yard below. A flight of stone steps, placed sideways to the wall, led down from this terrace, and at the foot of these steps was a woman mounted upon a beautiful bay mare, which pawed the ground, impatient to be gone. At a little distance a group of horsemen waited for her signal, which she was in the act of giving when the soldiers, with their prisoner in their midst, came to a halt not a dozen yards from her. The light from two or three torches held by servants who stood on the lower steps lit up her face, and Herrick saw again the woman who had ridden past the diligence a few hours ago, the woman who was destined to play so great a part in his life.

Captain Lemasle stepped to her side and saluted.

"Are you not to ride with us?" she asked. "We are waiting."

"Pardon, mademoiselle. I have just been rescuing a spy. The crowd had caught him, and it would have gone hard with him had we not taken him."

"If he is a spy, would that have mattered?" she said, loud enough for Herrick to hear.

"There is justice in proving a man guilty before he is hanged," Lemasle answered.

"Since when have you been so fastidious? I have heard other things of Gaspard Lemasle. Let me look at this spy."

"I seem better known than I imagined," the soldier muttered as he stood aside.

She rode toward Herrick, the men about him falling back, until she was close upon him.

"Look up," she commanded, "and let me see the face of a spy."

"Not of a spy, mademoiselle, but of an honest man," he answered, looking her straight in the eyes.

"Spy, spy," she contradicted sharply, "or what do you in Vayenne at such a time as this?"

"I am a traveller."

"So are they all," she cried. "There is a guest-room within these walls for you. Vayenne knows how to welcome such travellers. Ah! I could honor an enemy, but a spy——" And there was such utter contempt in her face that Herrick could find no words to answer her.

As she tightened her reins, her riding whip slipped from her fingers and fell at his feet, and before any one could prevent him he had shaken the loosened cord from his wrists, and had stooped and picked it up. In an instant half a dozen soldiers sprang forward to prevent his attacking her. She did not flinch, but waving them back, held out her hand for the whip.

"Thank you, mademoiselle," said Herrick. "At least you have generosity enough to know that I am incapable of such a thing as that."

She looked at him for an instant as she took the whip, a new interest in her eyes, and a slight lowering of her proud head thanked him. Then she turned the mare round sharply.

"Captain Lemasle, I am ready," she said, and as the soldiers closed round Herrick again, she rode out through the grim gateway, followed by the troop of horsemen.

CHAPTER III

ALONG dark stone passages, through many a doorway, and across two or three rough court-yards, half a dozen soldiers conducted Herrick to his "guest-room." The woman's pleasantry had caught their fancy, and they laughed boisterously as they went, hoping, perhaps, to put fear into the heart of their prisoner.

They halted before a low door, which one man unlocked with a great key. The immense thickness of the wall formed a narrow passage, at the end of which some steps descended into a semicircular cell of no great size, but of considerable height.

"There's straw for a bed," said the jailer, pointing to a corner, "though how it came here I don't understand, and you've got heaven's light itself for a candle." And he nodded toward a patch of moonlight. "There are honest soldiers who are worse lodged, I warrant."

"It ill becomes a guest to complain of his treatment," Herrick answered.

"Ay; that idea of a guest-room was smartly thought of," the man returned, "but maybe you hardly see the full humor of it. This is the South Tower, and it's usually the last lodging a man needs this side the grave."

"Is that so?" And Herrick's attitude had interest in it, but little personal concern.

"Yes; and it's a short walk from here to the last yard

we crossed. It usually happens there." And the jailer
made a suggestive downward sweep with his arm.

"Axe or sword?" asked Herrick.

"Sword. Unless they decide to make an especial
example in your case, then they're likely to hang you
over the great gateway."

"Am I sufficiently important for that, think you?"

"I've known a dead sparrow on a string scare away
much finer birds," the jailer answered; "but at any rate
you're no white-livered man, and I shouldn't grieve to
see you cheat both sword and rope."

"Thanks for your good will," said Herrick. "Who
knows, I may live to speak a comforting word to you.
I will be honest with you, I had not appreciated the full
extent of the lady's humor."

With something like a salute, deference to the prisoner's courage, the jailer departed, and the key grated
harshly in the lock as the bolts shot home.

High up near the roof there was a deep-set window
through which the moonlight came. The tower could
not be shut in by high walls, therefore, and probably
was one of the outer towers of the castle. From that
window possibly a prisoner might look into a free world,
reach it, perhaps, if age had worn the bars loose in their
stone sockets. A moment later Herrick felt certain
that only this single wall held him from freedom, for
the music of the carillon burst upon his ears. His fancy
made the moonbeams the path along which the music
travelled. But the window was unattainable. The
rounded walls were almost as smooth as if the surface
had been polished, and the cell was bare of everything
but the heap of straw in the corner.

"My first night in Vayenne," he muttered, and some
of the bravery with which he had addressed the jailer

was wanting. The moonlight was upon his face as he spoke, a serious face just now, although neither hopelessness nor despair was in it. It could hardly be called a handsome face, yet it was one to remember. They were good, steady eyes, and if the nose and mouth were not an artist's ideals of beauty, in the whole face the artist would have found attraction. It was strong, forceful, fashioned in an uncommon mould; it was a face apart rather than one of a type, a strong family possession which to strangers had often marked him for a Herrick.

"My first night in Vayenne," he repeated as he began to pace his narrow cell slowly. How long ago it seemed since he had first seen the city from the brow of the hills. How much had happened in the few short hours since then, and yet one incident stood out more clearly than all the rest, the woman leaning from her horse to look into the face of a spy. Even now her contempt hurt him. It was hateful to appear mean in her eyes. All else that had happened to him seemed of little account beside this. The moment his eyes had rested upon her there had sprung a desire in his soul to serve her. In that service he felt himself capable of much, yet she despised him. A little touch of sympathy had shown in her face for a moment when he handed her the whip, but it had no power to obliterate the contempt. That was her true feeling toward him, the other was but the passing pity which a woman may have even for a coward.

The carillon had sounded several times, and the direction of the moon ray had changed, leaving the floor of the cell in darkness; but buried in thought Herrick took no notice of the little rushes of music, nor was he conscious of the deepening gloom around him until a sudden shadow seemed to flit through the chamber, and a new stealthy sound startled him. Instinctively he drew back to the wall, that whatever enemy might be near should have to face him and not be able to take him unawares. Once to-night already he had been seized from behind.

Standing on the outside ledge of the window, holding on to the bars and peering into the cell, was a figure that might well startle the bravest. The opening could not be more than four feet in height, yet it was sufficient to allow this figure to stand upright. Head, feet, and hands were at least normal in size, those of a full-grown and powerful man, the body was that of a child, though its curiously twisted form might have abnormal strength in it. His hair was long, and a thick, stubbly beard and whiskers completely surrounded his face. He was ugly in the extreme, and even Herrick was pleased to think that solid bars were between them.

For full five minutes the dwarf stood there, uttering no sound, but moving his head from side to side, trying to pierce the darkness, and once or twice he leant backward at arm's length to look down on the outside below him. Then he took hold of one bar with both hands, and, lifting it out of its socket, laid it carefully along the window-ledge. From the breast of the loose smock-like garment he wore he took a length of rope, knotted one end round one of the bars, and let the other end fall into the cell. For a moment he waited and listened; then, with the agility of a gorilla, he swung himself down, and stood on the floor of the cell, the rope still in his hand, as though he were prepared to spring upward to safety again at the first sign of danger.

"Who are you, and what do you want?" said Herrick suddenly.

The dwarf turned quickly toward him.

"Hush! It's only friend Jean."

"I have no such friend."

"You do not know it, but yes, from this moment you have. See here, my knife; watch, I fling it across the floor! Take it, it is for your protection—to show my good faith. I have no other weapon. Now, let's come close and look at each other."

The knife, a formidable blade, came skimming across the stone flags to Herrick's feet. He picked it up, and walked into the centre of the cell to meet his strange visitor.

"You must bend down to let me be sure that you are the man," said the dwarf.

"You have seen me before, then?"

"To-night when she rode across the court-yard to look at you. Ah, yes, you are the man. You were so quiet I thought they had put you elsewhere. Did I frighten you?"

"Well, you startled me, friend Jean."

The dwarf laughed a little, low chuckle, and, silently clapping his hands, stood on one foot and scratched the calf of his leg with the other.

"Ah! So I startled you, friend Spy."

"Stop! Not that word."

"I must needs call you by some name. Give me another."

"Roger Herrick."

"Friend Roger, good. It comes to my tongue easily. Let's sit, and I'll tell you who I am." And doubling his legs under him he sank cross-legged onto the floor.

"I will lean by the wall, Jean, I find it easier," said Herrick.

"Ah, there are compensations, after all, for a man like

me. To know Vayenne is to know me; you can't help
it. They call me an innocent; you know what that
means?"

"Yes."

"But not all it means, I warrant," chuckled the dwarf.
"I get pity; I am not supposed to do things like other
men. Who cares where I go? In the castle, in the
church, in a house where there's feasting—anywhere—
I don't count. Who cares if I listen? It's only Jean; in
at one ear, out at the other. No one looks to me for
work, they'd sooner pay me for playing the fool, and I
let 'em, I let 'em." And somewhere in his strange, loose
garments he made the coins jingle. "So I go in and out
as I will. If I curled up to sleep on the rug at the Duke's
door they'd hardly trouble to disturb me, I count for
such a little. Generally I sleep in the church."

"In the church?"

"Ay; in the porch. They call me the dwarf of
St. Etienne. Listen! there's its music." And he remained silent with uplifted finger until the ripple of
the carillon had died away into the night. "I'm a
little fellow to have so large a church to myself, as I
often do at nights; and, friend Roger, I see things in
St. Etienne when the moonlight sends faint, colored
beams through the painted windows. There are legends
and superstitions about St. Etienne, and people are superstitious about me, too. They believe I know things,
and so I do, but not of the sort they fancy."

A strange little madman, Herrick thought, yet one
with a method surely, as the unbarred window
showed.

"An innocent, that's what they call me," the dwarf
went on, as though he answered his companion's thought,
"and though I am no more one than you are, it suits my

purpose. My wisdom would get any other man into trouble."

"That loose bar, for instance," said Herrick, pointing to the window.

"Yes; but I never thought of the use I should one day put it to. It is well to have more than one hole to creep into, and few would expect to find a man lodging in the South Tower of his own free will."

"I hear it has an evil reputation," said Herrick.

"Ay; the grave's anteroom. So I chose it as a hiding-place. There are times when I like to sleep here, to be alone and think of all I hear and see. I was many nights loosening that bar."

"And why have you come to-night—to sleep here?"

"No; to plot with friend Roger," the dwarf answered promptly. "The Duke died to-night; you know that? Out of his death will come trouble for many—for the woman you saw in the court-yard a little while since. Ah! That moves you. She is beautiful, friend Roger."

"Who is she?"

"Mademoiselle Christine de Liancourt, and might be ruler in Montvilliers, but that the law denies it to a woman. There are many who would overthrow that law if she would let them, but she will make no sign. The Duke is dead; his son must reign in his stead. This son is a poor sort of fellow, a lover of books instead of a man of affairs."

"The pale scholar of Passey," said Herrick.

"How learnt you that catch phrase?" asked the dwarf sharply.

"I overheard it to-night."

"Yes; they call him that," Jean went on slowly, "and

in truth he may make us a poor Duke, but Mademoiselle de Liancourt thinks otherwise. Count Felix—maybe you overheard him mentioned to-night?"

"I did. He would be Duke, and the old Duke wished it so."

"You have great knowledge for a casual traveller in Vayenne, friend Roger," said the dwarf with some suspicion, "but you shall explain it to me presently. Count Felix would be Duke; more, would wed with Christine de Liancourt, and she loves not either of these ideas. To-night she rides to Passey to carry news of the Duke's death to his son, and to bring him to Vayenne."

"A strange office for a woman to perform; stranger still that Count Felix should let her go and jeopardize his schemes," Herrick said.

"She has influence with the scholar, who has no desire to be a Duke, that is why she was determined to go. Count Felix thought it wise not to thwart her, since he would stand well in her favor, but he has arranged that an accident shall prevent the scholar ever reaching Vayenne. The escort will be attacked, and it is arranged shall be beaten, and no effort will suffice to save the life of the scholar. It is cleverly conceived, eh, friend Roger? A man who can plot so prettily will go far toward success."

"But you could have warned her," Herrick exclaimed. "Why didn't you?"

"I am an innocent. Who would believe me?"

Herrick glanced at the window.

"Of what think you, friend Roger?"

"That Mademoiselle sorely needs a swift messenger to-night."

The dwarf sprang to his feet.

"Truly, by the way one man gets in another may well

leave. But stay." And he put his hand on Herrick's arm. "I took you not for a spy when I saw you in the court-yard to-night, but how came you by your knowledge of the scholar of Passey?"

"As I dined to-night at the Croix Verte I heard a priest talk of him."

"A narrow, hatchet-faced priest, with never a smile, and eyes that look into you without blinking?"

"The same."

"Ah, Father Bertrand has his plot, too. When he talks, friend Roger, remember how easy it is for a man to lie. Come, you shall be the swift messenger Mademoiselle needs. That is why I came to-night. See, I have brought what shall pass you easily through the streets." And he produced a priest's cassock and cloak with a hood, which he had deftly fastened round him under the folds of his smock. "I borrowed them from St. Etienne." And then, as Herrick arrayed himself in the garments, he silently clapped his hands. "You are more like a priest than most of the real ones I know," he chuckled.

"I do not know how I am to travel to Passey, but, at least, I trust you, and there's the proof of it," said Herrick, handing the dwarf his knife.

"A little while ago you didn't know that the bar was loose in that window," said Jean, taking the weapon, "and you didn't know me. To-morrow is as far off as next year for all a man knows of it."

"That's true."

"There are those who would wed to-morrow, yet die to-night," the dwarf went on. "It's a world of minutes for us all. You come to understand these things when you roam through St. Etienne at nights. I'll set you on your way to Passey within an hour unless

3

'twixt now and then time ends for me. If so, you must needs shift for yourself."

He caught hold of the rope as he spoke, and swung himself to the window-ledge with the agility of an ape. Impeded by his unaccustomed garments, Herrick found it a more difficult matter; but he was strong and athletic, and in a few moments was crouching on his knees beside the dwarf.

The bars were placed midway in the thickness of the wall, so that on either side there was room for them both.

"We'll shut our door," whispered the dwarf when they had crawled through the opening, and he replaced the movable bar and drew up the rope. The next instant he had gripped his companion's arm to compel him to silence and to keep him motionless. Below was the sound of a heavy step, which came to a halt immediately beneath them, and from within the cell came a grating noise. It was the great key being thrust into the lock.

CHAPTER IV

THE ROAD TO PASSEY

THAT intricate calculations occupied Father Bertrand's mind as he slowly paced his room from end to end was apparent in his face. Ascetic in appearance, wont to present a calm exterior under the most trying circumstances, the fact of his restlessness proved that he had reached some crisis, that some part of his scheme was on the point of settlement. Father Bertrand was a power in Vayenne. Not greatly beloved, perhaps—he was too stern and unbending for that—his priestly office, nevertheless, appealed strongly to a people naturally superstitious, while his learning and political acumen made him forceful with those who ruled. He held no office; but even the late Duke, strong as he was, had sometimes been guided by his opinion, and Count Felix recognized long ago, that, in his claim to the Dukedom, the support of Father Bertrand would be of very real value.

If he is a weak man who cannot refrain from speaking his thoughts, the priest was a very strong man, for to no one had he betrayed himself. Count Felix felt confident of his support; Mademoiselle de Liancourt believed that he heartily shared her ideas of right and justice; while, as a priest, he spoke with authority to the great mass of the people, who believed his policy based entirely upon his religion. A few who fondly believed themselves in his confidence, but were in reality little more than his tools, knew at least that other schemes were working in his mind, and that, as a member of a secret order, his information was invariably correct and reached him long before it was known in the castle. In a peculiar sense he was all things to all men, yet really known by none. Such a man must needs walk warily, for his path is beset with snares.

Father Bertrand, moreover, was a man of wealth. His charity was known in Vayenne, yet he fared simply himself, it was whispered; and there were those who could tell of the mean, poor room he occupied in his house in the Rue St. Romain, a room little removed as regards comfort from that of the ordinary toiler of the city. But there were other rooms in the house in the Rue St. Romain, and there was no lack of luxury in the large chamber on the upper floor which the priest paced slowly from end to end to-night. It was evidence not only of wealth, but of taste, too, and had they known of it, many in Vayenne would probably have formed a different estimate of Father Bertrand's character.

Absorbed as he was in his calculations, the priest was keenly alive to every new sound in the street or in the house. Several times he paused to listen, and once drew aside the heavy window curtains to look down into the street below. The Rue St. Romain lay along the north side of the Church of St. Etienne, and was little frequented after nightfall. Any excitement resulting from the death of the Duke would hardly penetrate here.

There was a knocking at the door at last, and Father Bertrand immediately took his seat at a large writing-table, and, drawing some of the papers with which it was covered toward him, began to study them carefully. No matter how agitated he might be in thought, his visitor would only see him calm and self-possessed, and doubtless be more impressed than ever with the priest's strength of character.

A man entered and closed the door behind him.

"We have failed, father."

"Only a weak man admits that, Monsieur Mercier. Where is Nicolas Pigou?"

"At death's door. He is still unconscious, and the surgeon I got to him declares that half of his ribs at least must be broken."

The priest did not speak, but by a gesture asked the reason of this catastrophe.

"Our opportunity came when the stranger had passed through the arch of the great clock into the dark street beyond," said Mercier. "We had approached close behind him when he suddenly turned, coming into collision with us. We had planned to take him quickly, place him in a carriage which had followed us, and bring him here, but his unexpected action thwarted this. Pigou passed on, and to gain time I began to apologize. Then Pigou seized him from behind, and I immediately closed with the man. Pigou is strong, as you are aware, but he was a babe in the hands of this stranger, who, with a heave of his body threw him over his head into the roadway. I should have fared no better had I not slipped to the ground and, holding his legs, shouted 'Spy!' The street was alive in a minute; but I have bruises about me which will last for many a day to come."

"And then?" said the priest quietly.

"The crowd hustled him to the end of the street, and would have hanged him there, probably, but it seems they were met by a company of soldiers, and the stranger is now a prisoner in the castle."

"You saw the soldiers take him?"

"No; I heard that later," Mercier answered. "I slipped from the crowd, and went to look after poor Pigou. There might have been awkward questions asked had he been found in the street."

"I am sorry for Nicolas Pigou," said Father Bertrand, "but if a broken rib or two is all the payment, our enterprise is cheaply won. Why do you talk of failure, Monsieur Mercier?"

"Is it not failure then?"

"Surely not. There are more ways of reaching a place than by the high road. This stranger is no spy. I shall prove that to Count Felix, and we gain our end. Indeed, circumstances have favored us. The stranger will look upon me as his deliverer, and will be the more ready to be advised. I doubt not we shall have him in this house within a few hours. Were you recognized by the crowd to-night?"

"No. I am known to few in Vayenne."

"Then, my dear Monsieur Mercier, two desperate villains set upon this poor stranger in the streets; one is like to die, it is said—the other has succeeded in escaping. This is my story—a good and plausible one, eh?" said Father Bertrand, with a smile; "and since justice done quickly has the greater mercy in it, I will go to the castle at once."

"And Gaspard Lemasle?" said Mercier as the priest rose.

"He will dance to our piping, but we shall keep him always on the chain. Untrammelled he might be dangerous."

"Is the chain forged that will hold him?"

"My son, I never confide in a man of whom I am ignorant. My friends may rest assured that I treasure some knowledge of them, some episode, perhaps, which they have forgotten, but which in an emergency will compel them to remain my friends." And while he laid one hand on his companion's arm, he touched his own forehead significantly with the other. "Come with me into another room. My servant shall set before you wine of such a vintage that you shall forget your bruises. And do not leave, Monsieur Mercier, until you are rested. Indeed, if I find you asleep in your chair when I return, I will not quarrel with you."

As he followed the priest, Mercier's estimate of his companion possibly took a wider scope than it had done before, and he wondered which of the many episodes in his life which he was unlikely to talk of the priest knew most about.

It was conclusive proof of Father Bertrand's power with the late Duke and Count Felix that he was admitted to the castle without question at so late an hour; and that the soldiers bowed to his authority was apparent when his suggestion that he should see the spy before he saw the Count met with no opposition.

"Lodged in the South Tower?" he said as he followed the jailer.

"Ay, father; it's the safest cage we have."

"Too safe for an innocent bird, master jailer."

"Well, I know naught of his innocence," said the jailer as he thrust the great key into the lock, "but I'm not regretting that he should cheat death. There's no fear about him, and there's none too many brave men in the world that we should want to hurry them out of it."

The jailer had a torch, and he preceded the priest down the narrow passage in the thickness of the walls.

"Asleep, prisoner?" he called out. "Here's a reverend father to see you, and he comes as a friend."

There was no answer, and priest and jailer looked slowly round the cell, then at each other, and then at the barred window. No ray of moonlight came through it now, but the moonlit sky was clear without, and there was no one crouching on the ledge!

The measured tread halting suddenly below, and the sound of the grating key within, had had a paralyzing effect upon both fugitive and guide for a moment. Although prepared to make a fight for it, the position appeared hopeless to Herrick; but the dwarf, who had perhaps foreseen that they would have the sentry to deal with, was quick to grasp the situation and see the way out of the difficulty. The terrace, which was considerably above the level of the floor of the cell, was only some twelve or fourteen feet below them. It was comparatively narrow and bounded by a low, battlemented wall.

"That's our road," whispered the dwarf, pointing to a certain point in this wall a little to their right. "Jump, and make for it."

As he spoke he whipped out his knife, and tucking his legs under him suddenly let himself drop upon the sentry. The thud of the fall and a feeble, stifled groan were all Herrick heard as he, too, jumped from the ledge, and, trusting implicitly to his companion, ran to the spot he had indicated. As he looked back, the dwarf rose and came quickly after him, but the sentry lay under the window and did not move.

"You have killed him!" Herrick exclaimed.

"Sharp, after me," the dwarf said, springing onto the wall, and then, as Herrick followed him, he threw himself on his stomach, twisted himself round, and holding onto the rough stonework let his legs hang down on the outside of the wall. "That's it, do the

same. There's a rope here. Go steady! I'll go first.
Now let me catch hold of your feet, and get the rope
between them. The stones are rough enough to lower
yourself by until you get a grasp on the rope with your
hands. "

This was the outer wall of the castle, and in the angle
formed by a buttress a stout rope had been fixed.

Herrick found it no easy matter to follow the dwarf's
instructions, and had he paused to consider, might have
declined to make the perilous descent at all. But with
Jean's help from below he managed to get the rope
between his knees, and the rest was comparatively easy.

Some distance below was the roof of a house which
clung to the castle wall like a mussel to a rock. The
dwarf caught Herrick to steady him as he landed on
the roof, for it sloped at a sharp angle, and was dilapidated.

"Sit, and put your hand on my shoulder, and shuffle
down after me," he said. "Now carefully. Catch hold
of this rafter. Let yourself swing, and drop lightly.
It's barely four feet fall for your length of body."

Herrick did as he was told, and dropped into a dark
attic, followed by the dwarf.

"You please me, friend Roger," said Jean, chuckling
quietly. "My private road is not an easy one to travel
in a hurry, and the man who takes it is not likely to
wear a scared face and feel his knees tremble when
danger comes."

"I like not murder, friend Jean."

"You'd like being murdered less, I warrant," was the
prompt answer. "Besides it wasn't murder, for two
reasons. Killing a man in self-defence is not murder,
and you're likely to do it yourself before many hours
have passed if you would serve Mademoiselle; and

secondly, the sentry yonder isn't dead. I had to let his strength out of an artificial hole lest it should come through his mouth in a shout which would have betrayed us. He will be well on his way to recovery before a new moon, and, if not, there are plenty more sentries in the castle to take his place. Come, you are not out of Vayenne yet, and you must be on your way to Passey before the dawn."

The dwarf led the way down two flights of broken stairs, and through the door of the house, and passed into a narrow, deserted street.

"We'll go quickly," he whispered. "No one will suspect you in those garments. We shall meet few, and they will think that some one dying has need of a priest, and that I have fetched you. I have done it often before."

They passed through a perfect labyrinth of narrow streets in silence, and the two or three night wanderers they met took no notice of them.

Vayenne was asleep under the pale moon; that temporary death called sleep was in every habitation. The dead Duke in his chamber in the castle was hardly less silent than the sleeping thousands he had ruled.

Presently the dwarf stopped before the door of a house at the end of a blind alley.

"We go in here, friend Roger," he said, "but by a window. The door is locked, because they who own the place still hope for a tenant, which is a forlorn hope. The house grows more rotten every day, water rats make a retreat of it, and some mischievous person has said it is haunted by a horrible ghost."

"You are that mischievous person, I suppose."

"Why think so ill of me?" chuckled the dwarf. "When I don't wish to leave the city by the gates, this is the way I go."

He led the way to a room at the top of the house.

"From the roof we scramble onto the city wall, which is low here, and rough, for the river washes its base. Sometimes, I just drop into the water, and swim, but under a low arch there is an old boat, which we will use to-night. Have you money in your purse, friend Roger?"

"A little."

"You may want more. I came provided. Here is gold," he said, taking a small leathern bag from the folds of his blouse. "Put it away carefully. You can repay me another time. Remain a priest, it may serve you to get audience with Mademoiselle more easily, but although priest without, you must be soldier within."

The dwarf went to a corner of the room, and, wrenching up a board, knelt down, and thrust his long arm into the opening, from which he drew out a sword and a revolver.

"Strap this under your robe," he said, handing Herrick the sword, "and put the revolver where you may come at it easily. And listen, friend Roger. You must come at Mademoiselle de Liancourt as your wits serve you; tell her what I have told you. She will not easily believe the tale, but you must convince her; and for the rest, circumstances must guide you."

"Do you not come with me then?"

"A little way to show you the road, then I return to plot in the city. Were I a straight man as you are, I might not have come for you to-night. That's a dark saying—I wonder if you can read its meaning?"

"I cannot, friend Jean."

"Well, you'll want all your wits for your enterprise; it's a pity to waste them on riddles. But remember this, friend Roger: when I was made in this queer shape, an ordinary heart was put into me, and there was no strange twist given to my feelings.   We are not so very different, you and I, after all.   Come, we waste precious time.''

There was no great difficulty in scrambling onto the wall from the roof of the house, and, bidding Herrick wait, the dwarf climbed down the face of the wall almost as easily as the rough stones of it had been steps.   Working his way along a narrow stone course, or ledge, which was near the bottom, he reached an iron ring let into the wall, and, supporting himself by this, managed to drag out a small, flat-bottomed boat from beneath a nearly submerged archway.

Having carefully watched the descent of his companion, Herrick attempted to make as little of the matter as he had done.   The descent ended in a sudden and rather unsteady jump, which almost sank the rickety old craft, and Herrick would certainly have fallen sideways into the water had not his companion caught him.

A fairly strong stream was running, and they were carried down some two hundred yards in the process of crossing.   A belt of trees in a thick undergrowth screened the landing-place.

"I have a friend here," said the dwarf.   "We will not wake him to-night, but we will borrow his horse.   I will explain to-morrow."

There was a small house nestling under a clump of trees, and on the opposite side of a roadway a shed at the corner of a field.   To this the dwarf went, and it was evident that he knew every corner of it intimately, for in a few moments he had saddled the horse there and led it out.

"We don't want to wake the good man, so we'll walk the animal along the grass for a little way," he said. "There is a gate higher up.   You follow this road, friend

Roger; it runs without interruption for many miles. At a wayside Calvary it forks; take the right-hand road. Five miles will bring you to a deep wood, and I have heard of thieves there, so it would be well to have your revolver ready. Once out of the wood keep the left-hand road, and to your left you will presently see the Château of Passey on high ground. Perhaps it would be well to let your horse go free then, and enter the village on foot. A mounted priest might cause wonder, and the horse may find his way home. Here is the gate. Mount, friend Roger. Use your horse well, and you will be in Passey before noon."

"I may overtake Mademoiselle and her escort."

"You will be clever if you do, since they have gone by a different and a shorter road, one which might not be safe for you to travel. They will be in Passey by dawn."

"And how shall I let you know how I fare and where fortune may take me?"

"Success or failure, I shall hear soon enough," the dwarf answered. "Remember only that you serve Mademoiselle de Liancourt, and that all prison windows have not bars which may be lifted out. Farewell!" And without another word, he turned, and hurried back to the river-bank, where his boat lay.

So it happened that as Father Bertrand went back to the Rue St. Romain, and the alarm given by the jailer presently resulted in the finding of the wounded sentry, Roger Herrick was galloping through the night toward Passey and the woman he was destined to serve.

CHAPTER V

THE village of Passey, nestling in the shadow of its château, looked secure, had indeed been well protected in past times, but to-day little real resistance could have been offered to a determined enemy. The outer wall of the château had crumbled and fallen in pieces, no vigilant eyes kept ward and watch from its battlements, and the serving-men in its old guard-rooms and courts were not of the kind out of which stout soldiers are made. It had been in the hands of the Duprés for three centuries or more, given originally to an ancestor in return for good service, for the family had bred many a gallant warrior in the past; but in recent years misfortune and poverty had come, and the Duprés were too proud to make petitions in the Castle of Vayenne. Nothing is easier to forget than past service if there is no present need of favors, and the Dukes of Montvilliers had practically forgotten their once powerful subject of Passey. More and more the family had lived a retired life, and the last two heads of it had been confirmed invalids. The present owner was a man of weak physique also, barred from a life in the open and all manly sports. Thrown in upon himself he had found consolation in books and in study, and had little care how the world went so it left him in peace. The late Duke, a man of warlike character and iron will, had thoroughly despised the old man at Passey, and when his son evinced a love for dreaming over books, his father sent him to Viscount Dupré. The château would serve as a convenient place of isolation, the Duke argued, and the old fool might well be made useful as a jailer to the young one.

"I hold you responsible for him," the Duke had said to Dupré. "Teach him to hate the books you love and I will find means to thank you; let him become such a one as yourself, and rest assured the reins of government will never fall into his hands when they drop from mine. The good of Montvilliers is far more to me than any son."

The Duke rode away, hoping perhaps that banishment from Vayenne would cure his son, but the lad had been at Passey ever since. How far the old Viscount attempted to turn the boy from his studies, who can say? The fact remained that he did not succeed, and Maurice de Broux—now a youth of eighteen—had found peace and contentment in the crumbling old château and was as little concerned about the world as old Dupré himself.

To-day the quiet life had suddenly been broken in upon. With early dawn a company of horsemen, a woman riding in their midst, had clattered through the village street and in at the château gates. "The Duke is dead," one serving-man presently told another, and the news spread rapidly through the village, and out into the fields beyond, where bent-backed men and women hoed. One old man there looked toward the château, and pulling off a ragged cap cried feebly, "Long live the Duke!"

In a room in the château, a room of books and students' comforts, such a room as could not have been found in the length and breadth of the Castle of Vayenne, Maurice and Mademoiselle de Liancourt had been closeted for hours. There was no more important person in Montvilliers that day than the pale scholar of Passey, yet there was no excitement in his face. That he should mourn for a father who had been little more than a stranger to him was hardly to be expected. From time to time he moved restlessly about the room, letting his companion talk, and now and again her words brought a flush to his cheek. To no one would he have listened as quietly as he did to her, for, scholar though he was by nature, he had yet something of his father in him, a temper that might burst into fury were it pressed too far. No one knew this better than Christine de Liancourt, and if any words of hers would sting him into action she would certainly speak them. For this very purpose had she come in haste to Passey. In old days she had often stood between Maurice and his .ather's wrath. She had prophesied that when the hour came Maurice would rise to the occasion and make a wise ruler. He was, besides, the heir, nothing could alter that, and justice, coupled with her half-formed fear of Count Felix, drove her to espouse the young Duke's cause with all the strength that was in her.

"My dear Christine, you easily get angry with me," he said presently. "Try and see the whole matter through my eyes. I am eighteen, and I have never done a single thing to fit myself for ruling Montvilliers; more shame to me, you may say, but we are not all born with a desire to rule. Ever since I came to Passey I have practically been a prisoner—a happy prisoner. I have easily forgotten how near I stood to a dukedom, and, I warrant, have been as easily forgotten. Why remember me now when I only desire to be left in peace? Believe me, as a duke I should be an utter failure, a breeder of dissension and revolution, no blessing to the land, but

a curse. Let the power fall as my father wished it.
Cousin Felix will make a much better duke than I."

"Have you no sense of duty?" she asked.

"Truly I think my duty to Montvilliers is to let
some one else rule it," he said, with a smile.

"Duty is not a cloak a man can put off and on as he
wills," Christine answered; "it is part of the man himself. He is called to fulfil certain conditions of his
life, of his birth, and he cannot throw duty aside by
saying he is unfitted to perform it. Are you a coward,
Maurice, as well as a scholar?"

"No; I do not think I am a coward."

"It is only a coward who would not ride to Vayenne
and claim his birthright."

"If we come to such close argument as that, this
same birthright may be found to have little justice in
it," he said quickly. "Did my father become Duke by
right of birth? You know he didn't. He was a strong
man, while those who should have ruled were weak.
Montvilliers wanted a strong hand to guide her, and a
bloodless revolution raised my father to power."

"Has Felix any greater right than you?" she asked.

"By birth, no; by capacity, yes. Let him be Duke.
I will be the first to shout for him."

"Coward!" she said.

"Christine, there are bounds which even you must
not pass," he said, turning a stern face to her.

She clapped her hands at his sudden anger, nd
stepped quickly to his side.

"There spoke a worthy Duke. I have seen the same
anger rush blood-red into your father's face, and have
tr mbled for his enemies. You cannot hide your real
self; you cannot deny your real personality, even
though you would."

4

"It lies in peace among these books of mine," he answered. "We have talked of this enough."

"Not yet. Listen, Maurice. Felix is hated by many, and if he seizes the crown, there will be bloodshed in the streets of Vayenne."

"He will be strong enough to suppress rebellion," was the answer.

"And wise enough perchance to shed blood in this peaceful Château of Passey," she went on quickly.

"Why here? Passey does not trouble itself with politics. The harvest of the fields is Passey's concern, and it is of small consequence who rules in Vayenne."

Christine laid her hand on his arm. "Think you the golden circle of sovereignty will rest easily on your cousin's brow while you live? Deny your birthright, Maurice, and then, like a coward, flee your country for safety, for I warrant you will die a violent death if you stay in it."

"I cannot think so—so much evil of Felix," he answered.

"I know him far better than you possibly can do," she said. "He let me come to you only because he is convinced that you will not come to Vayenne. He despises you, Maurice. He will use your refusal for his own purposes, and in his own manner. He will easily convince many that you are a danger to the state and that there is righteousness in judicial murder."

"Will not a kingdom satisfy him, but he must have my poor life as well?" Maurice muttered.

"Has it ever satisfied, in any age, in any history? Felix will seek to make himself secure in every possible way. Since there are many who love me, he wishes to wed me."

"Perhaps he loves you?"

"It may be," she answered, "but not as he loves himself."

"And you would marry him?"

"For the good of Montvilliers I might be persuaded."

She watched him as he walked slowly across the room. Perhaps there was a vague, half-formed desire in his heart that she should not marry his cousin. She would be less his friend if she were Felix's wife.

"Perhaps such a marriage might be good for Montvilliers," he said after a pause.

"I shall serve my country more directly by persuading you to do your duty, Maurice," she answered. "It is not only internal strife which is to be feared, but danger from without. In the past Montvilliers has fought for, and maintained, her independence, but our neighbors have not ceased to long for the possession of our fruitful soil, and our dissensions are their opportunity. Only last night a spy was caught in the streets and brought to the castle."

Maurice went to the window, and for some time stood looking down at the peaceful village he had loved so well. Here he had found happiness and the life he longed for. But beyond were the fruitful fields and green pastures of his native land, dearer to him than any other land, though he had no desire to rule it. Did it not rest with him to save this land from the enemies who had so long sought to lay a conquering hand upon it? Immediately below him, lounging in the court-yard, were some of the soldiers of Christine de Lianconrt's escort, proof that there were men armed and ready to fight for their freedom as their fathers had done. Duty seemed to present itself with a new meaning to Maurice, and, as though Heaven itself would send him a messenger in this crisis of his life, just then a cassocked and hooded priest came slowly in at the gates.

"At least we will see what plots exist," he said presently, turning to Christine, "and also prove your cousin Felix. To-morrow I will ride with you to Vayenne. Leave me alone until then. A man does not break with so peaceful a life as mine has been without sorrow."

In an instant her manner changed. Stepping back she made a low curtsey. "Long live the Duke," she said quietly, and then left the room quickly.

She had conquered. He had promised to come to Vayenne. She could not tell which particular argument had forced him to this decision, she only knew that it had been far more difficult to persuade him than even she had expected. What would his answer have been had she told him that the fact of going to Vayenne was only one step toward success, and only a small one—if she had explained that he spoke no more than the truth when he had said that he had been forgotten? Vayenne was not going to open her arms and shout a welcome to him until he had proved himself a man. She was thrusting upon him a great task, would he be able to perform it? She could have wished him different to what he was, but at least right was his, and opposition might stir him to great things. Of herself she thought little. For Felix she had little love, yet, were it for the good of her country, she would marry him. She was ready to make any sacrifice for the land she loved.

At the foot of the stairs a soldier saluted, and said that a priest craved an audience with her.

"What should he want with me?"

"He would say no more than that he had a message of importance. He is not of Passey, and carries the dust of a long journey upon him."

"I will see him. Bring him to the small room yonder, and see that we are not disturbed."

Christine turned from the window as the priest entered. Much dust was upon his cassock and cloak, and the hood, which he did not remove, partially concealed his face.

"You have travelled far," she said.

"From Vayenne," he answered.

"From Father Bertrand?"

"No, mademoiselle; from one far humbler than Father Bertrand, yet one who is wiser, perhaps, in your interests."

"He chooses a strange messenger."

"No stranger surely than the messenger chosen to ride to Passey and bid the young Duke to Vayenne. Besides, a priest may enter where a soldier would be refused. These are perilous times, mademoiselle, and I come to tell you so."

"In this matter you can tell me little I do not know," she answered.

"Then you do not ride to Vayenne to-morrow?"

"Yes—with the Duke." And she watched the priest closely to see if he were astonished at this information.

"With the same escort as came with you to Passey?"

"I think I have sufficiently answered you," she said.

"Mademoiselle, I have travelled all night to serve you. You must not ride to Vayenne to-morrow. It has been arranged that your party is to be attacked by a strongly armed party of robbers, and defeated. Your soldiers will make a show of fight, but for the most part they are bought men. You will escape, there is no desire to hurt you, but the Duke will be slain."

"You shall tell this to the captain of our escort."

"One moment, mademoiselle," he said as she moved to the door.

"Ah! you are afraid to let the captain and his men hear your story," she said contemptuously.

"They would probably kill me, and that would hardly help you," answered the priest quietly. "Count Felix has determined that the young Duke shall not enter Vayenne. I had the story from one who is well known to you, mademoiselle—from Jean, the dwarf of St. Etienne."

"A fitting story from such a madman," she laughed. "How came he to persuade a priest to be his ambassador?"

"I am not a priest." And Herrick threw back the hood from his head.

Christine took one step toward him, and gazed into his face.

"The spy!" she said.

"Mademoiselle, do I look like a spy? Do I act like one? Last night I was locked in the South Tower, a place of ill omen, as you know. To be his messenger the dwarf released me by a way known to him alone. I have ridden hard all night to bring this warning to you. All roads were open to me; I need not have taken that to Passey were I not desirous of serving you."

"You shall tell this story to the captain," she answered. "It is for him to weigh its merit."

"As you will, mademoiselle. Heaven grant he is an honest man."

She went to the door, and, calling a servant, bid him fetch the captain of the escort; nor did she speak to Herrick until the captain entered the room.

"Do you know this man, Captain Lemasle?" she asked.

" *The Spy!* " *she said.*

Gaspard Lemasle was not a very observant man, and the priest's dress deceived him.

"No, mademoiselle," he answered.

"He comes to Passey with a strange story."

"I have no great love for priests," returned the captain, "and saving your presence, mademoiselle, have often known them to tell strange stories."

In as few words as possible, Herrick repeated his tale.

"Do you say that I and the men I command are traitors?" Lemasle burst out angrily when Herrick had finished.

"I say nothing against Captain Lemasle," said Herrick. "Not many hours since he toasted Mademoiselle de Liancourt with such enthusiasm at the Croix Verte, I could not believe him anything but an honest man."

"You are no priest, and there is something in your voice that I remember."

"No, I am not a priest; you took me for a spy last night."

"I thought you safely caged in the South Tower."

"I was, captain. I am here to try and save the Duke."

"But how could you escape?" said Lemasle in astonishment.

"That I can tell you at another time."

Lemasle was silent for a few moments.

"It is indeed a strange story, mademoiselle," he said presently, "and truth to tell there are some in our company who would not be in it had I had the choosing."

"If there is any worth in the story, you must judge," Christine said. "For myself, I do not believe such tales easily, and at all hazards we ride to Vayenne to-morrow. It might be well to take this man with us. Unless he can prove his honesty, the castle can surely hold him though he has escaped once."

"And from the South Tower," muttered Lemasle.

"I ask nothing better than to strike a blow in your defence, mademoiselle," said Herrick.

She looked at him curiously for a moment, as even she had looked at him last night when he had picked up the fallen whip.

"I have no mercy for spies and traitors," she said slowly, "but prove yourself honest, and I may find a way to reward you."

Herrick did not answer, but stood with bowed head as she passed out of the room.

CHAPTER VI

As soon as they were alone, Gaspard Lemasle shrugged
his great shoulders and looked at his companion.

"I've always said that ugly little dwarf was not half
such a fool as folk thought him," he remarked. "You're
the first man I've ever known to get out of the South
Tower. How did you manage it?"

"You would not have me betray the dwarf?"

"Faith, I'm at a loss to know what I would have you
do, and for the matter of that what to do with you. You
don't seem to have made much impression on Mademoiselle, and it's not often one finds an honest man
masquerading as a priest. How do you call yourself?"

"Roger Herrick."

"Well, Monsieur Herrick, for the life of me I know
not whether to treat you as friend or foe."

"Give me the benefit of the doubt and think me a
friend. At least be friend enough to give me food and
drink, for I have touched neither since I dined at the
Croix Verte last night."

"Come with me," Lemasle answered. "I wouldn't
starve my worst enemy."

Life without its dangers would have seemed a poor
existence to Gaspard Lemasle, and a man who could
make light of danger was a man he was inclined to take
to his heart. Herrick appealed to him. Somehow he
had got out of the South Tower, and he respected him
for that. Last night he had carried himself well, and

shown no sign of fear, even when an infuriated mob was
bent on hanging him to the first convenient lamp bracket.
Now he had voluntarily come to Passey to accuse a
body of men of being traitors, knowing that he ran the
risk of being delivered up to their tender mercies, which
might reasonably result in a harder death than hanging
would be.   He was no common man this, and Gaspard
Lemasle watched his companion anxiously as he ate and
drank.

"You will not tell me how you escaped from the castle,
will you tell me what you were doing at the Croix
Verte last night?"

"I did nothing but dine, but I intended to sleep there,
to stay there, a peaceful traveller, for some days.   Going
for a short walk after dinner I was attacked in the
street, for the purpose of robbery I suppose, but finding
the task beyond them, one villain shouted out, 'Spy!'
and I was soon in the hands of an infuriated crowd.   I
believe I owe you my life, captain, for had you not been
at the end of the street I doubt whether I should have
escaped hanging."

"What were the men like who attempted to rob you?"

Herrick tried to give some idea of their appearance,
and succeeded in making Lemasle thoughtful for a
time.

"And you heard me get talkative over the wine in
the Croix Verte," he said presently.

"There was only a partition between us, and Father
Bertrand's voice, even when he speaks low, is penetrat-
ing.   So long as I overheard the conversation his persuasion did not seem to appeal to you, Captain Lemasle."

"You left before the end then?"

"I did not return to the room after we all went into
the passage to learn that the Duke was dead."

"You noticed the priest and me, did you take no note of the other men?"

"No. I judged that in Father Bertrand's eyes you were of most importance, and truly I thought little of what I had chanced to overhear until afterward. Being suddenly locked in the South Tower instead of sleeping in comfort at the Croix Verte is apt to set one thinking."

"And your conclusion, Monsieur Herrick?"

"We seem friends—need I deceive you?" Herrick answered. "I thought that Captain Lemasle's duty held him to Count Felix, but that in his heart he was desirous of serving the scholar of Passey because of Mademoiselle de Liancourt. His final decision I did not hear, nor do I know it now, yet Mademoiselle seems to trust him."

"And with reason," Lemasle answered. "I care not much whether we have Duke Maurice or Duke Felix, neither one nor the other can really fill the old Duke's place, but I would give my life in the defence of Christine de Liancourt."

"Then we are comrades, captain. I, too, am willing to die in her defence."

"In the name of all the gods, why should you be?" Lemasle exclaimed. "You have seen her twice, and she has scorned you twice. Do men sacrifice themselves for women who treat them so?"

"Some men, captain; some for love, some because it is in their blood. For myself, circumstance has forced me into this service. Long ago, perchance, my fathers were knights-errant, and their spirit lives in me."

"I'm inclined to think you a friend," said Lemasle slowly.

"Then treat me somewhat as a prisoner to-mor.ow,

and for greater care keep me near you and Mademoiselle.
You spoke of having men in your company whom you
would not have chosen. You shall find me no laggard
when the time for action comes."

"Very well, and I will arm you for that purpose; but
mark you, if I find myself mistaken, if you are a traitor,
I shall have no hesitation in running you through the
back."

"Had I found Captain Lemasle a traitor, I should
have had as little compunction. I go armed, you see."
And Herrick drew aside his cassock to show his weapons.

Lemasle looked at him, measuring him with his eye
from head to foot and from shoulder to shoulder.

"There would be a satisfaction in meeting you face
to face and trying strength with you," he said. "For
aught I know you may lack my skill, but I do not doubt
your courage; and if your story be true we'll see what
we can accomplish side by side to-morrow. You shall
seem like a prisoner until then."

So that night the key was again turned upon Roger
Herrick.

"For form's sake," Lemasle said by way of apology;
"to the man who can escape from the South Tower in
Vayenne there is no chamber in the Château of Passey
that can really be a prison."

Did ever man find himself in stranger circumstances,
Herrick wondered, as silence fell upon the château. A
few hours since he had been free to direct his steps
whither he would, even to-day he might have ridden
toward safety, and yet he was here a prisoner, pledged
if need be to draw sword to-morrow in defence of a
youth he had never seen, and a girl who had treated
him with contempt. That he, a man of peace, who had
practised sword play merely as a healthy pastime,

should draw in earnest, staking his own life against another's, was strange enough, yet this aspect of the case he hardly thought of; the reason for the action was uppermost in his mind, not the action itself. Would he have entered upon this perilous enterprise for any pale scholar in the world? What was it to him who ruled in Vayenne? He knew it was because of the woman that his whole heart and soul were in this venture. She had looked into his eyes, and in that moment had entered into his life as no other woman had ever done. It was more than the spirit of the knight-errant which prompted him, and he knew it, even when he thus answered Gaspard Lemasle. At some turning in Life's road, Fate waits for every man. Herrick had reached that turning, and had found his fate in a beautiful woman who despised him. As he lay down to sleep her face seemed to watch him out of the darkness, and in his dreams she seemed to smile.

The woman stood long at her window that night, looking across the silent, moonlit land which lay below and stretched peacefully away to the dim haziness of the horizon. She, too, had her dreams. Deep in her heart, dominating all the other impulses of her life, was the love of this fair land which lay at her feet. It had suffered invasion, blood had watered its fields, the wail of misery had been heard in it, but it had never been wholly conquered. If for a time the invader had triumphed, some strong hero had risen and brought salvation. Its dukes to-day were independent rulers. What did it matter if in certain ways that rule was harsh? What did it matter if something were lacking in their civilization and manners when compared with other countries and courts she had visited? Was it not the very lack of certain luxury that fostered a warlike spirit in the people? To-day the country was in danger of civil strife, and that would be the opportunity its enemies waited for. Christine believed that only in the succession of the rightful duke was real trouble to be averted. In some ways Maurice was weak, she did not attempt to hide the fact from herself, but the love of his country was in him; while to Count Felix, love of country seemed second to his love of power. He was cruel, and had many enemies, not least among them the Church, and it was easy to believe that such a rule as his would be might drive the people to re-bellion and to a petition for help from one or other of those states which, through the centuries, had looked upon Montvilliers with greedy eyes. To prevent this, should Felix become Duke, she was prepared to marry him so that the people's love might be strengthened. Of herself she thought not at all, and little of the prisoner whose dreams she filled. Had he come honestly to warn her, or was he but a unit in some great scheme against her hopes and ambitions? If he were an honest man, he was a brave one, but was he honest? This doubt was her last thought before she slept.

Morning came with a thin mist hanging over Passey and the low country around it, which the sun would scatter presently. There had been noise and clatter in the court-yard from an early hour, for Captain Lemasle had decided to start sooner than he had at first intended. But it was a morning of mishaps, first one man and then another finding something wrong with his horse or its harness, now a shoe loose which the smith must needs see to, or a saddle-girth which had worn to breaking-point and must be repaired before a start was made. At first Gaspard Lemasle cursed

these ill chances as he cursed some such small matter
every day, but presently he became suspicious, so
piecemeal were the difficulties sprung upon him, nor
did they cease until close upon the hour originally
arranged for the start. This was surely more than
mere coincidence, and Lemasle determined not to
bring Herrick into their company until the last moment.
When Christine de Liancourt came from the château
ready for the journey Lemasle made an opportunity to
speak to her apart for a moment.

"I fear, mademoiselle, that our friend brought us
news which is only too true," he said.

"Our friend!"

"Indeed, I believe he has earned the name," Lemasle
answered. "As I told you last night, I had intended
to make an earlier start."

"True, and have kept us waiting, captain."

"So many little misfortunes have happened to delay
us, that I cannot think they have chanced honestly,"
he answered. "The men did not intend to move until the time first named. Have you told the Duke of
Monsieur Herrick's coming and his message?"

"Herrick, is that his name? Yes; I have told him,
and, if possible, he is more incredulous than I am," she
answered. "This masquerader goes with us—where
is he?"

"I have thought it best not to let him join us until the last moment," said Lemasle. "Some of these
fellows will grumble at having a priest in the company
unless I mistake not. I pray, mademoiselle, that you
will let me set the order of this march in my own way,
and that you will pretend a regard for this same priest
even if you do not feel it. I would have him beside me
if the worst comes, as I fear it will."

"So be it, Captain Lemasle; you are responsible _or our safety. I will tell the Duke."

"I shall do my best to bring you to Vayenne in safety," he said, saluting her.

The word to mount was given, and then Lemasle waited with his arm through his horse's bridle until the Duke and Christine were in their saddles, waited until they had bid farewell to old Viscount Dupré, who stood bareheaded upon the steps by the main door, and then he turned sharply.

"Where is this laggard priest?" he shouted.

"What priest?" said one man.

"We want none in our company," said another.

"That's true, comrades," Lemasle returned, with a pretence of grumbling with them, but speaking loud enough for Christine to hear. "Mademoiselle must needs carry a priest with us to Vayenne since we have not enough there already."

The sudden appearance of Herrick from an inner court-yard, mounted on a strong horse, prevented further words. His hood was drawn close over his head, and just raising one hand in a benediction, to emphasize his office, he rode to the side of Mademoiselle de Liancourt.

At a sign from Lemasle, Christine rode forward, the Duke and Herrick on either side of her, then vaulting to his saddle he placed himself at the head of the cavalcade, and followed them through the gates.

The old Viscount cried feebly "Long live the Duke!" and the cry was taken up by the few serving-men who were in the court-yard.

"Long live the Duke!" cried Lemasle in stentorian tones, and the company of horseman shouted in so genuine a fashion that Christine glanced at Herrick to see if this burst of loyalty had any effect upon him. He did not meet her glance and was apparently unconscious of it.

Most of the villagers, men and women, had already gone to their daily work in the fields, but the few who were in the streets also cried long life to the Duke, and bowed before him as he passed.

"It is a faint promise of what shall soon thunder out through the streets of Vayenne," Christine said, turning to him.

"It may be, yet my imagination does not seem to catch the sound of it," he answered. "In Passey they have learned to love me, that is why they shout, not because I am a Duke."

Once free of the village the pace was quickened, but the same order was maintained. Christine rode between the Duke and Roger Herrick, some little distance behind them rode Lemasle alone, the body of horsemen riding as many paces in the rear. However grave his suspicions might be, he showed nothing of it to his men.

"I ride 'twixt Church and State, comrades—a perilous position," he said to them, and he laughed as a man will laugh in a tavern when the wine flows freely and ribaldry is in the jests. He feigned a careless attitude that none might think him over-cautious.

It was Christine who really set the pace, and some miles had been traversed before the sun finally dispersed the mist. They went by the highroad, not by the way Herrick had travelled, but neither horseman nor pedestrian had been met. There were few who had business with Passey, and the road was ever a lonely one. At first it ran a straight and direct course across low, flat country, where there was no place for a lurking enemy to hide; then it wound round the foot of low hills to avoid steep ascents, and here were scattered trees, and undergrowths which descended to the roadway. Here it was that Lemasle lessened the distance between himself and the three leaders; and his eyes glanced sharply from side to side, while his ears were sharp set to catch any sound above the jingle of the harness of those who rode with him. Had he trusted a single man of his company, he would have sent him in front, but there was none he dared to send, nor could he go himself, since he alone was between the Duke and his companions and those whom Herrick had declared were traitors. If in truth the death of the Duke had been determined upon, it might most easily come from one of the traitors who rode behind him. . Lemasle, indeed, feared his own men more than the robbers who were to attack them.

From underneath his hood, Roger Herrick's eyes kept sharp watch, too. The road dipped gently for half a mile or so, and then ran darkly into a deep forest which stretched away on either hand. Herrick glanced back at Lemasle, and noted that he rode as one ready for emergency. It was evident that he was prepared to find danger lurking in the forest, and Herrick made sure that the revolver was ready to his hand and his sword loose in its scabbard.

Christine saw that backward glance, and noted every movement of her companion.

"Is this where you would have us believe danger lies?" she asked, turning to Herrick.

"I know not, but it is a likely place," he answered. "It is well to be prepared."

It was twilight in the forest, so closely were the branches laced overhead. Here and there a ray of sunlight struck downward into the gloomy aisles carpeted with the successive leaves of many winters, but it only served to make darker the distance beyond. Silence reigned, too, save for the jingling harness; even the sound of the horses' hoofs was deadened almost to nothingness at times, so deep was the road in leaves in many places.

Christine pulled in her horse to a walking pace. She had put her question to Herrick in a contemptuous tone. She meant him to understand that she did not trust his story, and yet her sudden action seemed to indicate that she was not so incredulous as she appeared to be.

For some time they went forward in silence, and then, as though it were at the end of a long tunnel, there was a patch of sunlight before them—not the end of the forest, but a wide clearing in its midst. When they were within a dozen yards of the opening, Herrick suddenly made his horse bound forward that he might be the first to come out into that open space. He could not have explained why he did so. He saw no more indication of danger here than he had seen at any other point of the journey, but an overmastering impulse seemed to compel his action, even while he was conscious that it might be misconstrued by those he had promised to serve. He had just time to note that several roads met at this clearing, when a bullet sang past his ear, cutting a piece of cloth from his hood. In an instant Christine turned her horse sharply aside as though to throw herself before the Duke, while Lemasle with a great shout to his men charged into the open.

"Forward!" he cried, for the clearing was now alive with men, some on horse and some on foot; and then as the troopers thundered after him, he spurred his horse dexterously to one side and let them rush past him. The next moment he and Herrick were beside the Duke

and Christine, while the robbers and the escort met
in the centre of the clearing.

"Be ready!" Lemasle whispered a moment later.
"You were right, Herrick. These scoundrels only
make a pretence of fighting, and these are no robbers.
This is rank treachery, and, by Heaven, some of them
shall pay the price in full."

No shots were fired; in such a *mêlée* that would have
been dangerous among men who had no desire to harm
one another, and never a blow was struck until he who
was struck at was ready to parry it. Lemasle cursed
underneath his breath, and Herrick waited, his naked
sword in his hand.

"It is the Duke's life you defend," whispered a voice
behind him.

"I know, mademoiselle," he answered, without turning his head.

"Ready!" shouted Lemasle.

The troopers were beaten down, some sorely hurt to
all seeming, while others fled into the woods. The robbers sprang forward toward the Duke and his companions, yet still they did not fire.

"Back, Christine—behind us!" the Duke cried. "We
three may yet teach these scoundrels a lesson." And
he struck the first earnest blow that had been dealt that
day, and the foremost man who rushed upon them fell
with scarce a groan.

"How long have you turned a thief on the highway?"
shouted Lemasle as a horseman came at him. "You
looked more honest when I last saw you in your soldiers'
dress in the Castle of Vayenne than in this disguise, and,
faith! I didn't love you even then."

The joy of fighting was upon Gaspard Lemasle, and he
laughed as he furiously struck this man from his saddle.

For one instant Herrick hesitated as the rush came. The first man who jumped at him to drag him from his horse, he struck at with his sword hilt, even as though his hand held no sword—struck, as an Englishman will strike, with his fist. For a moment there was a reluctance to shed blood, but only for a moment. Not far below the surface lies the fighting instinct in every man, the greedy lust for it, once the blood is up. This first adversary fell back stunned, but would rise again; the next fell with his head nearly severed from his body. How long he struck, now to right, now to left, hearing Lemasle's panting laugh as he got breathless with his work, and answering with laughter just as savage, he did not know; but suddenly there was a cry behind him—a cry, a shot, and an oath cut short in its utterance.

Some of their enemies had crept round to take them in the rear. One man had fallen on his knee, taking deliberate aim at the Duke, and even as his finger moved to pull the trigger, Christine saw him, and fired at him. The smoking revolver in her hand told the story.

"A dash for it and we may yet win through," said Lemasle in a hoarse whisper. "It's our one chance," and seizing Christine's bridle he spurred toward the road which lay opposite him.

The Duke and Roger Herrick spurred forward too, but a moment later, and in that moment the robbers managed to cut them off.

"The road to the right," Herrick whispered, wheeling his horse round sharply.

The manœuvre was unexpected by the robbers, and Herrick and the Duke found the road clear before them, and dashed along it. Then a shot rang out, and the Duke's sword fell from his hand.

"Are you hit, sir?" Herrick said.

"Yes. It's nothing," but even as he spoke he swayed in his saddle.

Herrick had caught his arm to hold him steady, when there was a second shot and the Duke's horse stumbled.

"Go on, and save yourself," Maurice said faintly.

The sound of galloping horses was now on the road behind them, the Duke's horse stumbled again, nearly to its knees. It was evident that it could go no farther. There was not a moment to lose. Slipping his arm round the wounded man, Herrick drew him from his saddle, and managed to lift him in front of him onto his own.

"We'll cheat them yet!" he cried as, in spite of its double burden, the good horse galloped forward.

CHAPTER VII

THE wounded man had fainted, and lay a dead weight in Herrick's arms. It was no easy task to hold him securely in his place and at the same time urge the horse forward at its topmost speed. Herrick knew that this must be a race for life, yet his heart leaped with excitement as the splendidly powerful animal he rode made light of its double burden, and with neck outstretched went on at a swinging gallop. To Herrick's surprise and relief no further shots were fired. The men who followed had only revolvers, probably, and the distance was too great for them to be effective. On they went, the trees by the wayside literally flashing past them, the long road before them with never a turning to right or left. Glancing back, Herrick saw that at least half a dozen men followed, all well mounted, and riding as though prepared for a long stern chase. For some time the distance between hunted and hunters did not seem to lessen at all. This was something, but it was not enough. There was no shortening in his horse's stride as yet, but the double burden would certainly tell its tale presently. How long was the race to last, and where was the goal of safety? Since they were upon a road at right angles to the one by which the cavalcade had entered the forest, Herrick knew that they might have many miles to traverse before they reached the open country. When they had entered the forest he had noted how it stretched away on either side, and that the chase should happen here instead of in the open had its advantages. If he could distance his pursuers sufficiently, he might chance upon some deep green glade down which safety might be found. In the open, it was true, some town, or village, or other place of refuge might present itself, but who could say that, for the young Duke, escape from one enemy might only mean falling into the hands of another? Though no fatalist, Roger Herrick had a creed that what was, was best; that come life or death, the circumstances mattered little so that honor was clean. Fear touches such a man with difficulty, and he is ever good friend or dangerous enemy, as the chance may be. And where there is no hampering fear, no vain longing for different circumstances and thought of what might be done in them, a man's resourcefulness has full play. This race was on a forest road, therefore Herrick's whole mind was concentrated on how this fact might be used to advantage. There was a turn in the road in the far distance that might be in his favor, since for a few moments, at least, he would be out of sight of his pursuers. Round such a bend in the road it might be possible to plunge suddenly into the depths of the forest. By the roadside, too, there was now a strip of turf, another point in his favor, for the sound of the beating hoofs of his horse would be deadened to those behind.

As Herrick turned his horse on to the turf he glanced back. It would seem that his pursuers were conscious that he had a chance of escape, for they were riding hard now, and the distance between hunters and hunted had lessened materially. One man, indeed, mounted upon a speedy animal, was overhauling him rapidly. In a few moments he would be close enough to fire. Such a risk must be avoided at all hazards. Herrick shifted the position of the unconscious man a little, so that he could

have his right arm free, but the movement had the effect
of slackening his horse's pace for an instant. The man
behind noticed this and shouted to his companions in a
triumph which was short-lived, for Herrick had turned
and fired at the horse, which reared up suddenly, beating the air with its forelegs for a moment, and then rolled
over with his rider. The shot startled his own horse, and
he plunged forward, sweeping round the bend of the
road with as gallant a stride as that with which he had
begun the race. The road turned again to the left, then
sharply around to the right to avoid a sudden shoulder of
rising ground, and beyond there was a dip in the forest, a
narrow, winding way going down into thick undergrowth.
It was not a path Herrick would have chosen, but the
winding road might lead the pursuers to suppose their
quarry was still in front of them, and he could feel that
the double weight was beginning to tell upon his horse.
His stride had quickly shortened after the sudden burst
on being startled by the revolver shot.

As Herrick plunged deeper into the undergrowth, he
heard his pursuers gallop past. There was no knowing
for how long they would be deceived. Two hundred
yards of straight road would betray his subterfuge at
once, and how near that piece of straight road might be
Herrick did not know. He rode his horse deeply into
the thicket, and then turned along a narrow green glade
which ran back parallel with the way they had come.
For some while he followed this path, scheming as he
went. When the disappointed hunters returned they
would almost certainly discover this way. How could
he deceive them? He urged his horse into a gallop
again.

"We will win now, my gallant beauty," he whispered.
He checked him presently, and turned sharply from the

path in the direction of the road, letting the horse walk carefully among the fallen leaves. When he saw the road, Herrick halted and listened. Save for the murmur of wind in the trees there was no sound. He walked the horse to the edge of the road, and looked to right and left. There was no one in sight, so he crossed it and plunged quickly among the trees on the opposite side.

All this while, so far as he could tell, the wounded man had neither uttered a sound nor made a voluntary movement. Herrick now began to wonder whether he had been carrying a dead man before him. The roadway was left far behind them, for a time at least they were safe; and coming to a small opening, across which a little brook ran its narrow, bubbling course, Herrick dismounted, and, laying the young Duke on the grass, began to examine him. The bullet had passed through his arm and torn an ugly wound in his side. It had bled freely, and Herrick did not think the bullet had lodged in the body. He had laid him down upon the bank of the brook, and made shift to cleanse the wound as best he could, with naught to hold water but his hands, held cupwise. He bathed his face, too, and contrived to get a little trickle of water between his lips.

With a sigh Maurice opened his eyes presently, but did not speak. He looked at Herrick without any recognition in his look, and then he closed his eyes again. The horse had gone to a little distance, where a break in the bank enabled him to get at the water and drink; now he came back, and nosed the prostrate man, perhaps looking for a caress for his part in the day's work. The touch roused Maurice again.

"Where's Christine?" he murmured.

"Safe with Gaspard Lemasle."

"Who are you?"

"Roger Herrick."

"I don't seem to remember," he answered feebly.

"You have been wounded," Herrick answered. "I will dress it as best I can, and then——"

"Yes; then call Christine."

Herrick tore out the sleeve from his own shirt. He could bind up the wound after a fashion, but what was he to do then? It was evident that his companion was not in a state to be carried farther on horseback, and where was he to get succor? They could hardly hope to remain there long undiscovered, and which way to go for help Herrick did not know. They had no food, either, of any sort. Even if the wounded man became conscious enough to know the dire straits they were in, it was doubtful whether he knew anything about the forest roads. Had he not been a virtual prisoner at Passey for years?

As he was binding the linen round the wounded arm he glanced at Maurice to see if he winced with pain. His eyes were open, staring not at him, but beyond him, in that uncanny fashion which compels one to turn and see upon what such a look is fixed. Herrick was turning when his arms were suddenly seized from behind and a cord drawn tightly round them, while rough hands grasped his shoulders and pulled him on to his back.

"Tie his feet, too," said a man, suddenly springing across the brook. "Whom have we here?"

"A wounded man," said Herrick, without attempting to struggle. He might want all his strength for that presently.

"Ay; and for a priest you're a poor hand with a wounded man," was the answer.

For a moment Herrick thought they had fallen into the hands of their pursuers after all, but as a score of men surrounded them he saw they were not those who had attacked them at the clearing. This surely was a band of real robbers.

The man who had stooped down to look steadily into Maurice's face suddenly stood upright.

"Quick! Fetch the old mother," he said excitedly to a youth near him; and then looking down at Herrick he said, "Who is he?"

"A wounded man. I never saw him before to-day."

"How came he thus and how did you come into his company?"

"An attack in the forest, and I helped him to escape. It was a small affair; but if you have skill in such matters, pray bind up his wounds without delay. He is weak from loss of blood."

The youth returned, hurrying forward an old woman with bent form, and chin and nose which nearly met, as they seemed to peck at each other continually.

"Mother, look into this man's face," said the man who seemed chief of this forest band.

"Ay, sore hurt he is," said the old hag, bending over him, "but I have salves—I have salves."

"But his face, mother; who is he?"

> "A wounded man
> In a forest lay,
> Who the fates decree
> Shall be Duke one day,"

chanted the old woman in a piping key. "I saw it all as the flame died out of my fire last night. I have salves; let me fetch them. There is money, much money in this."

"Mother, is it not he of Passey?"

"Who the fates decree
Shall be Duke one day.

"Let me go. Would you have him die when there
is so much money in the air?"

The robbers were evidently half afraid of this old
beldame, who probably found her pretended witchcraft
and doggerel rhymes profitable.

"The mother speaks truly," said Herrick.   "It is he
of Passey. Duke even now, and there is much money
for those who help him."

"You said you never saw him before to-day."

"I spoke truly also."

The man turned away, and, beckoning the other men
round him, talked eagerly for a few moments, and with
many gesticulations.   When the old woman returned,
some of the men went quickly into the wood, and the
chief turned to her.

"Quickly, mother, and so that he may travel."

"Whither?"

The man stretched out his arm.

"Cannot you see the money in that direction?"

"Ay, if you can reach it, plenty of it; but that is not
the road to Vayenne, and there is money that way, too,"
said the woman, bending over her work.

"As much?" queried the man.

"Why ask?   Is it not the Vayenne road he must take
so that he may be Duke one day?"

"Make up another riddle against that time, mother,
and read my fate."

"It would put the fear of God in thee, Simon; thou
art best in ignorance."

The man turned away with an uneasy laugh.   He,

too, feared the old woman, although he would not have it appear so. He stopped to look down at Herrick.

"What can we do with the priest?" he murmured to himself, but not so softly that another behind him did not hear.

"Why not knife him?"

"Ay; why not?"

"The mother loves not such," urged the man, "and alive he will be dangerous."

"I like not knifing a man when the blood is cold in me," Simon answered.

"I'll do it, I have no such sentiment."

"Time enough," Simon said. "Besides, since he helps this scholar of Passey, he's no friend to him of Vayenne." And then, turning to Herrick, he went on: "I marked you when you came to the brook; you rode not like a priest."

"What matter how I rode so we have fallen among friends?" said Herrick.

"Friends? Hardly that; but at least we would not let the wounded man die. Dead he is but carrion as any other man; alive he is worth much gold. There are those beyond Montvilliers who will pay handsomely for him."

"Beyond Montvilliers! You would sell him into the hands of his country's enemies? That were traitor's work indeed!"

"The country's rulers would hang me to the first tree if they caught me. To-day the game is mine; to-morrow——" And he snapped his fingers and laughed.

He walked away, and soon afterward the men who had gone into the woods returned with a rough litter. Into this the young Duke was carefully lifted, and

whether he were conscious or not Herrick could not
tell.   These traitors would keep him alive if they could;
at least there was more hope with them than with those
others who were bent on slaying him, and Herrick found
what consolation he could in the thought.

Lifting his head to watch what was happening about
the litter, he had not heard any one approach him until
he found the old hag bending over him.   Behind her
stood the man who wished to knife him.   They had
come upon him stealthily, so that Simon should not
stay their crime, Herrick supposed, and he gave himself up for lost.   Indeed, he saw the knife in the man's
hand.

"This one has no hurt," said the old woman, bending
over him.

"Not yet, mother.   Is he to live to tell of what we
do?"

"Give me a moment, my son," she answered, and
closed her eyes.

"Quickly, mother, or Simon will save him.   He likes
not the deed, but he will be glad enough when it is
done."

Herrick was conscious that a shout might save him;
yet he did not utter it.   The face of the hag seemed to
fascinate him with its closed eyes, so hollow that they
were almost like empty sockets, and its mumbling
mouth and pecking nose and chin.

"Quick, mother!" said the man impatiently.

"I cannot see him dead, my son, yet cannot I follow
his course.   Put up the knife.   He must be left to
chance."

"Curse the fates that mock you," said the man in a
rage.

"Mock me!" screamed the hag, striking him across

the face with her bony hand. "Mock me—me! Get you gone, or I'll set the finger of death on you or ever the year is out. Simon, I say, Simon! This sham priest must be left to the will of Fate. I have said it."

Simon, who had mounted Herrick's horse, made a sign and three men carried Herrick to a tree at the edge of the open. To this they bound him in an upright position, winding and knotting the rope tightly from his feet upward—so tightly that he could not move an inch either way. The end of the rope they wound round his throat but loosely.

"Fate must set you free if she will," said the hag.

Simon did not look at him. It seemed to Herrick that he would not willingly have treated him thus, but that fear of the old woman compelled him. He set the man who had wished to use the knife to be one of the litter-bearers, that he might have no chance of returning and doing the captive harm.

"March!" he said, and placing himself at the head of the band he led them through the trees, following no path but in the direction he had pointed, the way where much money lay, and which did not lead to Vayenne.

The hag stood by the brook watching them go, stood there for some time after the last of them had disappeared among the trees; then she entered the forest in the opposite direction, mumbling and gesticulating as she went.

Save for the wind in the trees there was no sound, and even the wind sank presently into silence. Twilight came, then darkness. A numbness crept through Herrick's frame, and there was a strange singing in his head. His throat was parched, for in ministering to his wounded comrade he had forgotten to drink himself.

Then came intervals of forgetfulness, then clear consciousness again, and a feeble effort to free himself.   In the little patch of night sky overhead shone a star, the North Star surely.   That way lay England—home—and in a moment all his life seemed to flash past him.   Was it his throat that swelled, or was it that the rope was tightening?   Then came oblivion!

CHAPTER VIII

INTO Herrick's oblivion there crept dreams presently. No longer was the rope tightening round his throat; his limbs began to lose their numbness, and a grateful sensation of warmth ran through them. There was movement about him; hands, gentle hands, touched him; and eyes looked steadily at him—not the eyes of one who was ready to strike with a knife, not the eyes of an old hag. These were beautiful eyes, with kindness in them, the eyes of a woman who had compassion. They were surely a woman's fingers, too, which had gently eased the rope tightening at his throat.

"His is more a weary sleep than exhaustion now."

The voice came suddenly to the dreamer's ears out of the darkness. Then for an instant there was light about him, dancing flames full of life, and huge, distorted shadows moving over him. Contentment was here, and sleep—sleep with no more dreams in it.

When he opened his eyes again, they fell upon a small square patch of daylight; then, turning his head, he saw a red glow a few paces from him, and the fragrance of burning peat was in his nostrils. He did not seem to be dreaming now, yet he knew not where he was, nor how he had come there. He remembered riding hard. Where? Why? Some run over difficult country with the hounds in full cry! He had been leading the field; that he recollected, and then—a rope at his throat. In a flash it came back to him—the escape, the recapture, the wounded man, the threatening knife, the bound, aching limbs, the star above him in the night sky. What had happened since? Where was he?

He raised himself on his elbow, and the movement disturbed a figure sitting near the peat fire.

"So you are awake at last?"

"Lemasle!" said Herrick as the man bent over him.

"Ay, the same; ready for another fight against odds, if need be, but sore weary of watching a sick man. The gods gave me not the gift of nursing."

"Is it the dawn coming in at the window yonder?" Herrick asked.

"Yes; and a plaguey wet dawn, too. You can hear the rain on the roof, hear it hissing as it falls down the chimney onto the peat. It rained all night and all yesterday."

"Yesterday? There was sunlight when we came upon the clearing, and——"

"That was the day before," Lemasle answered. "'Twixt fainting and sleeping you've lost full twice round the clock."

"Tell me," said Herrick.

"Have you all your wits?" Lemasle asked.

"Yes; and strength returning slowly. Let me lie here and listen."

"You remember how we dashed forward when the scoundrels began to creep up behind us?"

"Yes; and we were stopped from following you."

"For a time we were unconscious of that," said Lemasle. "There were galloping horses behind us, and without looking back I shouted to encourage you. When I did glance behind, I saw that we were pursued, but of you I saw nothing. I bade Mademoiselle ride on,

and then I turned, firing upon those that followed.
Faith, playing the traitor breeds cowardice in a man.
There were four of them, yet they halted. If they
wanted to make an end of me, now was their opportunity, I cried, and they hung back like curs from
the challenge. One man I hit, his hand went suddenly
to his face, where I think the bullet struck him, and he
pitched into the ditch by the roadside, what soul he
was possessed of going quickly to its judgment. The
rest turned and galloped back the way they had come.
Perchance they had no firearms, perhaps they saw that
the Duke was not with me, but the laughter I sent
after them should have made them fight had they been
men. I did not know the country reared such curs as
these. So I rode on to Mademoiselle. I would have
taken her to safety ere I returned to look for you, since
I hold that a man's first duty is toward the woman he
has in his keeping, but she would not. Faith, Herrick,
I think she still believed you half a traitor, and I did
you justice arguing your cause for full an hour as we
went carefully among the trees in search of you. But
I talk. It is you who should tell me your tale first."

"Finish, captain. I have wit enough to listen, but
hardly to talk much yet."

"Is the Duke safe?" asked Lemasle.

"Wounded, but not to the death; and I saw his hurt
attended to. Finish your tale, captain."

"We had to go carefully," Lemasle went on, "for the
scoundrels were still searching in the forest. More than
once we only just escaped their notice. Mademoiselle
took courage from this, for she argued that they had not
got the Duke. For none other of us would they have
troubled to look so long. Toward evening we came
upon a hag gathering sticks, and questioned her whether

she had seen or heard aught. The old beldame muttered that her eyes were bad and her hearing worse
and all she could see and hear were things that should
happen in the future. She held out her dirty palm
for silver that we might have our fortunes told, and
I was minded to let her tell them, for love would certainly have been in them and perchance set Mademoiselle thinking in my direction. Mademoiselle would
have none of it, however, and we got a shower of curses
instead of a blessing. It was growing dark when we
chanced upon the hut of a charcoal burner, this place
where we now are. It was empty, but the peat was
smouldering in the corner, so we waited, stabling our
horses in the shed without. The man would return
shortly, and he might have news. There were two men,
and when they came they made us welcome, but of news
they had none. They had been at a distance that day,
had neither seen any armed men nor heard the sound
of strife. But when I mentioned the hag, they immediately agreed that robbers had been in the neighborhood, for they knew this same old woman as being of
their company, a sort of mother witch among them,
and, more, knew the spot where they would most likely
have camped. One of the men stayed with the horses
lest in our absence they should be stolen, the other took
a lantern and led us to the place. There had been a
recent encampment, but we found nothing to help us,
and were returning across a little clearing when the
feeble light of the lantern fell upon a tree beside us, and
there was a man tied—dead, we thought. Your head
had fallen forward, Herrick, so that the rope, though
loose about your neck, pressed on your throat. Had we
not found you, I warrant you would have been past help
before morning. They were tender hands that lifted

your head and deft fingers that undid the rope about your neck. Faith, I was jealous of an unconscious man, and would fain have been in his place to have received such service. I quickly cut the cords that bound you, and the charcoal-burner and I carried you here; since when you have been faint and sleeping hour after hour till I wondered whether you would ever be yourself again."

Herrick got up slowly, stretched himself, and walked toward the fire.

"Is mademoiselle still here?" he asked.

Lemasle pointed to a rough door.

"There is a second room there."

As he spoke the door opened, and Christine entered.

"I rejoice to see you nearly yourself again. You have been most foully used."

Her face just then was like the face that had looked at him in his dreams. Herrick bowed somewhat stiffly and unsteadily over the hand she held out to him, for the ache was still in his limbs.

"Truly, mademoiselle, my service had come near to ending before it was well begun. Death has been hunting me more busily than I care for."

"What of the Duke?"

"He is alive," Herrick answered. "Mine is a tale you may well find difficult to believe."

"For unbelief, circumstances must be my excuse," she answered after a moment's pause. "There is yet time for repentance. Sit on this stool—you are still weak, I see—and tell us the story."

Herrick told what had happened from the moment Lemasle had made his dash across the clearing, repeated even the old hag's doggerel rhyme, and his own last consciousness of a star above him which pointed toward home.

"These thieves did not say to whom they would take him?" Christine asked him when he had finished.

"To the enemy who would pay highest. These robbers were in no doubt which direction to go. That a big reward would be paid for the Duke's person seemed well known to them. Have none been sent to spy in the enemies' borders, since it would appear spies are so frequent in Montvilliers?"

"We have ever fought our foe openly," she said, turning sharply from the fire by which she was standing.

"One must meet craft with craft," Herrick answered.

"Have you no word of advice, Captain Lemasle?" she asked.

The soldier shrugged his great shoulders, and walking to the fire, kicked back a piece of smouldering peat which had fallen from its place.

"Advice doesn't trip easily to my tongue at any time, and here there are so many considerations. Had the Duke fallen into the hands of those who attacked us, he would have been a dead man by now. I take it that our present position is an improvement upon that."

"They will certainly keep him alive," said Herrick.

"And therefore must travel slowly," said Christine. "We may overtake them."

"We are but two men, mademoiselle," Lemasle remarked. "To attempt the impossible is to court disaster. Besides, they have had many hours' start, and there is no certainty where they have gone."

Christine looked at Herrick, evidently asking his opinion.

"I should not shirk another desperate venture, mademoiselle," he said, "but there is wisdom in what Captain Lemasle says. To speak frankly, I do not know the real situation in Montvilliers well enough to give an opinion."

"And having heard it, you might have difficulty in understanding it," Lemasle muttered.

"At least you know that Count Felix has plotted the death of the young Duke," said Christine.

"That was the story which sent me to warn you," said Herrick.

"I have not believed that tale, I hardly credit it now," she went on, "but we know that the Duke's life has been attempted. Maurice dead, Felix becomes Duke. Montvilliers cannot be long without a ruler. Maurice in the hands of France or Germany is powerless; therefore this way Felix becomes Duke."

"Would not the people strike a blow for their rightful ruler?" Herrick asked.

"In their present mind they are more likely to listen to Count Felix. He is a strong man and has plenty of honeyed words when they fit in with his purpose. In Vayenne they hardly know Maurice, and the crowd likes a leader it can see; that is why I was so set on bringing him to the city."

"As the Duke is not dead, the Count may fear to move in this matter," said Herrick.

"You do not know him," Lemasle said.

"Even now some of these traitors have ridden back to Vayenne," said Christine. "While we talk, preparations may be going forward for Felix's crowning. Would I were a man!"

"What would you do, mademoiselle?" asked Herrick.

"Do! I would ride to Vayenne, throw this treachery in Felix's teeth, demand the Duke's rescue, set all the wheels of diplomacy turning, and, if need be, cry revolution in the streets."

"Mademoiselle might set the law aside that forbids women to mount the throne, and do all this herself," said Lemasle.

"I am no breaker of laws, captain; and even if I were, the citizens of Vayenne would not easily shout for me. A few—oh yes, there would be a few, but they would be of the rabble chiefly. I have no soul for such an enterprise."

"Yet you might go to the Count," urged Lemasle, "and demand justice for the Duke."

"And every courtier would urge my marriage with Count Felix," she said. "That way will they welcome me as Duchess, who would not draw a sword to place me on the throne. Such a marriage might bring peace. Were the Duke dead, I might be tempted to make it for my country's sake. As it is——"

"You hate such a marriage?" said Herrick.

"Yes; hate it. Only to save Montvilliers would I make it."

"Mademoiselle, if you bid me, I will go to Vayenne."

"You!"

"Think what you will of me, but at least have I not proved myself a man?" said Herrick.

"There was no mean thought in my mind," she answered. "But what would you do in Vayenne?"

"Why, even cast this treachery in the Count's teeth; let the city know that its honor is at stake, since the Duke is a prisoner; if need be, boast loudly of what I have done to save him, and perhaps ride at the head of that rabble you talk of."

"You would go to your death."

"If I care not, who is there to hinder me on that score?"

"It might be done," said Lemasle; "indeed it might,

mademoiselle. You and I could follow to the city. They will not harm you, and you would not go to the castle, where at present you might be unwelcome."

"I might go to the Countess Elisabeth, and——"

"And from thence let it be known that you were for Duke Maurice," cried Lemasle. "Faith, I see the Count 'twixt devil and deep sea already."

"We talk folly," said Christine.

"You must lend me a horse, Lemasle," said Herrick. "I must be there without delay. You must come slower, at mademoiselle's stirrup, unless you chance on a mount on the forest road."

"I'll see to it at once."

"No; it is folly," said Christine; but Lemasle had already gone.

"Won't you accept my service, mademoiselle?" said Herrick.

"You go to certain death."

"The death of a man has won a cause before this."

"But what part have you in the quarrels of Montvilliers," she asked—"you, a stranger? Why should you adventure yourself in such a cause?"

"Men are driven forward by all sorts of reasons," he answered carelessly. "The spirit of the wanderer brought me here; fate drew me into this quarrel, against my will, it is true, but I have a mind to see the end of it."

"You do not count the cost," she said eagerly.

"I do not think of it, mademoiselle."

"But you must. You shall not go!"

"You refuse my service?"

"Yes, because it is folly; there is no reason in it. Against your will you have played a part; they are your own words. Take one of the horses. Ride to the frontier. I will not have your death on my hands."

"It was against my will, mademoiselle, but it is so no longer. Would you have another reason for my service? A woman thought me a spy. I would prove her wrong."

"Believe me, I have already repented that such a thought was in my mind. Forgive me, and seek your own safety."

"Any other woman in the world may think or say what she will of me, and I shall not care," Herrick whispered.

Slowly she raised her eyes to his.

"So you looked at me, mademoiselle, in the Castle of Vayenne the other night, so you have looked at me in dreams since then. I would serve you to the death."

Lemasle burst suddenly into the hut. Talk of action excited him, and there were dangers ahead to appeal to him to the full.

"The horse is ready, Herrick—my horse. There is not a scratch upon him, for all the blows that were struck at him in the clearing. These good fellows, the charcoal-burners, have already a kettle bubbling over a fire in the shed without; you may scent the appetizing smell from here. Breakfast, and then——"

"But you are weak still," said Christine. "At least delay a day."

"I grow stronger every moment, mademoiselle. You have only to say you accept my service."

"I accept it for the Duke's sake," she answered, stretching out her hand; "for his sake and for my own."

There was a gentleness in her last words which made

Lemasle glance quickly at them, but Herrick did not notice the look as he raised Christine's hand to his lips.

In less than an hour Herrick was in the saddle.

"By good providence we shall meet in Vayenne," he said as the horse bounded forward down the narrow forest path.

"There goes a brave man," said Lemasle.

Christine did not answer. She stood at the door of the hut for some time after the horseman had disappeared among the trees, and there was color in her cheeks and tears in her eyes.

CHAPTER IX

FOR the great of the earth who die there is often less real mourning than for him who is of small account. To a throne there is always an heir ready, perhaps eager, to rule; but who shall step into the void of a sorrowing heart? The Duke lay dead in a darkened chamber in the Castle of Vayenne. Yesterday his word was law, to-day it was nothing. The very frown which had caused men to tremble, Death's fingers had smoothed out; and since love had played small part in the Duke's scheme of life, where should one find hearts that ached for him now? They would bury him presently with great pomp and ceremony in the Church of St. Etienne, where lay the dust of other Dukes, but to-day there was other business in hand. Outside the closed door two sentries stood, and there was silence in the corridor; but in every other part of the castle there was busy hurrying to and fro. To-day the new Duke must be welcomed. Count Felix had been issuing orders all the morning. From an early hour soldiers had been busy in the court-yards, and at intervals troops of horse-men and footmen had passed out of the great gate to take their appointed places in the city, there to wait long hours, and to grumble as men will who wait. In the great hall of the castle, where generations of fighters and feasters had quarrelled or made merry, a crowd of servants were making ready a great banquet; while courtiers, officers, and messengers passed to and from the suite of rooms which lay to one side of the hall. There was an air of expectancy about them all, anxiety and uncertainty in most faces. In one room sat Count Felix, at present the centre of this busy hive. To many it seemed only natural that he should sit in the place of the dead Duke, and they were careful that their manner should show what was in their minds. But there were others who made it clear that they looked on his commands as temporary, carrying authority only until the Duke came. Felix noted the attitude of every man, but to all his manner was the same. He was courteous, smooth-tongued, a little depreciatory of himself, and laid some stress upon the temporary nature of his position. He was a tall, dark man, dark eyes, dark hair, dark complexion; a strong and purposeful man with confidence in himself. The affairs of the state were at his fingers' ends; long ago he had gauged the character of every man, ay, and woman too, at the court; he knew both his friends and his enemies, and flattered them both, knowing well that such friends become slavish, while flattery may disarm the bitterest of foes. Very few had succeeded in reading the Count's character; he had been careful to conceal it from both friends and foes.

So he had done all that could be done to prepare a fitting welcome for the young Duke. If among the citizens there was no great enthusiasm for Duke Maurice, as some of his friends were careful to inform him, that was no fault of his; and neither by look nor gesture did he show whether he were pleased or not at this apathy on the people's part. His face was a mask, and only when he was alone for a moment did the anxiety and the excitement that were in him show themselves. His hands suddenly clenched, he took two or three rapid strides across the room, then sat down again, his eyes fixed on vacancy, deep in thought.

"Well! well!" he said as an officer came into the room.

"The sentry who was wounded last night is conscious, sir."

"I had forgotten. For the moment I thought you had come about another matter. Yes; I will come and see him. And the jailer, has he said anything?"

"Maintains that wings or a rope was necessary to reach the window, and therefore the prisoner must have had help from without. He declares there was no rope in the cell, and says he didn't notice wings on the spy. Those are his own words."

"It pleases him to be humorous over a serious matter," said the Count.

He had forgotten all about the escaped spy; now he remembered him, and began to speculate. Last night he had heard nothing of the arrest until they had come to tell him of the escape. Then he had been chiefly interested in the fact that a man had broken out of the South Tower. Examination had shown that one of the window bars was loose, but until the sentry could tell his tale, there was no certainty that the prisoner had escaped that way. Then the Count regretted the escape, because it robbed him of an opportunity of pleasing the people of Vayenne, whose hatred of spies was hereditary. It would have pleased him to gratify them by hanging this man high above the great gate. That would certainly have been his fate before ever he had chance to speak a word in his own defence. In the pressure of other thoughts the matter had slipped from his mind until the officer's entrance, and as is ever the case with an anxious schemer, he sought to fit this spy into the intricate design of his thoughts.

As the Count crossed the small court-yard toward the quarters where the sentry lay, he saw Father Bertrand, and ambling by his side was the dwarf of St. Etienne.

"Are we on the same errand, father?" said the Count.

"I am going to see the wounded sentry."

"Who is now conscious. We may learn something of this spy."

"Conscious!" exclaimed Jean. "Heaven be praised for that!"

"Why, what is it to you, fool?"

Jean looked at the Count with blinking eyes for a moment, and then said slowly:

"Much, truly. I am troubled this morning when I hear that a spy has half killed a sentry. I say to myself, 'That is one man less in the castle to defend it against its enemies.'"

The Count laughed at the dwarf's attitude and his air of wisdom.

"Ah, you say, 'What is one man?'" he went on. "The whole world is made up of one man after another. They all count. Why, to-day I'm worth more than the dead Duke yonder."

"There's truth in that," said the priest.

"And then when I come to the castle to see the poor soldiers, I——"

"Poor! Why poor?"

"Because they have to do what they're told and go where they're led, and God made men for better things than that. This wounded sentry, I find, is a particular friend of mine. He doesn't know it, but he is. That's the way of the world; we seldom do know our best friends. I've never spoken to him nor he to me, but I always look out for him, because his coat fits so badly. He's a poor figure of a man, your Grace, and an ill-fitting coat suits him. I will go with you and see how he does."

"Better run away, Jean, before I have you whipped."

"Whipped? For what, Lord Duke?"

"Silence, fool!"

"It may be, Count, that clearer insight is given to those the world calls fools," whispered Father Bertrand.

"That's a poor excuse for treason," said the Count; and then, turning to the dwarf, he went on: "The Duke comes to Vayenne to-day, Jean. Have you not seen the soldiers in the streets ready to welcome him?"

"Ah! what a fool am I!" laughed the dwarf. "I thought they were there to keep out any one else who might fancy himself Duke. I'll go and await his coming. But first, I pray you, let me see my ill-made friend. Nature has made such a mess of him. I doubt whether even the spy can have made him much worse."

"The fellow is an amusing fool, father. I've heard wise men talk more folly. Come if you will, Jean."

The sentry was conscious, but for all the Count's questions there was little to be got from him. He was standing with his back toward the wall when something fell on him and crushed him. He had no breath to cry out, and remembered nothing after the first thrust of the steel.

"Poor soldier!" muttered Jean.

"You saw no one run along the terrace?"

"No one," the man answered.

"And you heard nothing when you stopped beneath the South Tower?" asked the Count.

"No, sir," said the man faintly. He was weak, and

7

the Count turned away, followed by Father Bertrand and Jean.

"He is not such an ill-made fellow," the Count said, turning to Jean.

"Ah! but you and I see with different eyes," was the dwarf's quick answer. "You would call me ill-made."

"Strangely made," said the Count.

"Just so. Now I like twisted limbs, they're less common. Mark you, in a crowd there will be more turn to look at me than at you."

"And more will laugh at you," said the Count.

"Well, laughter's a good tonic," said the dwarf, and then sidling close to the Count, he went on: "Men such as I am see more than men such as you. I see ghosts in St. Etienne. I warrant you never saw them."

"Nor want to," Felix answered.

"See and hear them, eh, Father Bertrand?" Jean chuckled. "All the dead dukes who lie there, straight or with their feet crossed, have secrets to tell, and I listen. In the night St. Etienne is peopled with ghosts, and the great organ sings low to them, brave music, telling of great deeds done long ago, and of love that flowers and ripens into fruit beyond this world's time. Some day you'll hear it, only you'll have to lie under a stone effigy first, and maybe you'll tell me all your secrets then. I'll go and watch for the Duke, who is strangely late in coming."

The dwarf waddled across the court-yard, and presently passed out of the little postern beside the great gates. The soldiers laughed at him often, but none questioned his goings and comings. There was an old wife's tale among them that the presence of an innocent was lucky, and Jean had wit enough to be of service sometimes. He had carried a love message before now, and sometimes demanded that payment should take the form of a kiss from the maid. It amused him to see how reluctantly the debt was liquidated.

Outside the castle he went at a slower pace.

"One," he said, holding up a finger—"one, the poor sentry saw nothing, therefore I am still free to come and go. Two, the Count is clever making all this show for a Duke he never expects to arrive. Three," and he held up another finger for each number—"three, he's a fool because he thinks I'm a fool. Four, my uncanny talk of ghosts makes him shiver, so there's something of the coward in him somewhere. Five, the Duke is long in coming; has friend Roger failed, I wonder? I'll go and see what the crowd thinks of the new Duke. Truly he is coming to no rosebed, if the Count is to have a hand in the making of it."

The Count watched him as he went across the court-yard.

"Think you he is as great a fool as he seems, father?" he asked, turning to the priest.

"The crooked body may hold some wisdom which is beyond us. He may have visions."

"Even straight-limbed men have," was the answer. "Tell me, why did you come to visit the prisoner last night?"

"To make certain he was a spy. I know the breed, Count," said the priest.

"I would he were swinging over the gate yonder," said Felix.

"Ay; spy or no spy, it would have pleased the populace," said Bertrand.

"And served as a warning," returned the Count. "We shall have all sorts of wastrels begging favors of the new Duke."

"That depends."

"On what?" asked Felix.

"On the new Duke."

"True. He may be made of sterner stuff than we imagine." And the Count re-entered the castle.

"I trust not," muttered Father Bertrand as he went back to the lodging of the wounded sentry. "Pliability will suit us best just now, and a character which lacks resolution. Then——" His lips moved, but no uttered words came. He walked slowly, with eyes on the ground. Perchance he prayed silently.

Count Felix went back to his room, and sat there waiting. His attitude was expectant, and he listened for the shouting that might come in the city streets, for footsteps at the door which would surely come soon. He looked for a long time at a paper on his table—a list of names. He read each name carefully, calling to memory the man as he read it.

"Cut-throats all," he muttered, and then he laughed a little. "Why, the making carrion of them will bring me thanks. Gaspard Lemasle—he is different. He is ambitious. I must find a place for Gaspard Lemasle where he will easily make enemies. They shall destroy him."

Time passed slowly. The Duke was certainly late.

"Perhaps he refused to come," Felix murmured. "No; Christine would see to that. They cannot have failed; it was so easy a task."

The hours wore on toward dusk—long hours for those in the streets, for those in the castle, for Count Felix. The courtiers wondered and speculated. The Count's face was imperturbable. He had a dozen reasons to give for the delay. He gave them to friend and foe alike. No one hurried along the corridors, there was no need; all that could be done had been done. They could only wait and listen.

Lights were in the castle, and the Count was alone when hurried steps which he expected came to the door. A man entered, a swaggering giant at most times, but now travel-stained, with torn coat, and a streak of dried blood upon his forehead.

"Well, Barbier!" Felix cried, starting from his chair.

"Escaped."

"What!"

"They were ready," said the man. "We must have been betrayed. All fell out as we had planned, but Lemasle, and the Duke, and a priest——"

"Priest! What priest?"

"Some one Mademoiselle would bring to Vayenne," answered Barbier. "So Lemasle told us; but I warrant he lied, for this same priest was a fearless horseman, and wielded a sword that took its full toll of blood. We had surrounded them when Lemasle and Mademoiselle dashed through us, and we let them go, closing upon the Duke and this priest. In a moment they had turned, and were fleeing along the forest road. A shot wounded the Duke, another stopped his horse, but as it fell this priest lifted the wounded man before him on to his animal. We followed, but he outwitted us. He was no priest, I'll swear to that."

"A thousand curses on your blundering," said Felix. "He was wounded, you say?"

"Yes."

"To the death?"

"That I cannot tell," Barbier answered.

"I will tell you," said Felix. "He was. Do you understand? He was. He died in the forest."

"We searched. I have left them searching. We found nothing."

"Fool, you must find something. Is a man killed in

conflict always recognizable? Mar the face of some dead comrade, mar it effectually, and then come with your story to Vayenne. Trust me, it shall find easy credence. I will prepare Vayenne for it. Do you understand?"

"But this priest?"

"Curse him," said Felix. "Whatever may chance, I shall know that Barbier was one of the bravest in this forest fight. Having gone thus far, think you I shall turn back now? Here's to show you what a man may expect who is prompt in my service." And he placed a bag of coins in his hand. "Ride back. Answer no questions. Say 'The Count knows, ask him.' Do you understand, Barbier?"

"We shall find the body and bring it ere morning," the man answered.

"To horse, Barbier, Captain of the Duke's Guard. There is no time to lose."

The man saluted, and went quickly from the room.

For a moment the Count stood with clenched hands, and underlip tightly held between his teeth. Then he went out to meet the eager questions of those that waited.

That night there were again running feet through the streets of Vayenne, and men shouted as they ran: "The Duke is dead! The young Duke is dead!" And some were sad, while others rejoiced and spake no more of Count Felix, but openly called him Duke, and thought of the honors and rewards that should speedily fall to them. There were many who found no sleep that night in Vayenne.

CHAPTER X

AMONG those who found no sleep that night was Count Felix himself. A bold schemer of unbounded ambition, determined to allow no obstacle to stand in his way, he was at the same time both subtle and far-sighted. For years he had been preparing for this hour. He had ingratiated himself with the old Duke, who by word had virtually appointed him his successor. He had sought to draw to him all those who were prominent and powerful in the state. He had steadily besieged the affections of Christine de Liancourt. Had she been his wife, or had she even promised to marry him, he would at once have seized the throne, and any rising in favor of the scholar of Passey would have had poor chance of success. She was so well loved that she would have bound to him most of those who were at present his enemies. Christine, however, had persistently supported the claim of the Duke's son, in which Felix had applauded her; and when the time came, had urged that she should go to Passey herself to bring Maurice to Vayenne, since it was almost certain that he would refuse the crown unless strong pressure were brought to bear upon him. Such pressure Christine was certain to use, and not for an instant did Felix doubt that it would be used successfully. By supporting her in this way, Felix disarmed any suspicion she might have, and felt convinced that presently she would consent to marry him. In the meanwhile Maurice must not be allowed to enter

Vayenne. To aid him in this set purpose Felix had found a tool ready to his hand in Barbier, an adventurer who had enough crimes to his credit to hang him ten times over, and possessed of the doubtful virtue of loyalty to his employer, no matter how great a scoundrel that employer might be. It was Barbier who had chosen the men who should form the band of pretended robbers and those who should form Mademoiselle de Liancourt's escort. It was his own scheme, he declared to these men, but, as he explained to them, the Count would easily forgive such an affair, and the reward, if not openly given, would be ample. Some of the men may have had their suspicion that the Count knew of the plot, but it is certain that no one of them had a particle of evidence to justify any statement of the kind; nor had they any knowledge that their names figured on the list which Count Felix so carefully preserved.

To kill the young Duke on his journey from Passey to Vayenne seemed the simplest matter possible. That Christine had insisted on Gaspard Lemasle accompanying her as captain of the escort was a pity; but what could one man do against such a combination of enemies? Felix ranked Lemasle among his friends rather than his foes, and should the captain recognize any of his adversaries it would be easy to hang such traitors. It would not be difficult quietly to compass the death of Barbier himself if necessary.

So the Count saw no flaw in his plans. He felt secure, felt certain of grasping his ambition. Now the hour had come, and the unexpected had happened. Lemasle and this priest had succeeded in defending the young Duke. True, Maurice had been wounded, might indeed be dead, but there was no certainty. A body, marred past recognition, might convince the people, and the court, who had seen little or nothing of Maurice; it would be harder to convince Lemasle and Christine, but surely not impossible. This priest was the difficulty; he knew what had become of the Duke. Barbier had declared he was no priest. Who was he? Who was there who could have betrayed this secret to Maurice, or Lemasle, or to Christine? What tale had been told them? Certainly not the true one; only Barbier knew that. Count Felix still felt secure, but had he grasped his ambition? His fingers seemed to touch it, yet could they not grip it. Such success as this was worse than failure.

It was no time for hesitation. The news that the young Duke was dead was even now running through Vayenne like flame among dry sticks. In a few hours the people would have recognized fully that he, Felix, was Duke. The coming hours were precious, and no doubt of the truth of the news must be allowed to transpire. Lemasle and Christine would speedily return, and Lemasle had been captain of the escort and responsible for the young Duke's safety. Prompt orders were issued, therefore, that Captain Lemasle was to be arrested the moment he entered Vayenne, and orders were also given to arrest any priest entering the city, whether he came alone or in Lemasle's company.

Early in the morning father Bertrand came to the castle to protest against this second order.

"Many priests may enter Vayenne, coming and going about their duty," he said; "are they all to be arrested?"

"Yes, father, all," the Count answered. "They will easily clear themselves; but there is reason to believe that some miscreant—not a priest, probably, but arrayed as one—has had a hand in the young Duke's death."

Father Bertrand continued to protest, but the Count was firm yet courteous, and the priest returned thoughtfully to the Rue St. Romain. He, too, was a man of action, and the Count had raised his curiosity.

Soon afterward Count Felix left the castle on foot, and walked quickly to the Place Beauvoisin, which lay beyond the castle toward the North Gate. Here in times past the nobles had lived, but in these days the old houses there had meaner tenants—Jews who were accounted rich, and shopkeepers who either had made or were making money. There was an air of prosperity in the Place Beauvoisin except in one corner of it, where a faded house stood sideways behind a high wall. The Count entered the square by a narrow way near this house, which was his destination. His summons at a small door in the wall was quickly answered, and he entered without a word to the porter. Every one in the square knew that the beautiful Countess Elisabeth lived at the faded house in the corner, but probably no one knew that Count Felix was a constant visitor there.

The Countess rose from her seat to welcome him, and turned hastily to a young girl with whom she had been talking and laughing the moment before, telling her to go.

"I will send for you presently, Lucille," she said. Then when the door had closed she held out her hands to the Count. "I have been expecting you."

Felix bent over her hand for a moment.

"I come to you with all my joys and sorrows," he said, "with all my ambitions, my successes, and my failures."

"Yes; and I am glad. You know that, Felix," she answered. "To-day you touch your ambition."

"You have heard the news then? I sometimes wonder how news, bad news, can come into this sweet retreat."

"Bad news, Felix?"

"Is it not bad, since Maurice is dead?"

The woman looked at him for a moment, and then turned away.

"Why attempt to deceive me?" she said.

By common consent the Countess Elisabeth was pronounced beautiful. As a rule the beauty of really beautiful women is so marked in certain particulars that it excites criticism, and opinions will differ concerning it. But there is another kind of beauty, not so perfect, not comparable with any recognized standard, which nevertheless has something in it which appeals to all opinions. Countess Elisabeth was such a woman. She was fair, delicate-looking, and her coloring was wonderful; yet there was strength behind this seemingly fragile beauty—strength of purpose, strength of endurance. No one considered her of much importance in Vayenne. She seemed to live a retired life in the faded house in the Place Beauvoisin, her chief companion being a young girl, a distant relative, usually spoken of as Mademoiselle Lucille. Those who were inclined to be romantic gave the Countess a lover, some one in the past who had died or perchance proved faithless. They might have remodelled their ideas of her romance had they seen the color in her cheeks as she spoke to Felix.

"Does not the news spell fortune for you?" she went on after a pause. "All obstacles are removed by it."

"Yes. It seems so."

"Seems! What difficulty can remain?" And then she said suddenly, "You had no hand in his death, Felix?"

"No," he answered; "and yet your very question should show you something of the difficulty which still surrounds me. Others in Vayenne will ask that question, too, since the death occurs so opportunely for me."

"Why manufacture troubles?" she said. "Did ever a man yet step to a place of power without making enemies? I have always held that Maurice was not the man to reign in Montvilliers. His own father delivered the kingdom to you. Have I not urged you to take it when the time came, and chance a rising in Maurice's favor? It would never have come. Vayenne has looked upon you as the old Duke's successor too long."

"The way has always seemed easy when you have pointed it out to me," said Felix.

"Yes. I have been strangely generous," the Countess answered. "For your sake I have made no complaint when prudence suggested your marriage with Christine de Liancourt."

"You know, Elisabeth, that it is prudence a.one which suggests it."

"Yes; I have vanity enough to believe that." And there was the suspicion of a long sigh in her answer.

"Advise me, my dearest lady," he said, leaning toward her. "You are my strength, my living talisman. Shall I strike now or delay?"

"Delay! For what?"

"I have not seen Maurice dead. He may have escaped. There is always the possibility. If he were to return now, he would come wearing a halo of romance. Shall I strike or wait?"

"Strike, Felix."

"And Christine?"

"Is it necessary—now?" she asked.

"I fear so."

"Still I say strike, Felix."

"You give me courage," he said. "You give me hope. So it has ever been. An hour ago I was beset with doubts. They are gone. Love mocks at them."

He held out his arms to her, but she only gave him her hand.

"Nothing more at such a moment?" he said.

"It is a moment that there can be nothing more," she answered. "Remember, I do not urge your marriage with Christine now."

"It is necessary; believe me, I would not marry her if I could help it."

"So we come to the parting ways."

"But you have always known that such a marriage was inevitable if I would possess the throne in peace."

"Circumstances are changed, Felix; I do not know it now. My Lord Duke has chosen his Duchess. He may come to me for advice if he will; he must go to her for love."

"It is sacrifice. My love is here with you."

"Think so if it helps you, but it is my hand only, Felix."

"And for the first time in my life I find it hard and cruel," he answered, raising it to his lips.

She laughed, an unexpected laugh, as one may laugh at a grim jest which cuts deep into the very soul.

"I do not understand you," he said.

"Did ever a man understand a woman yet? Let it suffice that I have deeper learning, and understand you perfectly. Go, Felix. This is no time for such riddles as trying to understand a woman. Your strong hand is wanted at the helm of affairs now."

"Good advice again, but nothing more."

"Can a man have everything for the asking?" she

answered, and, laughing again, she passed from the room.

Felix went back to the castle, her advice ringing in his ears, all else forgotten for the moment. There was a subtle affinity between this woman and himself; he felt it, recognized it, bowed to it. She understood him, perhaps, better than any one else did. He felt better in her company, yet while he told her of his ambitions, there was much in his scheming which he dared not tell her. She was a good woman, and he had perception enough to think it strange that she should love him. Beyond that, his thoughts concerning her touched chaos, touched all that was most selfish in himself. He called it love, but there were moments when he understood himself well enough to know that such love as his, could she fully know it, might breed hate in her; and he would almost as soon have lost the crown as her good-will. Something of superstition there may have been in this; he had called her his living talisman, and the term had real meaning for him; perhaps deep down in his nature there were good inspirations which had never been granted an opportunity of rising to the surface.

To-day it was her advice that filled his thoughts. She, too, had called him my Lord Duke, even as Jean the dwarf had done. Was the spirit of prophecy in them both? Why had the dwarf called him so? Truly he was a fool, but might there not be method in such folly? He would see the dwarf and question him. So as soon as he returned to the castle, he gave orders that Jean was to be found without delay and brought to him.

The dwarf was sought for in the castle, in the Church of St. Etienne, and in the streets, but was nowhere to be found. He had been seen in the city during the morning, but no one could tell where he had gone. He was quite a public character in Vayenne, everybody knew him, but how he lived, or where he was to be found at any given moment, nobody knew. It was agreed, however, that there were times when he was not seen at all for days together. The failure to find him now only made the Count more eager to see him, and a diligent search went on throughout the day.

And all the while Jean sat in the corner of a room in the empty house by the wall, his legs doubled under him, his arms folded in his loose tunic, his head dropped forward upon his breast. He was as motionless as a squatting idol, and any one who had ever seen him thus might well believe that there was something mysterious about him. Jean was not hiding from the Count, he had no idea that he was being looked for; he had a problem to consider, and he had come into this solitude to solve it. He had heard of the death of the young Duke, had seen Barbier as he rode to and from the castle yesterday. He had heard of the Count's orders to arrest Captain Lemasle and any priest who entered Vayenne. Was the Duke really dead? How was friend Roger to be warned? The problem was evidently a difficult one to solve, for the dwarf sat for hours in the corner, never changing his position, scarcely making a movement the whole time.

Toward dusk, when the lights had begun to blink from windows, and the taverns and cafés were filling with men eager to discuss the news, he climbed to the roof, and clambered down the face of the wall to his boat hidden in the sunken archway. With a few vigorous strokes he sent it out into the stream, landing presently at the same spot where he had landed Herrick.

He made fast the boat, and went quickly to the house among the trees.

"Farmer Jacques at home?" he said as he pushed open the door.

"'Tis the limb of Satan," the farmer cried. "Come in. Art hungry? Here's provender."

"You call me a devil and give me the welcome of an angel," said Jean. "There are great things afoot, Farmer Jacques."

"To dreamers like thou art there always are."

"And the river yonder separates you from the world," said Jean. "When were you in the city last?"

"A week ago."

"That's an eternity when things are afoot," said the dwarf.

"True. I was minded to go the other day," said Jacques, "for things have happened on this side of the river too. My horse was stolen in the night."

"Stolen!"

"Ay; saddle and all; and next day, toward evening, came trotting home again. What he'd done with the thief I know not."

"I'm glad he came back," said the dwarf thoughtfully.

"He'd been ridden hard, I could tell that," said the farmer.

"And not by a thief, perhaps," said Jean. "The young Duke, they say, is dead, Farmer Jacques."

"What, the Passey scholar?"

"So they say yonder." And the dwarf nodded his head in the direction of the city. "It is said that some tried to rescue him and failed; and there are some who would arrest these men if they could. That's news for you, farmer."

"Bad news, Jean."

"It's good news to hear you call it so," said the dwarf, leaning toward his companion. "One of these rescuers was a priest, who will perchance come again to Vayenne. He might pass this way. If he does, Farmer Jacques, stop him, and say: 'All priests entering Vayenne are to be arrested.'"

"I'll do it. I don't hold with hangings over the castle gates. Would they hang a priest, think you?"

"This one they would; and for that matter all priests have necks as other men have," the dwarf returned.

"That's ribald talk," said Jacques, who was a religious man and had no liking for jests concerning priests.

"Crooked as my limbs, but a fact for all that, just as they are. I meant no jest. I've said what I came to say, and I'll get back. They watch the gate carefully to-night, and were I too late they might question me."

Jean's friendship with the farmer was not one of full confidence. Jacques knew nothing of the flat-bottomed boat and the dwarf's private entrance into Vayenne. So Jean started briskly along the road, and not until he was well out of sight did he turn aside and make his way back to his hidden landing-place. There he waited until near the dawn, listening for footsteps, or the beating hoofs of a horse, in the silence of the night.

They came some hours afterward, but Jean had re-crossed the river then. Herrick drew up in the shelter of the trees by the landing-place, and looked across the river toward the city. He was bare-headed, and no longer wore the priest's robe. He had thrown that aside before he emerged from the forest. It would mark him to those he had fought with there, some of whom had doubtless returned to Vayenne. How was he to enter the city? The sound of a heavy wagon crunching its way slowly along the road gave him

8

inspiration. Dismounting quickly, he led his horse round to the back of the shed Jean had plundered the other night. There was no one about, and he fastened the bridle to a staple in the woodwork.

"You're as good an animal as the one we stole, so that debt is paid," he said; and then he hastened after the wagon going in the direction of Vayenne.

CHAPTER XI

THE LAW OF THE LAND

THE driver pulled up his horses when Herrick hailed him.

"Are you going into the city?"

"Ay."

"Care to take a passenger?"

"Ay."

"A paying passenger?" said Herrick.

"Ay; they're the sort I care most about."

Herrick climbed up on to the wagon, which was loaded with straw.

"There's for fare," he said, putting money into the driver's hand as the horses moved slowly on again.

The man looked at it.

"I'll take you in and bring you out for this, if you like, and you've a mind to wait while I unload the straw."

"I don't want to come out again," said Herrick. "It's the getting in that's the difficulty. I'm for the new Duke, and there are some who plot against him. I might be stopped at the gate. I propose to lie buried in this straw, and once in the city, I will drop out of the wagon. Will you do me the service?"

The man looked at Herrick doubtfully and then at the money.

"But if there's trouble at the gate and they find you?" he said.

"Then I have climbed up into the wagon as you

came along, and you didn't know it. I warrant you've often given an unconscious lift to a free passenger that way."

"Ay; that's true. I'll do it," the driver answered, putting the money in his pocket. "Get you down in the straw."

They lumbered presently over the bridge, and were passing through the gate when the wagon stopped.

"Where from?" a voice asked.

"Farmer Jacques."

"That's a road that goes toward Passey, isn't it?"

"Ay."

"Met any soldier on the road this morning?"

"No."

"Nor a priest?"

"No. If you want a priest there's one up the street yonder."

"Only straw in your wagon?"

"Ay. Taking it to a man in the Place Beauvoisin. I go there with a load every month."

Then the wagon began to move again and to jolt over rough, cobbled streets. For some time Herrick did not move, but presently lifted his head cautiously to see where they were going, and to choose a moment when he might drop from the wagon without attracting undue attention. To do so unseen would be impossible, for at this hour of the day there were many people in the streets. Herrick chose a busy corner. There was nothing really remarkable in a man leaving a wagon as it lumbered slowly along. The chief risk was that some one had had his suspicions aroused at the gate, and had followed. Herrick dropped carelessly into the roadway close to an alley that led out of the main street, and which he immediately made for. He

wanted to take his bearings; he also wanted a hat.
The sooner he could lose himself in the life of the streets
the better. Fortunately he was well provided with
money, thanks to the dwarf, and he decided to take
a lodging at some third-rate café. He had formed
no plans as yet beyond the determination to get into
the castle, and into the presence of Count Felix somehow. Friend Jean might certainly help him so far,
and presently he would go to St. Etienne and look for
him. What was to happen when he did succeed in
seeing Count Felix he had not thought about. So far
fortune had favored him, and to fortune he trusted the
future.

The alley ran between a row of dilapidated dwellings,
into which one stepped down by two deep steps, and a
blank wall. A few dirty children were playing in the
doorways, but took no notice of him. He had nearly
reached the farther end, which opened into another
busy street, when a hand was suddenly laid upon his
shoulder. Herrick turned sharply, ready to fight for
his liberty if need be.

The man he faced smiled.

"I am a friend," he said, "who knows you are in
danger in Vayenne."

"What do you know of me?"

"I was looking for a priest who was with Mademoiselle de Liancourt's escort. Wisely you are a
priest no longer. There is an order to arrest all priests
entering Vayenne."

"Well, sir, and what then?"

"Some of these children are watching us," was the
answer. "There is anger in your face, and they hope
to see fighting between us. We are friends, let us walk
on."

"I have no proof of your friendship," said Herrick, walking on with the man.

"You would serve Mademoiselle de Liancourt, surely that is why you have returned to Vayenne. I would serve her also. I pray you trust me sufficiently to bear me company. If you are minded, as I believe you are, to strike a blow at Count Felix, who already makes preparations for his coronation, I have power to help you."

Herrick walked on for a few moments in silence. At the best this could only be an attempt to allure him into some plot against the Duke, which was probably more one of secret clamor than open action; yet he might learn something of the support a rising against the Count could depend on. At the worst—he pressed his hand to his side, and felt the revolver there.

"First help me to a new hat; I draw attention by going bare-headed," he said.

"That is easy; and afterward?"

"My good friend, I do not enter Vayenne in this fashion without having friends in the city. I warrant any hurt to me would be amply paid for. I will go with you, and treat you as a friend until I know that you are otherwise; then—— "

"Ah! leave all threatening for your enemies," the man answered. "You will find plenty of them."

The hat purchased, a soft one that he could draw down to conceal his face a little, Herrick went with his companion, carefully noting the way they took. For the most part it was by by-streets, and not the shortest way to their destination; but presently they came out close to the Church of St. Etienne. The carillon burst forth as they crossed by the great west doors set deep in a very lacework of stone, and ceased as they passed into the Rue St. Romain. Herrick's guide stopped and knocked at a small postern there, which was opened immediately by a man in a cassock, who, without a word, stood back to let them enter, and then closed the door.

"Will you wait here a moment, monsieur?" said his companion, leading Herrick into a small, barely furnished room. "I will return immediately."

He left the door open, as though he would emphasize his perfect confidence, but Herrick noted that the man in the cassock who had admitted them remained in the passage. A sudden movement Herrick made caused him to glance round quickly. He was evidently there by design to watch, and Herrick pressed his hand upon his revolver again.

In a few minutes his guide returned, and led him along the passage and up a flight of stairs. He paused before a door there, knocked, and, after waiting for a moment, opened it and motioned Herrick to enter. He did not enter with him, but closed the door, and was immediately joined by the man in the cassock. With a nod of comprehension to each other they took up their positions on either side of the door, an alertness in their attitude which argued ill for Herrick should he attempt to leave that room against their will.

Herrick walked boldly into the room, unconscious that his companion was not following him. His attention was immediately arrested by the man who rose from his seat at the table and came to meet him.

"I welcome a brave man," he said.

"This is not our first meeting," Herrick answered. "You were at the Croix Verte on the night I arrived in Vayenne. You are Father Bertrand."

"I am," said the priest, motioning his visitor to a seat.

"You can hardly know much concerning me beyond my identity."

"Very little more," said Herrick. "Subsequent events have made me remember a few words overheard at the Croix Verte that night which I took little notice of at the time."

"That is natural," the priest answered. "And you have assumed that we are both bent in helping the same cause."

"Captain Lemasle was at the Croix Verte with you. I saw him again at Passey. I found him honest, and I judge a man's companions are of his own choosing and after his own heart."

"I hope to prove myself a suitable comrade for so worthy a captain." And it was difficult to tell whether there was contempt in the priest's tone or whether he spoke in his usual manner. "Rumor has been busy with both of you in the last few hours, if, as I suppose, you were the 'priest' who fought beside Captain Lemasle."

"Rumor often finds it difficult to substantiate her tales," said Herrick, who was not inclined to admit anything until he understood his position more exactly.

"You are both to be arrested, and this I take to mean a short shrift and speedy closing of accounts. Justice in Montvilliers is inclined to be barbarous."

"Justice!" said Herrick.

"I am not considering the point of view," said the priest, with a smile. "Yours is the greater danger, for Lemasle has friends. You were received as a spy at the outset, and have no friends in Vayenne."

"I understood that I was brought here to find some," Herrick answered. "Besides, I have friends in this city."

"You mean those who helped you to escape from the South Tower?"

"That was a simple matter," said Herrick carelessly.

"Yes, Monsieur Herrick?" said the priest inquiringly after a short pause.

"Naturally I do not betray my friends," was the answer.

Father Bertrand smiled again, perhaps to hide his annoyance that his visitor would not speak more openly. He had so constantly found his suave manner a key to open hearts and loosen tongues, that he might well be disappointed now.

"Something more than your name is known to me, Monsieur Herrick—that, of course, was easy to ascertain —but first let me ask you one or two questions."

"I cannot promise to answer them."

"Where is the young Duke Maurice?"

"I do not know."

"Is he dead?"

"That I do not know."

"And Mademoiselle de Liancourt and this Captain Lemasle?"

"I last saw them in the forest which lies on the main road to Passey," Herrick answered.

"You do not look like a man who would lie," said the priest, regarding him intently.

Herrick inclined his head at the compliment. His answers were strictly true; he did not feel himself called upon to enter into explanations.

"Tell me, what made you come to Vayenne—originally, I mean?" said the priest after another pause.

"I came as any traveller might. From childhood Vayenne has always had a fascination for me. Long ago I determined to visit it some day, and truly it has treated me very scurvily thus far."

"Why this fascination?"

"Indeed, I cannot tell, but I do know it is being speedily cured," Herrick answered.

"And why have you returned to Vayenne now?"

"I hardly know," laughed Herrick. "The whim of an Englishman to see the game to the end. I might have been wiser to ride to the frontier while I had the chance."

"Perhaps; yet who shall say? Providence, or circumstance, call it what you will, determines these matters. I, too, have schemed, my son, schemed to bring about this very meeting, and after all it comes in a strange manner. It was I who on the night of your arrival arranged to have you captured—no, not as a spy, I never thought of that. I only wanted you brought here."

"Why not have invited me to come?" asked Herrick, who, although astonished at the priest's admission, would not show it.

"I did not know why you had come to Vayenne. I had reasons to be suspicious."

"I cannot congratulate you on your method," said Herrick. "Your fellows nearly succeeded in getting me hanged on the nearest lamp."

"You put such wholesome fear in them that they acted foolishly. One is still in his bed getting his bones mended, the other——"

"Faith, I'll give him some mending to do if he but gives me the chance."

"Poor Mercier," said Father Bertrand; "and you seem to have treated him in friendly fashion to-day."

"Was that he? The man who brought me here?"

"You may be anxious to thank him presently. That night," the priest went on, "I went to the castle, to your cell. I should have proved you were no spy, but you had gone. For the second time this interview was delayed."

"And this third time?" queried Herrick.

"Circumstances have changed. Duke Maurice is reported dead, is believed to be dead; you have said yourself that you do not know whether he is dead or alive. At such a time events happen quickly. Preparation is already active. Felix will be Duke, and once crowned——"

"That shall not be," said Herrick.

"How will you prevent it?"

Father Bertrand snapped out the question, and leaned forward, waiting for the answer. His whole attitude had changed. There was a tenseness about him that seemed subtly to convey itself into Herrick's blood.

"Show me the way," he said, leaning forward in his turn as eagerly as the priest had done.

"There is a mirror yonder, Monsieur Herrick," said the priest, rising suddenly. "If you have forgotten what manner of man you are, look in it."

Herrick had risen as the priest rose, and almost unconsciously turned to look at his own reflection. While he did so, he heard the rattle of a curtain being sharply drawn aside, and turned to see the priest pointing to a picture which the curtain had concealed until now.

"Do you know that face?" he asked.

"Surely, my grandmother—my mother's mother," said Herrick in astonishment.

"The likeness of the face in the mirror to this face leaves no doubt of close relationship. It is a distinctive face, as sometimes happens in families; it cannot be

hidden. I recognized it in an instant when I saw you
at the Croix Verte. That lady, your grandmother, was
sister to Robert VI. of Montvilliers. You did not know
that?"

"No. I only knew that she was a foreigner, a lady
of rank, who was content to become the wife of an
English country gentleman."

"Were it not for the law of this land, which forbids
the throne to descendants of the female line, your grandmother, or, failing her, your mother, would have been
Duchess of Montvilliers. There have been times
when the people have been inclined to do away with
this law. There are some now who would do away with
it in favor of Christine de Liancourt. I have been
tempted to wish it done away with. Her determination
is fixed, however; she will keep to the very letter of the
law, and lest she should loom too prominently in
this matter, it is her whim to use none of her many
titles, but to be called simply Mademoiselle de Liancourt."

"You mean that you would plot to do away with this
law now?" asked Herrick after a pause.

"The breaking of a law which has been long established, and has worked for the general good, is not wise,
my son," answered Father Bertrand, going to the table
and unfolding a rough pedigree chart there. "This will
show my meaning clearer. Here, you see, is Robert IV.,
dying without issue; Charles, his brother, who prede-
ceased him; and Marie, his sister, your grandmother.
On the death of Robert the crown went to Philip I., his
cousin, and at his death to his son, a dissolute man, who
was deposed in favor of Robert VII., the old Duke who
lies waiting burial in the castle yonder. The deposed
Duke, Philip II., died suddenly in the South Tower. He

had no friends to assist him to escape, and plenty of enemies to help him to his death.   Robert's elder brother Charles died before Robert seized the throne, leaving one child, Christine de Liancourt.   A younger brother, Conrad, died a few years since.   Felix is his son."

"Had Duke Robert no claim to the throne?" asked Herrick.

"You can trace it here," said Father Bertrand, pointing the descent with his finger; "through the male line all along you note until we come to Robert II., who had many children, of whom only the eldest and youngest survived—the eldest being the ancestor of your mother, the youngest of Duke Robert.   This was the Duke's claim, and putting aside the deposition of Philip II., for which the people had no quarrel with him, a righteous claim but for one fact.   You see what this youngest son was called."

"Called   The Bastard," Herrick   read   from   the chart.

"Nicknamed so in his own day," said the priest.   "His father's love for a young girl in his old age has entered into the regions of romance in this country.   You may find ballads which it has inspired.   No one has ever doubted the story until it pleased the people to forget it when they made Robert Duke.   Do you understand how the matter stands?"

"The story goes back so far, it may well be forgotten," Herrick answered.

"If Maurice came to the throne, yes; but not if Felix is the heir.   The law which forbids women to reign in Montvilliers, and under ordinary conditions excludes even their male descendants, has one important provision which is this: that failing a direct male heir, the son through the female line shall inherit."

"Then?"

Father Bertrand glanced at the picture from which the curtain had been withdrawn, and then looked again at his visitor.

"Have I made it quite clear to Roger Herrick, the real Duke of Montvilliers?" he said slowly.

CHAPTER XII

HERRICK looked from the priest to the picture, and then again at the chart lying on the table. He bent over it, his finger travelling from name to name as though he were carefully tracing the descent once more to satisfy himself that the priest was right. It was a ruse to gain time, to collect his thoughts, for they had leaped back to his mother, his youth, and his dreams. Now he understood why Vayenne had always had such a fascination for him. He was of it, a part of its life. The source of the blood that tingled in his veins lay far back in history. They were his ancestors who had kept Montvilliers inviolate as it was to-day, his fathers who had fought in the forefront of the battle, thrusting back their foes at the sword's point. Herrick did not remember his grandmother, and had only a faint recollection of his mother, who had died when he was young; but there certainly was a lady who came into his boyhood's life at intervals, and whom he remembered well. Perhaps she was a friend of his mother's or grandmother's, and he had often sat on her knee while she told him stories which stirred him, stories of Vayenne, so that the name of the city figured in his games of soldiers and doughty deeds, and sank deep down into his heart. One day he would go to Vayenne had been his determination as he dreamed lad's dreams of life and the future. That day had come. His finger had unconsciously travelled down the chart until it rested on his grandmother's name.

"There is no flaw," said Father Bertrand, and his voice made Herrick start, so lost was he in his thoughts. "This chart is no secret; it is copied from one which is common property, open to all who choose to study it, and in which every date is fully given. I am no maker and unmaker of dukes, no mere plotter for place and power. The late Duke, with all his harshness, was a just man in the main. Under his rule the country was at peace, and there was prosperity. His son, were he alive, would make but a poor ruler. Count Felix would assuredly prove a bad one. Is it not right that the reign of the usurping house should end here and now? I have only to bring this chart to date thus." And the priest took a pencil, and under the name of Herrick's grandmother drew a little vertical line, then paused, and said: "What was your mother's name?"

"Mary."

"Mary, daughter of Marie, and then Mary's son, Roger Herrick." And, perhaps unconsciously, he wrote the name more firmly and a little larger.

"And your plans, Father Bertrand?" said Herrick shortly.

"They are a tangled skein. How could they be otherwise until you came to help in the unravelling? But there are loose ends to catch hold of, and after the first few knots are unfastened, the skein is likely to fall easily apart. The Count moves swiftly; we must work swiftly too. Duke Robert is to be buried without delay. Courtiers and men of account have already been summoned from the country; and they come not only to a funeral, but to a coronation. Once Felix is crowned, it will be harder to foster a rising against him. Among those who will come to Vayenne is one Gerard de Bornais, a man of wealth, whose friendship

I have. He will bring a certain retinue with him, and you shall join yourself to his company. Events must decide our actions. For the rest——"

There was a single, sharp knock upon the door, given by the same man, Herrick thought, who had brought him hither. It was evidently an understood sign, for the priest did not answer.

"For the present you must be my guest," said Father Bertrand, drawing back the curtain from another door.

"I have friends in Vayenne. I must see them," said Herrick.

"My son, there is danger for you in the streets."

"Am I virtually a prisoner then?"

"If you would oppose Count Felix by the means I have shown you, yes, for yours is too tell-tale a face to be seen at present. If you decide not to claim your rights, yonder is the door you entered by, and you are free to go."

"I will stay," said Herrick after a moment's reflection. "One friend I have whose worth I know, and who may be of value to us among the people. Will you find and bring here Jean who is called the dwarf of St. Etienne?"

"Would you put your trust in a fool!" exclaimed Father Bertrand.

"There is more wisdom, strength, and cunning in that crooked body than lies in most of your straight-limbed men. I know. He is a hater of the Count besides."

"I should advise——"

"Either he comes, or I go," said Herrick.

"You quickly learn the part you are to play. You command, I obey. Jean shall be found." And the priest smiled, and led the way into another room. "I
9

will return to you as soon as possible. In the meanwhile Mercier shall attend to your wants. You have forgiven him for attacking you in the Rue de la Grosse Horloge?"

"Indeed, I have not."

"I petition that you do," said Father Bertrand. "I know him. He will be useful to us. A duke should grant so humble a petition when it is the first made to him."

"Send this Mercier. I will not harm him," said Herrick. "If I can mount the throne as easily as I grant the petition, we have no very thorny path to travel."

The dwarf, however, was not to be found that day, although Father Bertrand looked for him in St. Etienne and Mercier sought him at all the haunts he knew of. Jean remained in the house by the wall, and that night again crossed the river to make inquiry of the farmer. A wagoner was at the farm that night, and chancing to hear that he had been to Vayenne that day, Jean questioned him.

"Ay; sure they were on the lookout at the gate," he answered, "but I had seen no soldier or priest, as I told them."

He was an honest fellow, and remembering the coins in his pocket, held his tongue.

It was toward dusk the next day that Jean entered St. Etienne. Lights were burning dimly in one of the chapels where vespers were being said, and as he stood in the shadows of one of the great pillars, Father Bertrand, who was about to leave the church, saw him.

"Jean, there is a friend of yours at my house who wishes to see you."

"What friend? I have hundreds in Vayenne."

"The one who broke from the South Tower."

"What does he in your house, father?"

"For the present he hides, and waits for you. Go to him at once."

The dwarf shuffled down the long aisle. In the porch he paused, half expecting the priest to follow him. Was this a trap? Had Jean known of any way in which his capture could help Father Bertrand, he certainly would not have gone; and as it was, he stood before the small door in the Rue St. Romain for some time before he knocked. The door was opened almost immediately, and the man in the cassock stood back to let him enter, which Jean did, one hand upon his knife under the folds of his loose tunic.

The man closed the door, and bade the dwarf follow him. He led him upstairs, and at the end of a passage knocked at a door. The dwarf entered the room, and waited until the man had closed the door again and the sound of his retreating footsteps had ceased. Then he looked at Herrick, who had risen from his chair.

"They don't lock you in?" he said in astonishment.

"No."

"Why stay then?"

"I asked them to bring you here that I might tell you what has happened," said Herrick.

"Strange happenings, surely, to bring you to this place, friend Roger!" And as Herrick sat down again, Jean doubled his legs under him and squatted on the floor.

Herrick told him all that had occurred to the time Mercier had met him and brought him to the Rue St. Romain.

"Then the pale scholar is not dead," said Jean. "In Vayenne they believe he is."

"He was not dead when the robbers carried him away, and they would certainly do their best to keep him alive. How he will fare with those to whom he is sold I cannot say."

Jean expressed no opinion.

"And now, friend Roger, what happens now? You have come to tell the truth to the Count, and have fallen into the fox's hole on the way."

"Wait, Jean; let us consider the position for a moment. Had I gone boldly to the castle, what would my fate have been, do you suppose?"

"A dangle at the end of a rope over the great gate as likely as not," the dwarf answered.

"Exactly—and perhaps without a chance of seeing Count Felix at all," said Herrick. "Now Father Bertrand has promised to get me into the castle in the suite of one De Bornais, who comes to the Duke's funeral. In this way I shall attract no attention, and shall be ready when the moment for action arrives."

"What action?"

"That must depend on circumstances; but it shall be some action that shall prevent Count Felix being crowned Duke of Montvilliers."

"Friend Roger, you have proved yourself a brave man, but here is a task that would make a body of giants ponder and turn pale."

"Since we parted across the river yonder, I have learned strange things, Jean; so strange that I dare not speak of them yet. They will stir the very heart of Vayenne, and the Count himself shall be afraid."

"From whence heard you these things? From Father Bertrand?"

"Partly."

Jean shook his head.

"The fox enters the poultry run with a smile on his face and an air of harmlessness, but he brings death and destruction all the same."

"Listen, Jean. I am not trusting Father Bertrand without knowing that what he says is true," said Herrick earnestly. "Now I want to know who are my friends, whom I can trust; so I sent for you."

"The only friend you have in Vayenne," said Jean.

"You forget Mademoiselle de Liancourt and Captain Lemasle."

"Who are not in Vayenne, friend Roger, however friendly they may be. There are orders to arrest Captain Lemasle."

"Treachery must be met with cunning, and the time is short," said Herrick. "By this they are no doubt safe within the city. I will tell you the whole story soon, but there is no time now; there is work to do to-night."

Jean shook his head, one eye shut the while.

"Cannot you trust me?" Herrick asked.

"Not your wisdom. You talk of using cunning, but many as wise a man as you are has thought himself cunning, and been the victim all the time. I have no relish for pulling an oar in the same boat with Father Bertrand. I've been in Vayenne longer than you have, friend Roger, and know him better than you do."

"Listen, Jean. It is Father Bertrand who has told things to me, not I to him," said Herrick. "He does not know the whole story of the attack in the forest as I have told it to you; he does not know what has happened to Duke Maurice, nor of Mademoiselle, nor of Captain Lemasle. He knows nothing of what I want you to do to-night."

The dwarf was on his feet in an instant.

"Good, friend Roger, good! I see the smile of the fox on your face now. What is the work? I am content to hear the rest of your story another time."

"Do you know the house of the Countess Elisabeth?" asked Herrick.

"The outside of it."

"You must get in on some pretext, and see Mademoiselle de Liancourt."

"Faith! She has chosen as strange a hiding-place as you have."

"It was of her own choosing," said Herrick. "See her. Say you come from me. Say that she must remain in hiding until I send to her again; that Count Felix must be allowed to believe that Duke Maurice is dead. Tell her that since leaving her in the forest I have learned that which makes me certain that Count Felix will never be crowned. Can you remember the message?"

Jean repeated it, marking each item off on his fingers.

"And what have I to say to Captain Lemasle?" he asked.

"Tell him to wait for a message from me," said Herrick.

"You must have impressed him greatly, friend Roger, to command him in this fashion. He's a man more easily led than driven."

"And one thing more," said Herrick, who was too busy thinking of all it was necessary to tell to notice the dwarf's comment. "You will not say where I am. They do not know what has happened since I left them. They might not understand my being in Father Bertrand's house."

"Then we are all in the dark until it pleases friend Roger to open the door," said Jean. "Well, since you undertake giants' work, it is hardly strange you should set about it in queer fashion.   For all our sakes I pray your wisdom is as great as your courage."

At Herrick's summons the man in the cassock came and took Jean to the street door again, closing it gently behind him without a word.

It was quite dark now, and the dim lamps at intervals only served to cast deep, gloomy shadows across the Rue St. Romain.   The dwarf stood still for some moments, looking up and down the street, and his sharp eyes searched the shadows.   He was not certain, but one particular spot did not satisfy him; he thought a man stood there.   He expected to be watched and followed, for he had little faith in Father Bertrand. Jean was even surprised with himself for believing Roger Herrick so easily, for he placed small reliance on any man's disinterestedness.   He moved away slowly, and was soon aware that he had not been mistaken, that he was being followed.

"He must know Vayenne well if he hopes to keep me in sight," chuckled the dwarf to himself as he turned sharply into a narrow alley and began the task of losing his enemy.   For half an hour he dodged round corners, up dark alleys, and across small streets, returning at the end of that time to a spot close to the Rue St. Romain; and he chuckled to think of the dance he had led his follower.

Mercier did know Vayenne well, however, he was perhaps the very last man in the city to be deceived by such tactics, and no sooner had the dwarf set out on a more direct. route, than he came from a turning and went after him.

Jean was crossing one of the larger streets, which was well lighted, on his way to the Place Beauvoisin, when half a dozen soldiers suddenly caught sight of him.

"Well met, Jean," cried one, grasping his arm. "Where have you been roosting? The Count has been sending everywhere to find you to-day and yesterday."

"For what?"

"Nobody knows why—maybe to make a captain of you. But this we know, that he's promised silver enough to the man that finds you to pay for a merry night at the tavern. So you must come with us."

"That's certain," answered one of his companions, taking Jean's other arm.

Why should he be sought for? The wounded sentry must have gathered some of his scattered wits and remembered something of the spy's escape from the South Tower.

"The Count honors me," he said; "and if he makes a captain of me, we'll have merry times. I'll come with you; but at the top of the street yonder is the Barbe Noire, where is good liquor, and I have the wherewithal to pay. What say you? The Count is in no such hurry that he cannot wait another hour after waiting two days."

"The Barbe Noire let it be," they cried; and with Jean in their midst, they went up the street, Mercier following them.

But they drank no ale or wine at the Barbe Noire that night. Within a hundred yards of it there was a side street leading to the old markets, around which there was a perfect network of alleys and byways. As they came abreast of this street, the dwarf suddenly wrenched his arms free, dropped to the ground, and catching one of the soldiers by the legs, pitched him over his back among his comrades, and in a moment was rushing along the side street. In anticipation of

the drink, and believing that the dwarf had no desire
to get away from them, the soldiers were unprepared
for this manœuvre, and were utterly taken by surprise;
so that the dwarf had travelled some distance before
they took up the pursuit. For the second time that
night Jean's ingenuity was taxed to lose his enemies.

The pursuit was not long confined to the soldiers.
Mercier was the first to join in it, and then some idlers
about the corners of the old markets began to run, until
presently a mob of forty or fifty were making the streets
echo with their hurrying feet.

Jean had not enough advantage in the race to enable
him to deliberate which way he should take. He had
no desire to draw his pursuers into the Place Beauvoisin
where, even if he succeeded in eluding them, they might
watch for a long time, and prevent his gaining entrance
to the Countess Elisabeth's house. But presently there
seemed no other way for him to take with any reasonable hope of safety. He entered the square by a narrow
thoroughfare close to the high wall which surrounded
the house, and had a moment's respite before the crowd
turned the corner. Adjoining the high wall there was
a lower one, surrounding a yard. To run across the
square and escape by the other entrance would carry
him into well-lighted streets, where a hundred others
might join in the chase, and where he was almost
certain to be captured. His decision was taken in an
instant. With a spring, such as some great ape might
make, he was upon this lower wall, and another bound
took him to the top of the high wall. No light shone
upon it, and he lay down along it full length upon his
stomach. A moment later, the crowd was rushing past
underneath him.

A pause was made when no one was seen flying across

the square, and a dozen voices began to shout advice.
He had done this! He had done that! He had never
entered the square! He had managed to cross it before
they had got in! It was a babel of tongues, everybody
shouting, no one listening.

Jean had seen no one as he sprang on to the wall, but
the crowd saw a man in the square, and rushed toward
him.

"Which way did he go?" they cried.

Jean ventured to raise his head a little. He could not
hear the man's answer, but since the crowd did not rush
back to the wall, he concluded that either the man had
not noticed him, or had no intention of betraying him.

There was a moment's silence, and then a voice cried
out:

"We've lost the little game, but we catch the larger.
It's Lemasle, and there's an order for his arrest!"

In an instant there was a struggling mass of human-
ity. So closely and so suddenly was Lemasle pressed,
that there was no opportunity to use any weapon. The
dwarf ached to go to his assistance, but that would have
meant the capture of both of them. That would be
worse than useless. So Jean remained motionless on
the wall.

Lemasle said not a word. He struck out right and
left for a few moments, and one or two had reason
enough to regret that they had ever joined in the chase;
but numbers overpowered him. Then as they succeeded
in binding his arms, he laughed.

"Tell me," he said, "whom were you hunting when
you chanced upon me?"

"That devil of St. Etienne," said a soldier, with an
oath.

"Such a devil plays the saint sometimes, and perhaps

he'll tell all my friends where I am. Faith! half the city should be knocking at the castle for my release before noon to-morrow."

"Maybe you'll swing an hour or two earlier, and then they can have your body," said one of the soldiers brutally. He had felt the weight of the captain's arm a few moments earlier.

Lemasle had raised his voice, speaking clearly and distinctly. He had not seen Jean, but he guessed that he was not far off, and would perchance hear him.

The dwarf lay motionless as the crowd passed along under the wall, and he understood.

CHAPTER XIII

Some two hours ago the porter had opened the small door in the high wall, and before he could prevent her, or ask her business, a woman, heavily cloaked, had stepped hastily in, and bade him close the door again. He obeyed her command almost unconsciously, and then recovered himself sufficiently to ask the meaning of this sudden intrusion.

The woman laughed as she let the cloak, which she had held lightly across her, fall apart.

"Your wits move slowly, my friend. An enemy might enter while you were making up your mind to ask his business. Go and tell your mistress that Mademoiselle de Liancourt would speak with her."

Countess Elisabeth met her with a smiling welcome and outstretched arms, yet Lucille, who was with her when the message was brought, had seen an expression in her face which was certainly not one of pleasure, and was surprised at the sudden change as the door opened and Christine entered.

"Forgive me coming to you in this fashion, Elisabeth," Christine said. "I knew I should find a safe retreat here."

"Retreat?"

"Yes, or hiding-place if you will, for that is the true meaning of my coming. I would not have it known that I am in Vayenne for a while."

"Take the cloak, Lucille," said the Countess, lifting it from Christine's shoulders.

"Thank you; and Lucille, although it is a well-worn one, see that it is not thrown away, for it is borrowed," laughed Christine; and then when the girl had gone she went on. "I am travel-stained altogether, Elisabeth, and look strangely out of keeping with the comfort of this room. You will give me food presently, and perhaps lend me a gown; we are sufficiently of a size for that, I think. I have not had my clothes off for three nights."

"I do not understand," said Elisabeth.

"How should you? But you know that I went to Passey?"

"I have heard of that disaster and the death of the Duke," said Elisabeth.

"All Vayenne has heard of that, I suppose," said Christine.

"Such ill news travels quickly," was the answer; "if it is ill news altogether. Perhaps for the country's sake the death is not such an unfortunate one."

"You did not know Maurice," said Christine quietly.

"You must not be angry with me," the Countess went on. "I am thinking of the country, not of the individual, and I am sorry for the poor boy. But I do not understand why you should want to be in Vayenne secretly."

"A duke is not murdered without some upheaval in the state," said Christine. "The Duke's partisans may be the next victims."

"Is your life in jeopardy, Christine?"

"For three days I have been hiding in a charcoal-burner's hut. I should hardly have done so without good reason. Captain Lemasle saved me when we were attacked in the woods, and only to-night have I ventured to the city. I came by the North Gate, since it was nearest to your house, entering in the company of some market women, borrowing one of their cloaks to conceal myself as much as possible. How Captain Lemasle has fared, I know not. Let me see him if he comes, Elisabeth. He knows where I was bent on seeking sanctuary."

"But Felix——"

"I know. He will be Duke," said Christine, interrupting her.

"And powerful to shield you," said Elisabeth.

"He sent an escort to shield Maurice. It failed miserably in its purpose. Maybe Felix thinks, as you do, that Maurice's death happened fortunately for Montvilliers."

"Even then, I do not understand your position, Christine. Is not Felix to know that you are in Vayenne?"

"Not yet. He will know presently. As you love me, Elisabeth, let my being here remain a secret at present."

"But why?"

"Have you never heard that Felix wishes to marry me?" Christine asked.

"Yes; I have heard so. I know nothing of the truth of the story," said the Countess.

"It is true enough. Oh, there is no romance in it, Elisabeth. I have some power and wealth in the state. It might be a good marriage for Felix. There you have the whole truth of it."

"And you do not love him?"

"I do not think so. How can I tell? I have lived all these years on the earth without knowing what love is. Love, perhaps, finds no easy road into the Castle of Vayenne."

"Still, without love, you would marry him?" said the Countess.

"For the good of the country, perhaps; but if I do, he will probably live to wish that he had found another wife, even if she cost him a crown."

"Surely, Christine, if you have not learnt to love, you have learnt how to hate."

"Time enough for that when Felix and I are married. Will you keep me here for a while, and let it be a secret?"

"Yes; I promise. I will, even at the risk of Felix's anger. Am I not brave?" And she laughed light-heartedly.

"Then come and pick me out a gown, the prettiest you have, Elisabeth. I long to shake off the charcoal dust and the dirt of the highway. I want to feel just a woman, and look pretty again."

"Surely this Captain Lemasle—— Did you not say he might come to-night?" said the Countess.

Christine laughed.

"This old house gives you romantic notions, my dear. Let us call Lucille, and bid her help to choose the gown, for with such ideas in your head you may be jealous of me, and foist upon me some cast-off garment that no girl could possibly look charming in. You are so pretty yourself, Elisabeth, that I am inclined not to trust you in this affair." And with their arms about each other, they went out of the room, calling for Lucille.

Captain Lemasle did not come, and only the porter heard any disturbance in the square. It woke him from a doze, but not sufficiently to send him out to see what the cause of the noise might be. He was a sleepy old man at the best of times, and if there were any breaking of heads being done, he argued that he was safer in his little lodge on the inside of the wall.

They talked no more of politics that night. For one thing, Lucille was present, and this was a relief, for both Christine and the Countess were busy with their own thoughts. Countess Elisabeth had told Felix that they had come to the parting of the ways. She loved him, of that she made no secret, but she had been unselfish enough to urge his marriage with Christine. His good came before her desire. With the death of Maurice, it seemed to her that all reason why Felix should marry Christine vanished; and since circumstances had thus been kind to her, she looked for the reward of her great unselfishness. When Felix had come to her the other day, she had fully expected him to rejoice that all barriers between them were now cast down. He had not done so; he still saw a necessity for marrying Christine; and although too proud to question him closely, she had made him understand that for the future things must be different between them. Perhaps she understood his character more thoroughly, at this moment, than she had ever done; but she loved him. Hers was not that love which lies close to the borderland of hatred; wounded, it yet found excuses for him. To-night she had learned something of Christine's feelings toward him. She might marry him, but time could never bring love into that union. Christine had declared that it would bring hatred. Felix must be saved from this, and the Countess tried to persuade herself that she thought only of him in this matter. She would keep Christine's secret. Felix should not know that she was in Vayenne; more, if necessary, she would keep Christine a prisoner for a time, so that Felix might understand how easily he could do without her, that he was free to marry where he would. This Lemasle was Christine's lover, surely, since she had not denied it. Elisabeth might presently betray this secret to Felix. "Yes, I may do that," she said as she came to this climax of her thoughts in her room that night, and the expression on the fair face which her mirror reflected almost startled her. For an instant she saw deeper into her own soul than she dared to look as a rule. She was frightened, but not repentant.

And Christine had been silent that evening, too. She knew nothing of Felix's visits to the Place Beauvoisin. She knew that he did not really love her; she believed that he did not love any woman. She had come to Countess Elisabeth for refuge and with the intention of telling her the whole truth of the attack in the forest; but Elisabeth's evident partisanship of Felix had stopped the tale. Christine had to give some other reason for her desire to remain concealed. The fact that Felix wished to make her his wife, and her reluctance to such a union, seemed a reason that would be most likely to appeal to another woman, and the introduction of Lemasle's name added force to the argument; so Christine laughed and spoke no words of denial. But there was little laughter in her heart as she locked herself in her room. Lemasle had not come. He had said he would, and she knew him well enough to understand that he was unable to keep his promise. He had not succeeded in entering Vayenne without being seen, and she dreaded to think what his fate might be, once he fell into the hands of Felix. There was something strange about Elisabeth. Her welcome had been forced. She had been under some restraint all the evening. It was doubtful if this house was a safe refuge after all. What had Roger Herrick done? How had he fared? Brave man as he was, what could he hope to accomplish against Felix? Herrick and

10

Lemasle might both be taken, and they would both die a speedy death. Felix could not afford to let such men live, for they knew the truth.

"God grant he does not silence me before I have called him traitor!" she cried passionately; and then her mood changed suddenly, and a soft look came into her eyes. "I was wrong to let him ride back to Vayenne," she murmured; and for a little while she sat thinking, her mental vision reaching far beyond the four walls of her chamber, seeing the rough hut, the smouldering peat fire, and a man kneeling to her, swearing to serve her to the death.

Suddenly she shook herself free of such dreams. This was no time for visions. Even now Felix might be planning the death of this man—and of Lemasle. They must be saved. She would go to the castle to-night. The room seemed to have grown hot and stifling, and she threw open the window to fill her lungs with the cool night air.

Below her, the garden was in darkness. The night was overcast, but the trees were whispering together, and from the distance came the faint music of the carillon.

"I will go," she said, turning quickly from the window. "In some dungeon that music may penetrate to him as he counts the hours to dawn—and death. Felix shall listen to me."

The borrowed cloak was lying on a chair. She hastily wrapped it round her, and her hand was upon the key in the door when she stopped and turned round sharply.

"Mademoiselle!"

There was a face at the open window, a shaggy head that might well startle any woman, and two knotted hands grasped the window-frame, the muscles straining as the man drew himself slowly in.

"Pardon, mademoiselle. I have waited a long time. I knew no other way to get to you."

"Jean!"

"At your service, mademoiselle," said the dwarf as he got into the room and fell on his knee before her, a strangely grotesque figure, yet surely an honest man.

"What do you want with me?" Christine asked.

"I have a message from friend Roger. You are to remain in hiding until he sends to you again. Count Felix must believe that Duke Maurice is dead. Since leaving you in the forest, friend Roger has learnt strange things."

"What has he learnt?"

"That Count Felix will never be Duke of Mont-villiers," Jean answered.

"But tell me why? What makes him say this? Come, Jean, tell me quickly. I have no wit to-night to think of questions to drag out your story."

"There is no story to be dragged out, mademoiselle. That is all the message, all I have to tell."

"I must know more," said Christine.

"I know no more," the dwarf answered. "Friend Roger was mysterious. He would tell me more present-ly, he said, but to-night there was work to do; and I have done it, although 'tis a marvel I am here at all. I have been hunted half over the city like a rabbit, and for longer than I care to remember have lain on my stomach on the wall of yonder garden, so still that a cat climbed over me and found nothing strange with the wall."

"Where is Roger Herrick?" asked Christine.

"That he bade me not tell you. He said you would

not understand. I do not understand either. It is a place I should not choose to hide in. But there, it's a good thing all animals do not make for the same hole."

"Is he in danger?"

"He doesn't seem to think so."

"Has he been to the castle?"

"No. Friend Roger would hardly be such a fool as that."

"He spoke truly; I do not understand," said Christine.

"So far then he is wise, for he said you would not," Jean answered. "I had a message for Captain Lemasle, but he is not here. He also was to wait until friend Roger sent for him."

"You have seen Captain Lemasle?"

"Yes; but had no word with him. First one man followed me to-night, and I lost him; then presently half a dozen soldiers pounced on me, saying Count Felix had need of me. I was in a strait how to break loose and deliver my message. I said I was willing to go to the Count, but why should we not drink first; and as we went I got free. It was a long chase, mademoiselle, and presently I turned into the square here, and leaped on to the wall, and lay there. The crowd rushed by, and fell upon another man in the square—the captain."

"And took him?" said Christine.

"He fought as a man should, but there were fifty against him. Then he asked who they had been hunting, and when they told him, he shouted out that I might tell his friends. He guessed I was not far off, and I understood."

"They will hang him before to-morrow," said Christine.

"There are many hours yet before to-morrow," Jean

answered. "I dropped into the garden, and have waited a long time. I did not want to climb to the wrong window. I was just going to break into the house, and bring my message, though I had to wake you from sleep to give it, when you looked down. In that moment the garden grew light, mademoiselle. You have your cloak on. Were you thinking of going out to-night?"

"Yes. To the castle to beg life for——"

"For Lemasle? I will do that."

"You! Who will listen to you?"

"Few know the castle as I do, mademoiselle. Friend Roger escaped from the South Tower, and the Captain shall not hang to-morrow, or, if he does, I will hang with him."

"That would be of small use to him," Christine said.

"It would be company. Shall I take word to friend Roger that you will obey him?"

"Obey?"

"Indeed, he sent the message as though it were a command."

Christine slowly let the cloak slip from her shoulders.

"Yes. I will obey. He sent no other message?"

The dwarf looked at her.

"No, mademoiselle. He was full of business to-night, he had no thought for anything else. Is your —your obedience all the message I carry back?"

"Yes. And tell him of Gaspard Lemasle."

"I will tell him. The captain shall not hang." And Jean began to get out of the window. "The creepers are strongly grown here; where a friend can enter an enemy may. Shut the window fast, mademoiselle."

Christine stood by the window as the dwarf let himself hang by the creeper.

"A still tongue, mademoiselle, will make this place safer than it otherwise might be."

"I know, Jean."

"Good-night, mademoiselle."

"Good-night, Jean."

The dwarf paused in his descent, and Christine leaned from the window.

"Jean," she whispered, "you may say to Roger Herrick that I trust him."

"Obedience and trust," murmured the dwarf as he dropped into the garden, and the ghost of a laugh floated up to Christine as she closed the window.

CHAPTER XIV

THE towers and spires of the city were silhouetted against the early grey of the dawn when Jean stood knocking at the postern beside the great gates of the castle.

The dwarf had hurried through the dark and deserted streets from the Place Beauvoisin to the Rue St. Romain, and had watched Herrick closely as he gave him the message, the promise of obedience and trust. By neither look nor word did Herrick betray whether the promise were more or less than he had hoped for; he seemed entirely absorbed in the events which must shortly come to pass. First with Herrick alone, and then with Father Bertrand, who joined them, Jean sat through the night discussing revolution and the fighting spirit that was in the people of Vayenne. At dawn he was at the castle to learn what was to happen to Gaspard Lemasle.

"You!" exclaimed the soldier as Jean stepped in.

"I've come to see the Count. It's no good to laugh and refuse me admittance. He wants to see me; has sent all over the city for me, I hear."

"That's true enough, and last night when they found you, you slipped away."

"And that's true, too, comrade," answered the dwarf.

"The Count heard of it, and you'll find him in no good mood this morning, I warrant."

"He'll listen to reason, and there was no reason in last night's affair," Jean returned. "Come, comrade, think of it yourself. Here was I, peaceably walking along a street, counting the moments that brought me nearer to my love, when——"

"Love!" laughed the soldier.

"Did I not speak plainly, or is it that your head is full of sleep yet and you are somewhat deaf?"

"Do you mean a girl?"

"Faith, friend, this is full early to be full of liquor," answered the dwarf. "What should a man love but a girl?"

The soldier nearly choked with laughter, and this brought two other men out of the guard-house to see what it was that so amused him.

"A girl! He says there's a girl who loves—who loves him," spluttered the soldier.

The dwarf looked from one to the other, an expression of blank dismay on his face.

"He laughs because a man courts a girl," Jean said to the other men. "Where is the humor in it? What goes he after when he goes courting? A talking parrot in a cage or a cat mow-wowing on a wall?"

"How long have you called yourself a man?" asked one of the soldiers, laughing.

"About as many years as you have. I warrant there were not many months between the time that you and I began to run alone," answered the dwarf; and then as though a reason for their mirth had only just occurred to him, Jean looked down at his deformed limbs. "Ah, now I see! That's the humor of it!" And he began to laugh uproariously too.

"You'd forgotten what you were like, eh, Jean?" they said in chorus.

The question only made the dwarf laugh the more, and his companions were astonished into seriousness.

"To think—to think that you are such fools!" Jean cried. "Do you suppose all girls love such men as you? Why, set you in a row, marching in step round the court-yard, and there aren't a dozen women in Vayenne who could pick out their own man. You're all alike. comrades, there are girls, mark you, who favor men more distinguished, men there is no mistake about, and care not a jot for just a sample of the ordinary kind, which look as though they had been turned out of the same mould by the dozen. My girl's of that sort."

"Pretty, Jean?" asked one.

"What's the color of her eye?" asked another; "for surely she can only have one, and that defective, if she looks with favor upon you."

"Last night I climbed to her balcony," said Jean solemnly. "My lady looked down from her window, as an angel might from an open door in heaven, and all the world seemed flooded with silver light. There was music in the air, music that thrilled my soul, her voice and her laughter. There was a sense of holiness about me as when incense rises from before an altar, and the prayers of saints meet sinners' prayers and, mingling, float upward to the throne of God. Her eyes were twin stars, afire with truth, to guide me in the way that leads to the hereafter; her hair an aureole like to the crown that I may win; and her breath, the essence of all the perfumes that cling about the fair fields of Paradise."

The men were silent, and laughed no more, for the dwarf looked almost inspired as he spoke.

"'Twas in St. Etienne. Surely he saw a vision last night," whispered one man to his companions.

"Wouldn't you have rushed from half a dozen miserable soldiers when such a love was awaiting your coming?" asked the dwarf, turning sharply to them. "It was not that I minded visiting the Count. He is hardly out of bed yet, eh, comrades, and I scent the perfume of coffee through the doorway there. Will you welcome me? The chill of the morning is in my bones."

"Come you in. I'll risk it," said the soldier who had opened the postern. "I ought to lock you up lest you escape again. Look you, Jean, the Count's in the mood to hang me if you run away."

"You shall not hang, comrade; my hand on it."

"They lost you last night, but they captured a bigger prize," said one man.

"That may easily be," the dwarf returned. "There are men of more inches than I am in plenty. Who was it they captured?"

"Captain Lemasle."

"Ah! a truculent man, but a brave soldier," said Jean. "What's his crime, and what will they do with him?"

"I know not the crime, but he's like to end there," was the answer as the man pointed to the top of the gate.

"That will be waste of good material," said Jean. "I must speak to the Count about it. Meanwhile the smell of that coffee haunts me." And he moved toward the door.

The man who told Count Felix that the dwarf had come to the castle, told him also that Jean was strange and talked of visions he had seen.

"Bring him to me here, at once. I will see him alone."

It was in a superstitious frame of mind that Felix

had had the dwarf searched for. Deep in his schemes, with enemies constantly about him, and living in hourly uncertainty of what might happen, he was in the mood to augur good or ill from dreams and visions.

"I have sought for you everywhere," he said when Jean entered and the man who had brought him had gone.

"You were unfortunate in not finding me," said the dwarf, with a grotesque bow. "I am always at the Duke's service."

"Tell me, Jean, why do you call me Duke? You are in advance of time. The crown has not yet touched this head of mine."

"We speak of to-morrow ere the sun has risen upon it," the dwarf answered.

"True; but it might never dawn."

"Ah, my lord, one cannot stop to consider possibilities if life is to be lived."

"The other day you spoke of visions, visions in St. Etienne in the night. Is it true that you have been dreaming again?" asked Felix.

"I always dream; so do other men, only with the light they forget. I remember. Half our life is a dream, visions of things we long for, yet never attain to. Love, hope, ambition, they are all dreams, sometimes turned to realities, yet seldom fulfilling expectation."

"Have I entered into your visions?" asked Felix, and eagerness was in the question in spite of his efforts to conceal it.

"Often," answered the dwarf, quick to catch the trend of the Count's question. "Often, as lover, as a man of hope, as a slave of ambition."

"How say you? Slave!"

"Truly we are all slaves in varying degree; slaves to love, slaves——"

"Since when have I been slave to love?" asked Felix.

"Since the day a woman first said you nay," was the quick answer. It was a general answer enough, applicable to any man, yet the Count, remembering Elisabeth and Christine, found it easy to apply it forcibly to himself.

"And for the others, hope and ambition, what of them?" he asked.

"They stand with one foot on the steps of a throne," said Jean.

"And shall I mount it? Have your visions told you that?"

"Who can stop you?" asked the dwarf. "Is not the pale scholar of Passey dead? You did not know that when last we talked together, nor did I. Did I not leave you to go and welcome him at the gate of Vayenne? Yet I called you Duke then. I am but the dwarf of St. Etienne, a fool; yet maybe I sometimes utter prophecies."

There were steps outside the room, and then a soldier entered.

"Stand you here, Jean," said Felix. "You shall see how I deal with traitors."

"Have a care that you mistake not friends for traitors and traitors for friends," said the dwarf. "They have a habit of looking and speaking much alike." And, doubling his legs under him, Jean sank into a sitting posture by the Count's chair.

With chains upon his wrists, Gaspard Lemasle was marched into the room. He glanced at the dwarf, who did not meet his look, and then he fixed his eyes upon Felix.

"We looked upon you as an honest man, Lemasle," said Felix.

"Duke Robert ever found me so," was the answer.

"He is dead," said Felix, "and his son, who should have been Duke, was placed in your keeping. Where is he?"

"I do not know."

"He, too, is dead," said Felix. "His mangled corpse has been found in the forest yonder. How dare you come to Vayenne, Duke Maurice being dead?"

Lemasle was silent. He had no intention of being tricked into answering questions which might give the Count information.

"I will tell you," said Felix slowly. "You deserted him in his hour of need, not from actual cowardice it may be, that I will not accuse you of, but because you trusted in another man, and devoted yourself to Mademoiselle de Liancourt."

"I acted for the best," said Lemasle. "Should I have been welcome in Vayenne if Mademoiselle's body had been found mangled in the forest?"

"A loyal soldier obeys orders," the Count answered. "Your orders were to bring my cousin safe to Vayenne. There are plots in the city. I suggest that you never meant the young Duke to enter the city alive."

"You suggest—you——"

The dwarf raised his eyes for a moment, and Lemasle stopped.

"Well?" said Felix. "Have you an answer?"

"I was privy to no such plot."

"This priest in whom you trusted, where is he?" Felix asked sharply.

"I do not know, Count."

"Who was he?"

"An honest man, for he fought side by side with me,"
Lemasle answered. "I do him this justice, for the
troopers can bear me witness that I complained loudly
that he was of our company."

"You mean that his being there was Mademoiselle
de Liancourt's wish?" said Felix. "Where is Mademoiselle?"

"She did not return with me to Vayenne," Lemasle
said.

"Yet you know where she is?"

"I have said, sir, that we parted before I returned to
the city."

"Answer me," said Felix, bringing his hand down
heavily upon the table beside him.

Lemasle remained silent.

"You will not speak? Then I will see to it that you
cannot. We have spies and traitors enough in Vayenne.
They shall have warning of the fate in store for them.
You shall hang at noon."

The Count, the prisoner, and the soldiers suddenly
started, for at that instant the dwarf broke out into a
howl of laughter, rocking himself from side to side until
it seemed as though he must lose his balance and roll
over.

"Peace! fool, peace!" Felix said angrily.

Jean only laughed the more.

"Did I not tell you that traitors and friends were
often alike?" he cried. "When you hang that man as
a traitor, hang me too, for company."

"It were easily done," said Felix.

"Easy enough," laughed the dwarf, "so there be wood
sufficient for gallows, and hemp enough to break our
necks. I warrant there's no lack of either in the castle.
But two dangling in mid air is a poor sight; three

would cover the great gate far better, and there's another may well hang with us—the jailer who let the spy escape the other night."

"That is a good thought," said Felix.

"And noon's an excellent time," said Jean, laughing still. "Send out and let the city know of the show. It would be a pity if none should see your warning."

"Never fear, they shall see it."

"And then hide yourself, Count—mark how I call you Count—hide yourself in the darkest hole you can find in the castle, and even then I warrant they'll find you out, and perhaps——" And then again Jean howled with laughter.

Felix sprang to his feet.

"Take this miserable fool out and whip him. Let strong arms get well tired before they cease and let him go."

Two soldiers hoisted the dwarf to his feet.

"Of your mercy, one word," he said, becoming suddenly serious.

"Speak."

"Was there not a Count once who dangled over the gate? I have heard it was so in Duke Conrad's time," said the dwarf.

"Take him away," Felix thundered.

"A moment," said Jean, exerting his full strength and throwing off the hands which held him. "A warning, Count. Mark the word: the people love not the breaking of laws, and it is unlawful that any man should hang over the castle gate but by order of the Duke of Montvilliers. To-day there is no Duke, only Count Felix."

The Count's teeth savagely bit into his under-lip. Jean was right, and Felix had no wish to incense the people.

"Be wise, wait," said Jean. "This man may be a traitor, but he can wait a day or two. He may confess if you give him time, and let him know that he may perhaps win life by confession. He had accomplices without doubt; he may name them if he has a little time for thought. In a few days when you are Duke, you may hang a whole company of soldiers, if you will, and if I help to choose them, may lose nothing by the sport."

"You are indeed a fool," said Felix, hiding his anger under a boisterous laugh, as men driven to bay often will.

"With wisdom enough to save you from folly," whispered the dwarf as he shuffled to the Count's chair and sat on the floor again.

"The fool has saved you, Lemasle," said Felix. "You hear what he says? I may be lenient if you decide to speak openly."

"I thank the fool," Lemasle answered.

"Keep him close," said the Count as the captain was taken from the room.

Jean turned slowly toward Felix when the door had closed.

"You will never mount the throne if you make such mistakes," he said. "To have me whipped was nothing; but to hang a man!"

"Be your own judge: do you deserve such punishment?"

"Yes; surely. Be as honest, Count, do you?"

"You are good for sad hours," laughed Felix. "You shall have a dress, Jean, a dress of bright colors, and a toy of bells in your hand to jingle. You shall gossip with me as you will, speak to me as no other shall dare to do though he boast the greatest name in Montvilliers. You shall come to honor, Jean."

"You do not answer my question," said the dwarf solemnly.

"Why should I be whipped?" said Felix.

"Because there was never man born yet that didn't deserve it. Have I your leave to go?"

"For a while, yes; but you shall come to honor, Jean. There shall be honor in the title of 'The Duke's Fool.'" And Felix struck a gong which stood on the table. "Jean has my leave to go anywhere in the castle," he said to the soldier who entered. "See that this is known—anywhere, at any time, and may come to me without hindrance when he chooses. But he may not leave the castle on any pretext whatever. See that a lodging is found for him."

Jean rose to his feet, and bowed low.

"Some men never reach their ambition," he said, "but I soar far above it. Have the colored tunic and the bell toy made. My highest hope was to wander at will in God's house of St. Etienne, but behold I live to be the fool of a Duke!"

And that night, when the castle slept, Jean had to leave it by the way he had taken Roger Herrick.

11

At dawn Jean was in the castle again, but Herrick and Christine had heard what had happened to Lemasle. To Lemasle's cell the dwarf also gained admittance, for the Count's orders had been peremptory. Jean had a part to play, and he meant to make the most of it.

"The making or marring of you is in my hands," he boasted in the guard-rooms, "so if you're wise you'll make much of me. The Count and I are brother gossips, and when I get my robes of office, you'll hardly tell one from the other."

So Herrick was able to send his message to Lemasle, and the plot against the Count ripened to its gathering.

Two days later the castle was full of guests and their suites, come to the burial of the Duke, which was to take place on the morrow. There were signs of mourning in the streets through which the cortége would pass, and the great Church of St. Etienne was draped in black. In a few hours men would be busy packing away these death trappings and making ready festive trophies to grace the coronation; such is the kaleidoscope of existence.

The morning broke, heavy and cloudy, and rain fell at intervals. There were those who spoke of the dead man as the great Duke, and these saw a fitness in the sombre day on which he should pass for the last time through the streets of Vayenne.

Jean, by permission, had left the castle to-day, and

stood near the great west doors of St. Etienne.   Above
him tolled the great bell, rung only when a duke came
to his last resting-place; and across its solemn sounding
the joyous music of the carillon burst out at frequent
intervals.   The cadences seemed to fall from high
heaven, the dwarf thought, as though there were joy
there, no matter how great a sorrow there might be upon
the earth.   Dim lights gleamed in the great nave, low
music tumbled from the misty darkness, sad music, yet
ever and anon a wave of harmony that had triumph in
it, a sudden certainty that to life was the victory though
for a while the pageantry of death was supreme.

Into the church came all who were great and powerful in Montvilliers, men whose fathers had fought side
by side with other dukes, men whose names and honors had been handed down through the centuries.
Among them came the de Bornais, his suite halting
on one side of the great doors.   Jean's sharp eyes
scanned each man that stood there, resting at last upon
one whom he watched until the end.

Presently came the cortége—nay, two—drawn by
horses in waving plumes and black trappings.   Only
yesterday was it known throughout Vayenne that the
marred body of the young Duke had been found in the
forest and brought to the city by Captain Barbier.
One great funeral for father and son—the solemnity of
the occasion appealed to the people.   A silence was in
the streets and tears on some faces.   To-day the Duke
is dead—and buried; to-morrow, "Long live the Duke."
Before nightfall there was laughter in the castle halls
and corridors.   Men must eat and drink though dukes
die, and women's eyes will sparkle even though tears
were in them a little while since.

Felix moved from group to group, solemn, yet

smooth-tongued.   His ears were keen to catch whispers, his eyes quick to note each man's expression.

"Felix."

His name was whispered as he passed through the entrance of the great hall, and he turned quickly.

"Elisabeth."

"I must see you alone," she said.   "I have that to tell you which you ought to hear without delay."

"Christine?" he asked.

Elisabeth nodded, and then as the Count turned and led her away, the dwarf came from a dark corner where he had stood watching the Countess.

"This means mischief," he said, and went quickly down the corridor.

Many had looked for Mademoiselle de Liancourt at the castle that night, and marvelled that she was not present.   Felix recognized only too well that her absence was unfavorable to him, and, if necessary, would certainly have used force to bring her to the castle had he known where to find her.

But for the promise given to Herrick, it is doubtful whether Christine would have remained in her hiding-place to-day.   Her uncle had been very good to her; had loved her, perhaps, more than he had loved any one else in the world; had listened to her pleading when none else dared approach him, and many a man had her to thank for saving him from the Duke's anger. Christine's heart was heavy because she could not pay her last respects to the dead, and there was rage, too, in her soul that Felix had dared to take some marred corpse and bury it in pomp and state, declaring it to be Maurice's body.   She longed to rush out into the street and proclaim his treachery to every passer-by.

To-night Christine stood by the open window of her

room deep in thought, yet attentive to any sound in the garden below. Many things might have happened to-day, and Jean might bring her news at any moment. The tolling of the great bell at St. Etienne had ceased long ago, only the faint music of the carillon wove itself into her thoughts. She glanced back into the room where Lucille sat bending over a book. The girl had been with her ever since Countess Elisabeth had gone out. Christine had thought nothing of this fact at first, but when Lucille so persistently stayed with her, following her if she went from one room to another, she began to wonder if the girl were not carrying out some instructions she had received. Christine felt that there had not been a true ring about the Countess's welcome the other night, and since then there had been many signs of uncertainty and effort in her conversation and in her actions.

"Are not your eyes weary of reading, Lucille?" Christine asked suddenly.

"No," answered the girl, looking up; "but I would rather talk."

"Talk! Of what? Prisons and death?"

"Oh, but there are other things. Why should we talk of death or a prison?"

"Come here, Lucille." And Christine put her arm round her, and drew her to the window. "Isn't the city quiet to-night? It seems a sentient thing, awestruck and keeping silent because it knows that death is in it."

"I have known it as quiet other nights," the girl answered.

"What were your dreams then?"

"The Countess called them a silly girl's dreams, because I told her," said Lucille, a blush dyeing her fair face.

"Tell me. Perhaps I shall understand better."

"I wonder if you would! You know my little history —that I am the last of a family once rich and famous in Montvilliers. Long, long ago some ancestor of mine displeased some ancestor of yours, who was Duke then, and we lost honor and estates, and we have never risen again. Yet there has always been a legend that we should come to honor once more, and, strangely, that it should come through a woman. I am the only one left, so I dream."

"Of what?"

"Sometimes of a great deed that I shall do, and perhaps suffer for, but which shall make my name famous through all the world. And sometimes it is different."

"Well, Lucille?"

"Sometimes it is love," the girl whispered, "and I dream of a prince who shall come, who shall pass by all the rich and beautiful women, and kneel to me. So we may win back honor that way. Do you call them a silly girl's fancies?"

"No. Youth will dream of love, it cannot help it."

"Do you?" Lucille asked.

"That, I should confess to you, was not in the bargain," said Christine. "Some day perhaps I may help you to your ambition."

"Will you?" was the eager question.

"We will talk of it another time. To-night I can only think of death and a prison—death in the city, a prison in this house."

"This house a prison!" exclaimed the girl.

"I have a mind to go out for a little while."

"The garden is dark and wet. It has rained much to-day."

"The garden will not satisfy me—I mean in the streets. Yes, I think I will go."

"Oh, no, you must not," said Lucille.

"Why not?"

"The Countess said——"

"That I was not to be allowed to leave the house," Christine said. "Was that her command?"

"She meant for your own sake."

"Did she? Are you clever enough to read all that is in Countess Elisabeth's mind?"

"She has been very good to me," the girl answered. "I would not disobey her."

"I am not blaming you. You shall keep me prisoner. I will not go out to-night."

"Thank you; and you will——"

Lucille stopped. There was a knocking at the door, and a servant entered.

"Mademoiselle!—I mean Mademoiselle Lucille."

"What is it?"

"A man would speak with—with you."

"Or with me?" asked Christine sharply.

"With—with——"

"Bring him here," said Christine. "We will see him together."

"I cannot—I—— Ah! He is here already!"

From the darkness of the passage without a priest advanced into the room. His cloak was wrapped closely round him and the hood drawn low over his face.

"Leave us, Lucille," said Christine. "A priest may enter anywhere, even to a prisoner."

"The Countess said——"

"Go! You may lose the friendship of the Countess to find a better one. Christine de Liancourt has still power in Vayenne. Go! You shall have excuse. See, I force you from the room!" And she gently pushed her out, shut the door, and locked it.

As she turned Herrick threw back his hood, and let the cloak fall apart.

"Again as a priest I come to you, mademoiselle."

"But this house is dangerous for you. Only to-night I have learned that I am virtually a prisoner in it."

"To-night I believe Count Felix has learned that you are here," said Herrick.

"From whom?"

"From the Countess Elisabeth. Jean saw her approach the Count, heard your name mentioned. That is why I have come. I thought it might be that as a priest I should more easily gain admittance, and Jean borrowed the cloak for me."

"But they may be here at any moment if the Countess has betrayed me."

"That is why I have come," Herrick answered.

"You must not stay. Felix will not really harm me, but you——"

"Have no fear, mademoiselle. I go armed, as you see. This dress proclaims me in the suite of De Bornais, and to-day no one has recognized the man they took for a spy in it. I have come from the castle. I am lodged there—a guest."

Christine turned again to the door to make certain it was looked, and then ran to the window, and closed it.

"I am afraid," she said, a color in her cheeks; "Jean climbed in this way, and bid me remember that an enemy might do the same. Oh, why have you come! Could you not have sent a messenger, could you not have sent Jean?"

"No, mademoiselle. I could trust none with my message to-night."

"Tell me," she said. "Tell me quickly. Every passing moment makes me more afraid."

"In three days Count Felix will be formally proclaimed Duke," said Herrick. "The blow we have planned will be struck then. It is a desperate venture; it may fail, but it is the only way."

"And if it fails?" said Christine.

"To-night the Count is almost certain to send for you," Herrick went on, as though he did not hear her question. "If you will not go willingly, he will probably have ordered that you shall be taken by force. No one knows better than he does how much questioning there is at your absence from the castle at this time. Your presence must help him, and I could have wished that you had not been there until the day he is proclaimed. As it is, you must go willingly."

"And then?"

"Wait, mademoiselle."

"What part have I to play?" said Christine.

"Ours is a scheme in which little can be arranged beforehand," Herrick answered. "Much of our action must be decided by the events of the moment. If I fail——"

"Yes; if you fail?"

"Who can tell, mademoiselle? Even then luck may show me a way out," said Herrick. "A man who hopes to achieve never allows himself to consider what may happen in the case of failure. It would make a coward of him."

"But those who—others--his friends may think for him," she answered.

"We will not think of failure."

"Let me judge. Tell me the whole plot."

"Mademoiselle, I came myself to-night, so that you might understand. In the hut yonder in the forest you accepted my service. The other night when I sent you a message which must have sounded strangely like a command, you sent me an answer, obedience and trust. Even as Jean gave it me I could see you smile at the promise to obey."

"I did not smile. I meant it. Witness that I am here to-night."

"And trust, did you mean that too?" asked Herrick.

"Yes."

"I am going to try your trust to the utmost limit. I cannot tell you the plot. I cannot tell you what I intend to do."

"Why not?"

"Do not ask me. I cannot answer."

"The trust is to be all on my side," said Christine slowly.

"And it may be strained to breaking point. You may—indeed, I fear you will—find it difficult to believe in me. I am here to-night to tell you so. For no duke am I doing this thing, but for you—you. There will be plenty of tongues to fill your ears with evil thoughts of me; then remember what I have said to-night. Circumstances have forced me into this part that I must play, circumstances and a woman—you."

"Circumstances; yes, I understand that; but——"

"But the other you cannot understand," said Herrick quickly. "Is it anything to me, do you suppose, who rules in Montvilliers?"

"Did I not urge that upon you in the forest?" said Christine.

"Yes; and I gave you an answer. My whim compelled me to see the game to the end. There was truth in that answer, but not all the truth. Did you guess that?"

"I thought of it afterward," she answered.

"Circumstances I might break through," Herrick went on. "They may still be looking for a priest in Vayenne, but this dress of the De Bornais would pass me out of the gates. In a few hours I might be across the frontier."

"Why not go?" she asked, looking suddenly up into his eyes.

"Because you hold me."

"And Captain Lemasle, who is a prisoner, trusts you," said Christine. "You are not the man to leave a comrade like that."

"For the moment I had forgotten him," said Herrick. "You reprove me in kindly fashion; but after to-night we may never speak again as we are now, you and I alone—man and woman. It is nothing to me that you are the greatest lady in this land; to me you are only the woman I love, the lady I worship. I am dedicated to your service. The avowal is wrung from me to-night because—because failure may bring death—at the best flight, and success may bring your contempt."

"Death!" she said slowly.

"That were better than your contempt," he answered.

'I shall not easily hate you," she returned.

"I shall remember always that you have confessed so much," he said quietly, kneeling to kiss her hand.

Into Christine's thoughts came the memory of Lucille's dream and the prince who knelt to her, bringing the fulfilment of all her desires.

"Far from hating you, I might confess more," she whispered, bending over his bowed head.

"Christine!"

The next moment Herrick had sprung to his feet. There were heavy steps in the corridor without, rapidly approaching the room.

"Quick, the window!" said Christine.

"Open it wide," said Herrick, pulling his hood over his head, and noiselessly drawing his sword from its sheath. His cloak was a heavy double one, and the inner part he fastened to conceal his dress, the outer folds he drew together to hide the drawn sword.

"What will you do? Go. No harm can happen to me," said Christine.

The door was rattled sharply.

"Open! Open!"

"Go," Christine whispered. "They will kill you."

"They might insult you," he answered. "Open the door."

"For my sake, go," she said, pointing to the window.

"Open the door," Herrick repeated.

"Open! Open!" came from without as the door was rattled fiercely again.

"Go," she said, her arm stretched out to him. "Just now you said—I thought you meant you——"

"I did mean it," Herrick answered. "Christine, I love you. Now open the door."

She hesitated a moment, then unlocked it, and threw it open, and Felix strode into the room.

"What is the meaning of this intrusion?" she asked.

The Count did not answer her, but advanced toward Herrick.

"Whom have we here masquerading as a priest?"

"You have been looking for me, Count; now you have found me. You came to speak to Mademoiselle. You could hardly have expected to find me here."

By a sudden movement Christine placed herself between the two men.

"What do you want with me, Felix?"

"You will go with me presently to the castle."

"I will go with you now."

"Presently," said Felix.

"Mademoiselle, summon the young girl who was here with you just now," said Herrick. "You may go together to the castle."

The Count's sword rang from its scabbard as a fierce oath left his lips.

"Stay!" Herrick said, his sword's point flashing instantly toward the Count's breast. "Would you fight in the presence of this lady?"

Lucille hurried in with a pale face.

"You must be my maid to-night and come with me to the castle," said Christine.

"Go quickly," said Herrick.

"Felix, you shall go with us," said Christine.

"I will follow," he answered, his eyes fixed on Herrick. "Go. No one will stop you. You are expected at the castle."

"Obedience and trust," said Herrick quietly.

For a moment Christine hesitated, then she went out quickly with Lucille, closing the door.

"Now, Count, I am at your service," said Herrick. "What is our quarrel?"

"It lies too deep for words," said Felix, attacking his adversary hotly. "Say it concerns a woman's honor, if you will."

"Say rather that it springs from the Duke Maurice, whom you have buried in St. Etienne to-day," Herrick answered sternly.

Had he sought to put his adversary off his guard, he

could have chosen no better way than the sudden utterance of these words. Mad with rage, and with the consciousness that it was in this man's power to betray him, he rushed upon Herrick wildly, bent on silencing so dangerous a foe at once and forever. The next instant his sword clattered to the floor, and a moment later Herrick had tossed it through the window into the garden.

"This is not to be a fight to the death, Count," he said. "Yours is a small hurt. I will leave you to bind it up."

"Curse you!"

"Curses fall lightly on honest men," Herrick answered, retreating backward to the door, his sword still in his hand. "You would not have come alone had you expected to find me here; therefore I am fortunate, and in your present humor, mademoiselle is fortunate too in not having your escort back to the castle. There you will hardly dare to insult her."

While Herrick spoke he had opened the door, and fitted the key into the lock on the outside. Now he went out quickly, and locked the door after him.

"Good-night," he called out. "When you have bound up your wound, no doubt some one will come to your shouting."

"Curse you!" came the answer. "The future shall make you regret your present luck."

Herrick laughed, and went quickly down into the hall.

"There is a sword in the garden," he said to the sleepy porter, who was still wondering at the sudden coming and going. "Take a lantern and find it. Count Felix, who is up-stairs, will be calling for it presently."

Once out of the house, Herrick walked rapidly away, and a little later walked in at the castle gate; but no longer a priest. The cloak lay behind the wall of a

He rushed upon Herrick wildly.

garden near the old markets, and was destined to cause much wonder when it was found next day.

Jean shuffled along near him as Herrick went to his quarters.

"Mademoiselle came to the castle not long since. Is all well?"

"Yes."

"And the Count?"

"I left him binding a cut in his wrist."

"Good, friend Roger, though it might have saved trouble if you had made a slit in his heart which could not be bound."   And Jean turned aside, and was lost in the shadows.

CHAPTER XVI

On the terrace below the western tower the sentry slowly paced his appointed round, looking down over the city at intervals, and once or twice glancing up at the tower above him, where, clad in his motley of scarlet and green, Jean sat perched upon the battlements. The dawn was two hours old now, and for full two hours the dwarf had sat there, his grave face sadly at variance with his gay dress, and grinning bauble furnished with jingling bells, which he had stuck under his arm. From this western tower was the widest view of Vayenne, and Jean looked over the city and beyond it to the far hills as though he would imprint the picture upon his memory. Only that morning he had put on his motley for the first time. "The Duke's gift, Jean," Felix had said last night. "Who hurts the fool shall henceforth have to reckon with the Duke." And it would almost seem that the dwarf had come to this exalted spot to show himself to the new day. The sentry smiled at the fool's pride; and some sensation of showing himself to the earth and sky of a new dawn may have passed through the dwarf's mind, but there was no pride in it. He played a part; under the motley was the same Jean, wise, cunning, and alert. He had climbed to the battlements for a purpose, and thoughts had come into his mind as he sat there which had made his face grave as he looked over the city, and to the distant hills, which shut in all the world he had ever known.

It was the third day since Christine de Liancourt had come to the castle, and twice Jean had had speech with her. She had questioned him concerning Roger Herrick, but he could tell her nothing, because Herrick had commanded silence. The hours had been busy for the dwarf, and fortunately for Count Felix also. Jean had not been wanted, and could go about his own affairs unmolested. His work lay in all directions in Vayenne; in the smaller streets and alleys behind St. Etienne, where men lived poorly and nursed discontent in their hearts; in the network of narrow ways about the old markets; in mean cafés and taverns; and in some houses of a better sort where grievances sheltered. Some work, too, there was in the castle itself among the soldiers, who found it unnatural to speak of Felix as the Duke, or who were more than ordinarily superstitious and still marvelled who the spy who had escaped might be, or were suspicious concerning the death of the young scholar of Passey. For each there was different treatment, wisdom here, cunning there; and hardly had Jean slept these few nights past. Last night, indeed, many in Vayenne had not slept, for all signs of mourning had to be folded away, and the city must be decked with wreaths, and colored bunting, and flags, and prepare itself to shout "Long life to the Duke!" So workmen were busy all through the night, and the sounds of hammering faintly ascended to Jean's ears now. He had been in and out among these workers last night, and whatever else he told them, he whispered this in their ears:

"To-morrow! To-morrow! Justice shall be born to-morrow, toward evening, when the Duke mounts the steps of the throne. Then be ready to shout what you have been bidden to shout. All else shall happen

12

as I have told you. I play my part, a mean part, the part of a fool, clad in gaudy coloring with jingling cap and bells. Look for me at dawn at the summit of the western tower. There shall you see me, and what manner of part it is I play. It is the sign that all things are as I have told you."

Thus it was that the dwarf sat long upon the battlements, knowing well that many hundred eyes had turned to look in his direction since daybreak. He had looked down into the streets to see men stop and stare upward; he had looked to this side and that where he knew men were waiting eagerly for light; he had looked toward the high-pitched roof of the great hall of the castle, running lengthways to the great square, and he pictured the scene that a few short hours must bring, the climax to the work with which he had been busy night and day. Still he sat there, looking now to the distant hills, which wrapped themselves about the city, and instead of eager expectation in his face, there was grave contemplation, even the look that he might have worn when in St. Etienne he saw visions. The dawn would break again to-morrow. The morning star would pale in the quivering, golden beams up-springing from behind those sheltering hills. What would another new day lighten in Vayenne?

"Failure," murmured Jean, "and then swift death for us all. Success, and even that must mean rebellion and carnage in her streets once more."

He rose suddenly, and with an impassioned gesture spread wide his arms as if he blessed the city that he loved, a strange, uncouth little figure, ugly as an ancient gargoyle of some great Gothic church. Who shall chronicle all the thoughts that were in him as he stood there? Then he swung himself from the battlement to the roof of the tower, and slowly descended to the court-yard, where busy men greeted him with roars of laughter.

"Your commands, my Lord Fool! Your will, Sir Jester!" they shouted.

"You shall know through your captains, my good fellows," said Jean grandiloquently as he passed on his way to Count Felix.

There was much coming and going in the corridors of the castle, and the dwarf had to run the gauntlet of much chaff, good-natured banter for the most part; and for every one he had an answer, which if not witty passed for such and drew its measure of laughter. It is easy to see humor even in the commonplaces of a licensed jester. No one questioned Jean's right to go where he would, and he passed through the ante-rooms, where many were awaiting an audience, and entered the Count's private apartment unannounced.

Felix looked up, and then burst out laughing, the first time he had laughed since he had returned from the Place Beauvoisin with his hand bound up; and Barbier, who was standing by the Count's table, arrayed in his new uniform as Captain of the Duke's Guard, laughed too.

"So we are three gossips, but only two of us are dressed in our new clothes yet," said Jean. "Haven't they sent yours home yet, friend Felix? Grant they may not come too late."

"Little fear of that now," said Felix, but he became solemn again, and turned to Barbier. "There is nothing more, captain. See that the sentries are doubled everywhere. See that a special guard of honor is given Mademoiselle de Liancourt to-night, and make it clear that neither she nor any of her suite has permission to leave the castle. And remember no priest may enter the Castle of Vayenne but Father Bertrand."

"Had I my will, I would keep him out, too," said Barbier.

"That is impossible," Felix answered. "Every detail of ancient custom must be observed. Go, Barbier, I depend upon you."

"We trust you, Barbier," said Jean. "You are earning your new dress very creditably."

The captain shrugged his shoulders contemptuously at the dwarf as he went out. Barbier had little appreciation of such humor, and perhaps he was not so comfortable in his new uniform as he pretended to be. The Count's wounded hand troubled the Captain of the Guard. Somewhere, undetected, in their midst was a man who knew their secrets.

The wounded hand also troubled the Count. Who was his adversary? What had he to do with Christine de Liancourt?

"No more visions, Jean?" he said, turning to the dwarf, who had seated himself on the floor beside his chair.

"None."

"We travel swiftly to the goal."

"Ay; straight to the goal," Jean answered. "I saw carpenters and servants putting the final touches to the great hall as I passed. It will be a grand spectacle."

"I would it were over," said Felix, "or that we could do without it."

"Why so? The Duke is dead, young Maurice is dead, and Montvilliers must have a duke."

"I have enemies, Jean, and they trouble me. What can I do with them?"

"Bury them quickly, just as we buried the old Duke and his son," the dwarf answered.

"That would be easy could I find these enemies," answered Felix, "but they are secret foes, striking in the dark."

"At your hand," was the quick retort; "your heart is whole. It puzzles me why your enemy did not run you through the heart the other night."

"It puzzles me, too, Jean."

"It would have saved a lot of trouble," the dwarf went on in a musing manner, "and you would have gone to your account proclaimed as a martyr. There would have been pilgrimages to your tomb in St Etienne, and Vayenne would have become famous."

"Since he did not kill me, he must mean other mischief," murmured Felix, following his own train of thoughts and paying little attention to the dwarf.

"Ay; you will lose much by being a duke instead of a martyr," said Jean.

Count Felix roused himself with a sudden effort. This was not the time for fears or dismal forebodings, and he struck the gong upon his table. He had much to do, many persons to see, many things to arrange; and Jean sat there while all this business was transacted, welcoming and dismissing each person with a little musical shake of his fool's bauble. Most of them laughed at him, a few were angry, but it made no difference to the dwarf.

Presently the Count rose.

"Play the fool where you will, Jean, until evening; I go to see the Countess Elisabeth, and I will not take you with me."

"Are you jealous?" asked the dwarf.

"No."

"I'll go and see Christine de Liancourt," said Jean. "I warrant I shall have a hearty welcome. Art jealous now?"

"A little, perhaps."

"She might have liked you as a martyr," chuckled the dwarf. "Oh, I grant you, being a fool has its advantages." And he shook his bauble as the Count passed out of the room.

Then Jean seated himself thoughtfully on the corner of the Count's table, and for a few moments was busy with his seals and wax.

"Since the sentries are doubled, we must take double precaution," he murmured. "Chance is a very useful mistress sometimes, but it does not pay to leave too much to her."

Count Felix went quickly to the suite of rooms Countess Elisabeth occupied for the time being in the castle. He had requested her not to return to the Place Beauvoisin until after he was crowned Duke. He wanted his talisman beside him, he said; and the Countess, perhaps hoping that she would never permanently return to the Place Beauvoisin, remained.

She received him now, as she always did, with a smile of welcome, and he bent over her hand in silence before seating himself beside her.

"I would it were well over, Elisabeth."

"To-morrow at this time it will be," she answered.

"Had I dared to do so, I would have altered the ceremony," he went on; "I would have curtailed some of these absurd customs, and made my coronation far more simple and direct. It should have been swiftly done, and I would have had the reins firmly in my hands before any had time to question me."

"Who can question you?"

"I fear even the voice of one starveling about the court, or even of some soldier who mayhap has begun his revelling too early."

"Your fears are groundless, Felix."

"Are they?" And he held out his bound-up hand to her.

"That was but the stroke of a lover mad with jealousy," Elisabeth answered. "When I sent you to Christine that night I little thought you would find her lover there."

"Who is this lover?"

"Indeed, I cannot tell; but being a woman I read another woman easily. As I told you, I thought she loved this Captain Lemasle; in that I was mistaken, but I was not at fault when I said she was in love. That you must know now."

Felix was silent. A lover of Christine's this sham priest might well be, but he was something more—he was the man who knew his secret. This he could not tell to the Countess without betraying himself.

"Would you still marry her, Felix?" she asked.

"Only for the good of Montvilliers," he answered.

"She will hate you, Felix, even though she be your wife. They are her own words."

"I must risk even that for the good of Montvilliers."

"Ah, your love is a small thing beside your ambition," she said, turning away from him.

"Your love is the dearest thing I have in life, Elisabeth," he said quickly. "Do not turn from me, even for a moment, in such a time as this. I am like a child stepping in the dark who holds out its hands for guidance and protection. After to-morrow, who can tell what action of mine may be best for Montvilliers? If Christine hates me so much, she may show it now, and

give strength to my enemies; she has that power, I cannot rob her of it. Let me once feel that I am firm
without her, and then——"

"Well, Felix?"

Her face was raised to his, and he bent and kissed
her lips.

"For the present know that I love you," he whispered,
"and give me strength for the ordeal through which I
have to pass."

"You ask so much and give so little."

"Wait," he answered. "After to-morrow, I may give
all."

"Yours are, indeed, a child's fears," she said. "Come,
tell me them one by one, and like some good nurse I
will try and show you how foolish they are."

All his fears he could not tell her, perhaps she recognized that he did not, but many he could talk to
her about, and she comforted and strengthened him.
All the ghosts that conscience sent to harass him were
powerless to annul the Countess Elisabeth's work altogether, and it was with firm step and steady eye that
presently the Count met his friends and foes.

Meanwhile Jean went about his work, but it did not
include a visit to Mademoiselle de Liancourt. He
passed slowly through the ante-rooms, where men were
still waiting.

"The audience is at an end," he said. "We have too
much to attend to to-day to see any more of you. The
Count is tired; and has gone to rest a little."

"My Lord Misshapen, won't you attend to us?" said one.

"My unique limbs also require rest; still, what would
you have? We know nothing against you."

"A high place at court, to which my love for you
entitles me," said the man.

"What say you to a rope over the great gate?" said Jean. "It is the most prominent place I can think of."

The man's hand went suddenly to his sword hilt.

"If you draw sword on me," said Jean, tapping him on the arm with his bauble, making the bells jingle, "you are likely to earn your high place rather easily."

The laugh was turned against the man, and the dwarf passed on.

"It is very well to jest," mused Jean as he crossed the court-yard, "but I'm likely to hang yonder over the gate myself if anything goes wrong in the next few hours."

He entered a low doorway, and going slowly along a dark passage, was challenged at the end of it by a sentry. There were two sentries standing there.

"I have come to see the prisoner."

"We have no orders," answered the sentry.

"I go everywhere under a general order," said Jean. "You should know that, blockhead; it has been shouted loud enough in every corner of the castle."

"It does not apply to-day, Jean."

"Who has been telling you fairy tales, that cock-sparrow Barbier?"

The sentry smiled. The new Captain of the Guard was no great friend of his.

"We shall have to cut his feathers," said the dwarf. "Did he tell you that all prisoners were likely to be released to-morrow in honor of the Duke's coronation?"

"No; he did not tell us that."

"And I'm a fool," said the dwarf, "for I was told to keep it secret when I was ordered to bring this release to one of the prisoners to-day." And Jean held out to the sentry a paper, an order of release forthwith, signed and sealed by Count Felix. "You see the name, Pierre Briant, the jailer who let the spy escape. Now, block-heads, are you going to let me pass?"

There was no disputing that order, the sentries stood aside, and one of them proceeded to unlock the cell door.

Pierre Briant looked at the paper and then at the dwarf.

"You are free, jailer Briant," said Jean, "but you are dismissed the Duke's service. You'll have to turn 'prentice to some pedler in the town."

"I'm sorry for that," said the sentry.

"I'll see you on your way to the gate," said the dwarf, and then, when they were out of hearing of the sentries, he went on quickly: "All goes well. Those in the square to-night will follow you. You know what you have to do. Here, put this order of your release in your pocket, walk boldly to the gate, you will not be questioned. Say 'Obedience and trust,' that's your password, and make all speed you can to the Cheval Noir in the Rue de la Grosse Horloge. You will find friends there."

He stood watching the retreating figure across the court-yard, and saw the jailer pass safely through the postern by the great gates.

"That's one deed that would serve to hang me," he muttered. "Barbier is no fool; it is well I had the papers."

He entered the castle again, taking a different direc-tion this time, but again before the door of Gaspard Lemasle's cell two sentries barred his way. Not until he had produced another order of release would they let him pass.

Lemasle walked away with the dwarf in silence.

"What now, Jean?" he whispered when they had passed out of earshot of the sentries.

"Lie low until dark.   Then make for guard-room C. They will be all friends there, stout men, captain, that wait their stout leader.   'Obedience and trust' is our password to-night.   You understand what you have to do?"

"Never fear, Jean; and grant there's a skirmish of some sort, for I have several scores outstanding."

"We had better both hasten to cover then."

"I know a likely hole," Lemasle answered, and he turned quickly into a side passage, and was gone.

"I'll hide, too," muttered the dwarf.   "I have no great desire to meet Barbier until I see him to-night in the great hall."   And he, too, turned into a dark corridor and silently disappeared.

CHAPTER XVII

Darkness crept slowly over Vayenne. Lights shone in the wider thoroughfares, and blinked dimly in the narrower streets. The taverns and the cafés were full, and although there were some who went about their business as though this night were as other nights, there were many who had waited eagerly for the close of day and knew that the hour of action was at hand. Only a few, perhaps, had any clear notion what was to happen; the majority would merely follow where they were led, do what they were told, without question, and without knowing to what end their actions tended. Whatever that end might be, they understood in a vague manner that it would be to their own individual advantage, and in every city there are large numbers who want no greater incentive than this to make them turn out of the ordinary course of their daily routine. They will eagerly follow a possibility without pausing to weigh probabilities. So they waited in the taverns, in the cafés, and at street corners for their leaders, who were discussing the final plans with Pierre Briant at the Cheval Noir.

Within the castle all was life and movement, all men working toward the same purpose it would seem, and if there were an undercurrent which set in an opposite direction, none but those interested in it had time to notice it. Even the lynx-eyed Barbier surveyed his preparations, and found little wanting. For the Duke must be crowned with all ancient customs, and it was so long since a duke had been crowned in Vayenne that some of the usages had been almost forgotten.

The custom had come down from ancient times, and Count Felix dared not alter it. To-night was the civil crowning. In the great hall stood the chair of state, mounted on a platform of six steps; and here in the presence of the nobles of the land and representative burghers of the city, must Felix claim to mount that throne as rightful heir, or by the power given him of the people. If any choose, now might they question him, and he must answer, but being once seated in the chair of state, all right of question was over; only could petition be made then, which the new Duke might answer or not as he willed. Then a priest, placing a golden circle upon his brows, proclaimed him crowned Duke of this land of Montvilliers, and bade him consecrate such crowning on the morrow according to all rites and customs. Then must the representative nobles and burghers, each and individually, bow the knee and swear fealty to their sovereign, making oath to keep the realm inviolate with their lives, and to hold their swords and revenues at the Duke's service for the defence of the state and of his person. Thus was the Duke crowned by his court and by his people. To-morrow in St. Etienne must he be crowned by the Church. Here for a space he must wear the iron crown of Montvilliers and make his vows before the altar in the midst of gorgeous ceremonial and splendor.

There had been occasions when the religious crowning had not followed the civil one immediately, but this was only when stress of state affairs intervened, or an enemy thundered at the gates. Count Felix had decreed that it should follow at once. To-night the civil, to-morrow morning the religious ceremony. When darkness fell again the double ordeal should be over.

The dwarf squatted upon his doubled-up legs in the deep embrasure of one of the windows in the great hall which overlooked the square. He was lifted well above the heads of those who were rapidly filling the hall from end to end, and no one entered without Jean's keen eye noting them and the particular position they took up. Yet to watch him, one would not have supposed that he took any very keen interest in what was going forward. He sat in a more huddled-up fashion than usual, his eyes half closed, as though he might fall asleep at any moment. His bauble was tucked under his arm, and held there so that the little bells on it might not jingle; and although several men looked up at him and made some passing jest, he had no answer for them. The lights in the hall left this window somewhat in shadow, and the dwarf seemed to have chosen it in order to draw as little attention to himself as possible. Beside him lay a small, unlighted torch.

The chair of state stood on its raised dais at the upper end of the hall, and the space around it was at present empty. The less important folk came into the hall first, soldiers and retainers, those who held office about the castle, and others who held civil offices in the town and who by custom had a right to be present at this ceremony.

Captain Barbier, still ignorant apparently of the release of the prisoners, was the most conspicuous person in the assembly at present, and Jean gave more than a passing glance to him. He noted how he placed the company of guards who presently tramped into the hall, noted that, for all his fine appearance and buoyant camaraderie, the captain was no great favorite; a sneer met him here, and a look of contempt followed him yonder. Barbier was quite oblivious of the one and the other. He could afford to smile and strut in his gay new feathers, for was he not trusted by the new Duke, was he not a man in authority, one it would be ill considered to offend? Barbier knew the full strength of his position, and was unlikely to let any of its advantages slip. Jean was quick to recognize the tact and wisdom there was in this man, and to understand that with a few more like him Duke Felix's throne might stand firmer than it did at present.

Next there came into the hall representatives of the suites of the nobles who had come to Vayenne for the funeral of the old Duke and for the coronation of the new. Some of these nobles had been lodged in the castle, some in the town. For the most part they had brought few retainers with them, having, indeed, few to bring. There were rich men in Montvilliers, but not many of them were of noble descent, and some of the most ancient families were comparatively poor. De Bornais was one of the exceptions, and besides loved to uphold his dignity. He had come to Vayenne with a considerable retinue, and although all his followers did not find a place in the hall to-night, he had a larger representation there than anyone else. Jean looked at these men keenly as they were marshalled to their places at the very edge of the open space which surrounded the raised dais. They were fewer in number than he could have wished, but they were stalwart men. One, who fell into his place behind the others, and who, while Barbier was near, kept his hand over his brow, hiding the upper part of his face, glanced presently toward the window where the dwarf sat, and their eyes met. No heads were turned to look at this man particularly, yet for Jean the most important person who would find place in that assembly to-night had already come. It was Roger Herrick.

And now from the side doors which led from the great hall, nobles entered, and took up their positions in the vacant place around the chair of state, and there were many ladies, their wives or daughters, or those who in their own right held high place in the land. The beautiful Countess Elisabeth drew all eyes to her as she took her place at the foot of the dais. Jewels were at her throat and in her hair, and there was no woman fairer to look upon in all that great assembly. After her coming there was a pause, and then, followed by Lucille, Christine de Liancourt entered the hall. A murmur of welcome, like a ripple of low music, greeted her, and the eyes that had rested upon the Countess turned to rest on her. Jewels were at her throat, too, and on her brow a jewelled diadem; almost it seemed as though for her all ceremony was at an end, that already she was crowned Duchess. It was the first time Herrick had seen her arrayed in all the splendor of beautiful womanhood, and that beauty and her position seemed to lift her far beyond his reach. All that had happened in these last days, the ride through the forest, the desperate encounter, the charcoal-burners' hut, their last meeting in the house in the Place Beauvoisin, all seemed to sink far back into the past, to fade and take indefinite outline, to wrap themselves in the dim mantle which belongs to dreams. The present, and all thought of the things he was to do in it, was for the moment forgotten, and fascination riveted his eyes on this woman as a man may look upward and gaze spellbound at the beauty of a distant star. Was it true that only a few nights since she had almost confessed that she loved him? That such a thing could be, seemed impossible now.

Christine was pale, but her eyes shone, and the little firm mouth was brave and determined; yet Lucille, who stood beside her, knew that she was nervous. Christine spoke to her companion, looking into her eyes as she uttered some commonplace. She paid no heed to the girl's answer, her only desire was to steady herself. To-night something was to happen, in a few moments it might be. What was to happen, how it was to come, she did not know; she was only certain that whether came success or failure, bloodshed must assuredly follow. What part had she to play in this rebellion? Then growing steady, she turned and looked to where de Bornais' men stood close behind their master, and saw how Roger Herrick's eyes were fixed upon her. If she read any message at all in them, it did not help her to understand what was to occur. She did not glance at the window in the shadows. She had no knowledge that Jean was there. "Obedience and trust," the dwarf was muttering to himself and wondering how it was friend Roger had succeeded in making her promise so much. Truth to tell there was something like resentment in Christine's mind at that moment at being kept so entirely in the dark. What could happen to-night? What power had this one man, who stood, insignificant, behind de Bornais?

Suddenly there was movement in the hall and shouting, loud shouts of welcome rising sharply above a low, murmuring accompaniment which might be a welcome, differently expressed, or might not. At least there was no harsh and unruly cry of dissatisfaction, nothing that broke upon the ear as actual discord. Those at the back stretched themselves and stood on tiptoe in an endeavor to look over their neighbors' heads; and even Jean from his exalted position could not see clearly what

13

was going forward, for the crowd had closed in at the upper end of the hall for a moment. Then it fell back a little, to show that Count Felix stood at the foot of the dais, and that Father Bertrand had mounted it and stood by the chair of state.

There was a moment's pause, during which the shifting feet became silent, and Jean, leaning backward in the shadow of the embrasure, stole a glance down into the great square below.

"It has ever been our custom to crown the Dukes of Montvilliers according to certain peculiar rites and customs," said Father Bertrand, speaking slowly and in a tone which carried his words clearly to the utmost limits of the great hall. "You know, most of you, what these ancient rites and customs are, how your future Duke, claiming this throne, must stand to answer your questioning before he seats himself to receive your homage. There have been occasions when the claim has stood more by might than by right, when your voices by common consent have bid a warrior, or a deliverer from oppression, to wear the crown and rule over you. This is no such occasion. Since Maurice, son of the late Duke, is dead, Count Felix stands before you, the legal heir to Duke Robert. I have then but to ask him those questions which every Duke that has reigned in Mont- villiers has been asked, solemn questions which here, in this old hall of Vayenne, each one of them has been required to answer. Count Felix, I demand by what right you claim to ascend this throne of Mont- villiers?"

"By right of birth," came the answer, spoken quickly and in a loud voice.

There was a pause, but no sound broke the silence which followed.

"Count Felix, I charge you, is there any reason known to you which makes your claim a false one?"

"There is no such reason," said the Count. Again he spoke quickly and in a clear tone, and he looked at Christine. Her eyes met his for a moment, but hers were the first to look away. Whatever she knew or believed, she was not going to speak.

Again the silence remained unbroken.

"Count Felix, do you swear to govern this land according to the same laws of right and liberty by which it has heretofore been governed, and to hold the welfare of your people as a sacred trust?"

"All this I swear to do," answered the Count.

"My lords, knights, burghers, and men of Montvilliers, those are the questions I have to ask, and which you have heard the Count answer. Now question him as you will," said Father Bertrand.

Count Felix stood on the lower step of the dais, and turned to face his questioners. He was pale as a man facing such an ordeal well might be, but he smiled bravely. He felt that the worst was over. Christine had not spoken. The time for the questions which he had dreaded most seemed to be passed. Christine did not look at him. Her eyes were fixed upon the group of men behind de Bornais. One of them no longer kept himself in the background. His companions had made way for him, and he stood almost at de Bornais' side. Why had Roger Herrick not spoken? Had fear kept him dumb at the last moment?

For some little time no question was asked, and then a burgher, stammering in his words and half fearful of the sound of his own voice, prayed for an alteration in some civic law, a mere triviality it seemed to break so momentous a silence. Yet it set others asking questions, and Felix answered them, promising future grave attention where no immediate relief could be given. Such questioning served to stimulate the Count, and a color gradually stole into his face. A new courage was in his soul as may come to a man who feels himself whole, and knows that the danger he has so much dreaded is past.

The questioning was over. A long pause had come, and not a voice was raised in the hall. The dwarf silently put down his bauble by his side, careful that the little bells should not jingle, and took up the torch. Matches were in his hand, but his eyes were fixed upon the dais. No movement below caused him to look away for an instant.

"Count Felix," the priest's voice rang out clearly, "you have answered my questions, you have answered the questions of your people as represented by this assembly. To this throne you must now ascend."

Count Felix turned, and his foot was on the second step of the dais when a loud voice cried:

"Stay!"

Felix, white again suddenly, and to his very lips, looked down into the face of the man who had dared thus to approach the throne and stand even with his foot upon the first step. He wore the uniform of the de Bornais, but Felix hardly noticed this. It was the face of the man that riveted his attention. He recognized it. How could he forget it, since when last he looked into those eyes it had been across keen, naked blades. Does a man ever forget a face seen thus?

"Your interference comes late," said the priest, "yet is it not, I think, against the ancient custom. Until the Duke is seated he may be questioned. What is your question?"

Christine bent suddenly forward almost as though she expected the question to be asked in a whisper. But the words rang out clearly.

"It is no question I would ask, but a demand I make, not to Count Felix, but to those assembled in this hall. I, Roger Herrick, claim my right by birth to ascend this throne as the true and lawful Duke of Montvilliers!"

CHAPTER XVIII

As the moment after a catastrophe is ever one of silence, a hush before the piteous wail of anguish rises or the tempest thunders out its fury, so was it now. Herrick's words were followed by utter silence.

Then the tempest broke suddenly. With a hiss of rage, Felix raised his arm to strike his adversary, but Herrick sprang up to him, and gripped it before the blow could fall.

"I stand sponsor for this man's claim!" de Bornais cried, and the men who had stood behind him drew their swords as their chief did, and ranged themselves with him at the foot of the dais.

Other swords leaped from their scabbards in a moment, and women screamed and scattered, fleeing to the side doors of the hall, men pressing back to let them go. Only Christine stood immovable, and Countess Elisabeth made a sudden step forward as though she would go to Felix's help. So round the dais men waited ready to attack or to defend, but no one moved to strike the first blow.

At the end of the hall by the great doors it was different. There was Barbier with his guard, and at a sharp command from the captain they began to move to Felix's rescue. At that moment Jean sprang to his feet in the embrasure of the window, a lighted torch, which spluttered and flared up, in his hand. There was the crash of broken glass, and as he flung the burning torch into the square below, he shouted in a voice that rang high above the tumult:

"Long live Roger the Duke!"

For one instant the cry seemed a solitary one, doomed to die in its own echoes, but the next an answering roar came from the square below, such a rage of sound that even Barbier's men paused.

"Cut down that grinning fool from the window," shouted Barbier, "and forward to the Duke!"

Whatever his faults, Barbier was a brave man. Had Felix had more like him, the situation might have been saved even at this eleventh hour. But his men hung back, and did not strive with a will against the pressure of the crowd. Barbier alone fought his way through all obstacles, and threw himself, sword in hand, upon de Bornais' men. One stumbled, wounded slightly in this onslaught, and then Barbier's sword rattled to the floor, and with a catch in his breath he flung out his arms and fell backward through the crowd which pressed aside to let him go—dead.

"So he pays for his attack on Maurice," whispered Herrick to the man whose arm he still held.

Few moments had elapsed since the Count had raised his arm to strike, and since Barbier had fought and fallen, other swords might well have been crossed in anger had not the roaring from the square held men back. There was a force around them which there was no withstanding, and the cry of "Roger the Duke" now rang in the castle itself, in the court-yards, and in the corridors. Armed men, shouting the cry, rushed into the hall, headed by Gaspard Lemasle, and in the court-yard was a compact throng of men of Vayenne with Pierre Briant at their head. Barbier was dead in the hall, and one or two who had attempted to defend the castle had been struck down, killed or grievously hurt, that was all. The success of the conspirators was complete.

"Treachery triumphant," Felix said as Herrick let go his arm. "The day is to traitors, Christine."

He had stepped from the dais, and stood beside her, but neither by look nor movement did she show that she had heard his words. Her eyes were fixed upon the place where Barbier had staggered back and fallen through the little lane that pressure on either side had formed for him. It had closed up again immediately, but somewhere behind there he lay, perhaps trampled underfoot. It is not to be supposed that the terrible suddenness of his death had not shocked her, but there was a sense of relief that the whole hall was not full of fighting and death. Beyond this her thoughts were unable to focus themselves. Fear had not held Roger Herrick back, but, as yet, she hardly realized what had happened. She neither looked at Herrick standing on the steps of the dais, nor took in the words of Felix, who was standing beside her.

The shouting was still loud in the court-yards, but in the hall there was silence after the coming of Lemasle and his men.

"Your claim must sound strange to many here," said Father Bertrand. "Is it your will that I explain it?"

"Speak, father," said Herrick.

"So you, then, are chief conspirator, old fox?" sneered the Count. "This farce tires me. Have I permission to retire while you prove to these, my lords and loyal men of Vayenne, how false a claim is made by this man?"

"No. Stay," said Herrick.

Felix glanced at the faces of those about him. A

single sign would have sufficed to make him their leader in an immediate attack upon their enemies, but no sign was forthcoming. Even those who were his friends, whose hope of future advancement lay with the Count, were afraid to move with those shouts from the court-yard and the square ringing in their ears.

Speaking very deliberately, Father Bertrand recited the history of the last Dukes of Montvilliers, even as he had explained it to Herrick in the Rue St. Romain, showing that although the late Duke, having deposed his predecessor, had ascended the throne by the will of the people, even then there existed one with a prior claim.

"This Roger Herrick was alive then, a child in England, the rightful heir to the Dukedom," said Father Bertrand. "The descent of the late Duke is known to you all, and all that I have said you can verify at your will. Might, and the people's will, set the late Duke upon the throne, and it is in your power to set Count Felix in his place, but not by right of birth while this man Roger Herrick lives."

While the priest had been speaking Christine turned to look at Herrick, but he would not meet her eyes. His glance wandered from face to face in the hall as though he were absorbed in the thought of how far the people were with him. To Christine it seemed that his own ambition possessed him entirely.

"Is Vayenne gone mad that it will believe such a tale as this?" said Felix.

"Let the Duke speak!" cried a voice in the hall, the voice of Lemasle, and there was a shout of applause, which showed the Count how many there were against him.

Then Herrick looked at Christine, and their eyes met.

Something he read in them showed him that what he
had feared had happened in spite of all his efforts to
prevent it. The knowledge forced him to a sudden
determination. There were friends about him, but there
were many enemies, too. Any indecision would be his
ruin; he saw that in the faces which turned to him
expectantly. Circumstances still drove him forward,
and he dare not say all that it was within his heart to
speak. The occasion demanded strong measures.

"Father Bertrand has told you my legal claim,"
Herrick said, "yet that should hardly suffice without
the will of the people. For the moment let might be
my right, and understand why that right has been
exercised. That success has followed organized rebellion, shows how ready the people were to do away,
not with law and order, but with a man unfit to reign
over them. For this reason I have pressed my claim,
and for no other. Count Felix has friends amongst
you, some innocent, some bought with his promises for
the future, but the true value of that friendship rested
on his becoming Duke. Those who were taken utterly
into his confidence I believe to be few, but at all hazards
he meant to be Duke, and to achieve this the Duke's
son Maurice must be got rid of. The manner in which
this was done was clever, worthy of the man who conceived and carried out the treachery. An escort was
sent with Mademoiselle de Liancourt to Passey to bring
Maurice to Vayenne, an escort that had only one honest
man in it, Captain Gaspard Lemasle; the rest were the
creatures of Count Felix, paid assassins. This escort
on returning to Vayenne was attacked by a strongly
armed band of robbers, who were no robbers, but other
creatures of the Count, led by the man Barbier, who
only a few minutes since so justly paid the penalty of

his crime. A mock skirmish took place in a clearing in the woods. The result you know. Maurice's body was found and brought to Vayenne, and the Duke and his son were buried at the same time in St. Etienne. My lords, is such a man a Duke you would willingly have to reign over you?"

"Is such a lie to be easily believed?" the Count burst out.

"I fought beside Captain Lemasle in the young Duke's defence," Herrick cried, "and Mademoiselle de Liancourt can prove the truth of my words."

All eyes turned to her.

"They are true," she said, and then looking at Herrick, she asked: "Is that all there is to tell?"

It was not. The very tone in which she asked the question showed that there was more to be said, and that she knew it. All eyes were turned to Herrick again expectantly.

"There is no more to tell," said Herrick slowly and firmly, looking at Christine with a challenge in his glance. "What need to speak of the silent and careful plotting which has resulted in this night's success? There has been no treachery against the state."

"Long live Duke Roger!" cried Jean, who still stood in the embrasure of the window. "Long live the Duke!"

The cry was taken up by Lemasle and his followers in the hall, and immediately was roared along the corridors, now filled with the men who had followed Pierre Briant into the court-yard. It was no uncertain sound, and not a dissentient voice made itself heard. Even Felix remained silent, and he remembered with sudden fear how Jean had spoken of a Count once who was hanged over the great gate.

"It is the voice of the people," said Father Bertrand,

standing by the chair of state in which every Duke of Montvilliers had been crowned. "Roger Herrick, I demand by what right you claim to ascend this throne."

"By right of birth," he answered, his eyes upon Christine.

"Roger Herrick, I charge you, is there any reason known to you which makes your claim a false one?"

"There is no reason," he answered, still with his eyes upon Christine.

"Roger Herrick, do you swear to govern this land according to the same laws of right and liberty by which it has heretofore been governed, and to hold the welfare of your people as a sacred trust?"

"I swear to do this," said Herrick, and then facing the excited crowd he cried: "Is there any here who would question me?"

The sudden silence remained unbroken, and with a firm step Herrick ascended the dais, and seated himself in the chair.

"Roger Herrick, I crown you Duke of Montvilliers," said Father Bertrand in a loud voice, placing the golden circle upon his head. "Presently in St. Etienne must you wear the iron crown, and there receive Heaven's blessing upon this high estate to which you are called."

Then once again the roar went up from a multitude of throats: "Long live Roger the Duke! Long live the Duke!" And an instant later came the first angry growl. "Down with Felix! Death to the Count!"

The Countess Elisabeth with a sharp cry sprang to Felix's side. Christine did not move, but she looked at Herrick as though she wondered to what lengths he would go in the pursuit of his ambition. The Count's death seemed only the natural sequence to the events of that night.

Herrick sprang to his feet.

"Stop!" he cried, and he looked a leader of men as he stood there, his arm outstretched in command. "Stop! No revenge shall have my sanction. Count Felix may yet live to make a good subject. All we need guard against is his becoming a dangerous rebel. You are free, Count, only for a term you must limit your freedom to Vayenne. You are not permitted to leave the city nor to enter the castle. Lemasle, see that the Count has safe conduct through the streets."

The Countess touched Felix on the arm. Whether she believed what had been said of him or not, this was not the time to desert him. Felix bowed his head, and they passed out of the hall together. It would have gone hard with the Count in the corridors and court-yard but for the men who marched beside him to the gate and presently escorted his carriage to the Place Beauvoisin.

"My lords, I would not ask too much of you," said Herrick, when Felix and the Countess Elisabeth had gone. "Here is no trap to catch your loyalty and obedience. You were not bid to my coronation; those who will are free to depart. No harm shall be done you in Vayenne, only within seven days shall you promise me service, or you will be reckoned amongst my enemies."

There was a pause, and then an old man stepped forward.

"My Lord Duke, I have ever been a loyal servant to my country. My name is amongst the oldest in the land, and, therefore, it becomes me, perhaps, to give words to what many here must feel. This that has happened to-night has come without warning. You are a stranger to us, and we cannot know whether all that we have heard to-night, either of yourself or of Count Felix, is true, or whether there is not something held back from our knowledge which might give a different complexion to this affair. It is only just, therefore, that we have time for consideration, only just that no suspicion should fall upon us though we do not bow the knee and take oaths upon us to-night."

"Your contention is reasonable," Herrick answered. "I have given you seven days."

"I would be the first to wish your Grace long life, and herewith I proffer my service," said de Bornais, kneeling for a moment at the foot of the dais.

A few followed his example, some honestly enough, since they hated the Count, others making haste to put themselves forward prominently. But the greater number chose to take the seven days for consideration, and passed from the hall without kneeling.

De Bornais and his men, still with swords drawn, stood round the dais, the Duke's guard of honor, as the hall slowly emptied. Gaspard Lemasle had cleared the corridors, with the promise that the Duke should come presently on to the terrace above the court-yard and speak to his loyal subjects. The nobles passed to their lodgings in the castle, or waited in ante-rooms until they could be taken through the streets in safety. The murmur of the great crowd, like the distant ocean breaking on a rock-bound shore, could still be heard, but the excitement had died down. The thing that these men had come to do was accomplished.

Jean leaped from the embrasure of the window, and, waddling across the hall, seated himself on the lowest step of the dais, close to where Christine still stood immovable.

"Has Mademoiselle de Liancourt no word for

us?" said Herrick, when the last of the nobles had gone.

She started at the sound of her name, but sne did not speak.

"You gave us a certain promise, mademoiselle, which I warned you it would be hard to fulfil."

"So hard, sir, that it has already passed from my memory," she said.

"I feared so," Herrick returned quietly. "Later, perhaps, you will understand. Mademoiselle, with you I make no bargain. Take time for consideration, as long as you will. Though you hate me, I swear never to number you among my enemies."

"I understand," she said, turning to him quickly, "and I want no time for consideration. I shall never recognize your title to sit on the throne of Montvilliers. You have cleverly realized your ambition, and in a measure I have unwittingly helped you to it. Count me as you will, but I make no secret of my enmity. It shall last to the end, and those who plot against you shall find me a willing tool. It is not for nothing that I have loved this land, for the good of it I am prepared for any sacrifice, and am I, Christine de Liancourt, to bend the knee to an English adventurer, who, with the help of a fool and a mob and his own mother-wit, seizes the throne? To-night madness has run riot, the reaction has to come, and be very sure it will come. What real value is the support of a mob? To-day it shouts for you, to-morrow it will as easily shout for another. Live out your little dream, I promise you a rude awakening. To-night is yours, and I bow to circumstances which give you power to-night. Have I your leave to depart?"

"Whither, lady?"

She looked at him defiantly.

"Though we have sworn never to count you amongst our enemies, we are not ignorant of the power of so fair a rebel. There was an order issued by Count Felix that Mademoiselle de Liancourt was not to be allowed out of the castle, that order I endorse."

"Am I a prisoner?" she asked.

"No mademoiselle; an honored guest in my Castle of Vayenne. De Bornais, I deliver our guest into your keeping. And, Lemasle, see that the password is changed presently. 'Obedience and trust' have little meaning."

Christine looked at Herrick once swiftly, and then passed out of the hall, followed by de Bornais and his men. Herrick, the golden circle upon his brow, leaned back in his chair like a tired man. Father Bertrand stood beside him. Lemasle stood at the foot of the dais, and Jean sat on the lowest step. They were alone.

"You look too glum for a successful man, friend Roger," said the dwarf.

"Success leaves a bitter taste upon my lips."

"It will pass with morning," said the priest.

"It shall last to the end," said Herrick, repeating Christine's words.

"I fear you have been too lenient," said Lemasle, letting his sword fall with a rattle into its scabbard.

"He, at least, has found the payment sufficiently high," said Jean, and the bells on his bauble jingled as he pointed it at the dead body of Captain Barbier.

CHAPTER XIX

THE conviction that the new Duke had been too lenient was more firmly impressed upon Gaspard Lemasle each day, each hour almost. In the captain's conception of life and duty there was much that was primitive; a blow for a blow, treachery for treachery, seemed to him amongst the first laws of existence. Failure would have meant certain death to the conspirators, success naturally ought to mean death to those against whom they had conspired, to Count Felix and all who had aided him.

"A man who holds his power at the hands of the mob cannot afford to be lenient," he said to Jean.

"Is that friend Roger's case?" said the dwarf.

"At present, yes. The few soldiers we can command would hardly serve to crush an organized rising in the Count's favor. I would he were dead."

Lemasle did not speak without reason. The people had come together for a purpose, but that purpose accomplished, the mob was not to be easily dispersed. Such men in rebelling threw law and order behind them, the thought of riot and plunder filled their hearts, yet at the very outset restraint had been put upon them. Nobles had been allowed to pass through the streets and leave the city, strict orders being given that they were not to be molested. Some of the bolder spirits had refused to obey these orders and immediately found themselves confronted by soldiers, their carbines loaded,

14

their swords drawn. The sharp orders from the officers left no doubt in the mind of the crowd what the result of disobedience would be. There had been some looting of shops, and swift punishment had fallen upon the robbers. The command to desist, if not instantly obeyed, was likely to mean sudden death. The crowd was disappointed, and grew quarrelsome. What had been gained by setting this Duke Roger on the throne? The question once asked, there were many quite as ready to fight against Duke Roger as they had been to fight for him, and the mob was split up into factions. Serious street fighting became general, and had to be suppressed with a strong hand. To the Count and his allies, Herrick may have been too lenient, but it soon became evident in Vayenne that the man who had been raised to power was capable of ruling with an iron hand. His prompt action somewhat appeased Lemasle, but it was evident to the captain that the dissatisfaction was not stamped out, but lay hidden, smouldering, waiting its opportunity.

The seven days which Herrick had given the nobles to decide whether they would serve him or not, had passed, and comparatively few of them had submitted. Some asked for an extension of time, some would fain have remained neutral, and others boldly declared their inability to accept his claim as a just one. There was little doubt that Christine de Liancourt's attitude, which had certainly become known in many quarters, had something to do with the position taken up by the nobility; and the people of Vayenne, whose idol Mademoiselle was, were silently, if not openly, opposed to the new Duke in consequence. There was another point which told against Herrick. He refused, for the present, to be crowned in St. Etienne, and people were quick to declare that he was afraid to go through such a ceremony because he knew that his claim was an unjust one. Lemasle urged him to wear the iron crown, pointing out how valuable an effect it would produce, but Herrick remained obdurate.

"Not yet, Lemasle," he answered. "When the iron crown is placed on my head the whole nation shall shout for joy, or the crown shall never rest there."

"You occupy a thorny seat, sir," said the captain, who had easily fallen into his place as a loyal subject of the Duke.

"I care not so long as such men as you, and those you command, love me."

The overbearing and insulting manner of Barbier had proved of great service to Herrick. The best soldiers and men-at-arms, who loved Gaspard Lemasle, were for the new Duke to a man; and if Herrick did not hold his power by the will of the people exactly, he certainly could not have held it without Lemasle. The fact was not unrecognized in the Place Beauvoisin, where Felix still remained, and elsewhere. Lemasle might be bought presently, it was argued; for to men who are not scrupulous themselves every man has his price. Those who hated Roger Herrick could afford to wait.

Herrick issued his orders from the same room whence Count Felix had issued his, and Jean squatted beside him as he had done beside Felix. Herrick had wished to do away with the gaudy raiment and the cap and bells, but the dwarf had pleaded that he might retain them.

"They have proved useful, they may prove so again," said Jean.

Herrick was busy, and the dwarf had not spoken for nearly an hour, when the door opened, and two men were ushered into the room. In an instant the dwarf's fingers were upon a revolver which he carried underneath his fool's garment, for Jean had constituted himself the Duke's special body-guard. His eyes were ever keenly watching those with whom the Duke conversed. An unfortunate movement might easily have cost a man his life.

Herrick signed to the men who had remained near the door to come forward.

"Do you recognize me?" he asked.

"No, my lord; but I know you are the Duke," answered one.

The other was not so certain.

"One of you helped to cut my bonds one night when I was bound by robbers to a tree in the forest near your hut," said Herrick.

The men remembered at once.

"You little thought your services were given to the Duke of Montvilliers, who does not forget them. We would find you better service in the Castle of Vayenne; but not at once. We have other work for you to do. You remember our speaking of an old, toothless hag who was with those robbers?"

"Yes, my lord."

"She must be found. Can you find her?"

"We can try," was the answer. "We are more likely to be able to trace her than anyone else perhaps."

Herrick struck a gong, and sent for Pierre Briant, who was instructed to take half a dozen men and go with the charcoal-burners.

"This hag must be brought to Vayenne," he said. "Tie her up as you will, but do not injure her. She has a secret, and we shall find means here to make her tell it."

Jean looked at Herrick as the men left the room.

"This mission is a secret, Jean; I would have no one told of it."

The dwarf nodded.

"Vayenne would be alive with rumor in an hour, and that we cannot afford."

"Will you tell Mademoiselle?" Jean asked.

"Why should I tell my enemy?"

"To make her a friend," was the answer.

Herrick laughed, but there was no mirth in his laughter.

"You have changed a good deal, friend Roger," said the dwarf after a pause.

"Is that wonderful? Does a man become a duke without changing? To be nobody particular is the happiest condition, Jean. When you climb up into the seats of the mighty, you get a wider view of the world and the men and women in it. The sight is not pleasant, and the heart and head grow quickly sick of it all."

"Why climb then?" asked Jean.

"We are children of circumstances, and our own inclinations count for little," Herrick returned.

"Twice, at least, you might have ridden to the frontier and left Montvilliers to settle its own quarrels. Why didn't you?"

"Ah! Why didn't I?" said Herrick, asking himself a question rather than making a reply to the dwarf.

There was a long silence, and presently Jean rose to his feet, and going to Herrick, touched him on the arm with his fool's bauble sharply enough to make the bells jingle.

"I alone wear the uniform, friend Roger, but maybe I am not the only fool. There are different kinds of fools. Dukes may be of the brotherhood, and perchance women like Màdemoiselle de Liancourt. You might find the world a less disagreeable place if you deigned to explain yourself and tried to understand others. Men have become wise before now by following the advice of a fool."

Herrick laughed again, still mirthlessly, as he passed out of the room. His days were full of arduous business. A few stanch friends he had, but mostly enemies surrounded him, enemies who were silent because they feared him. Was it a marvel that he had changed? A man forced to hold his position by inspiring fear must necessarily live apart and take care to show no weaknesses. Sentiment is not for him, and any kindness he may do must be begged for, not given freely. Such a man must own to no mistakes, cannot confess to an ill-judged action, theoretically he must be incapable of doing wrong.

From her window Christine saw Herrick cross the court-yard, and drew back as he glanced up. He had made no attempt to see her, had sent her no message, since that night in the great hall, and not wishing to meet him she had remained in her rooms, although she was at liberty to wander anywhere in the castle. Lucille was her constant companion, and although she was not allowed to go abroad in the city, she did go about in the castle, and from her Christine learned much of what was happening. She heard that many nobles had refused to submit to the new Duke; that rioting had been suppressed with a quick and heavy hand; that the coming and going to and from the castle and the city were under strict supervision.

"They say everywhere that the new Duke is a strong man," said Lucille.

"Has he captured your fancy?" asked Christine.

"Do you see in him the prince who, passing all others, was to come and kneel at your feet?"

"Oh, mademoiselle, of course not," the girl answered, blushing. "I have passed through such excitement since I told you my dream that I had almost forgotten it. Besides——"

"Well, child?"

"Ah, you will be angry, but I thought—I really thought you loved the Duke."

"You have strange fancies. Am I likely to have any feeling but hatred for a tyrant and a usurper?"

And then Christine had wished to be left alone, and Lucille wondered whether her anger was as great as it seemed.

Who shall understand the heart of a woman? Truly, not even her lover. Christine told herself that she was glad Roger Herrick had not been to see her, yet she watched from her window at those times she expected to see him in the court-yard. As Duke he might be nothing more than an ambitious tyrant, but she could not altogether forget what manner of man he had been in the charcoal-burners' hut and at the house in the Place Beauvoisin.

She was alone, and Roger Herrick filled her thoughts, when the door opened, and Herrick entered. He came unannounced, the door was closed behind him, and they were alone. Jean's advice had not passed unheeded. Herrick had come determined to make an explanation. A slight color stole into Christine's face. Perhaps she was glad he had come, yet she resented the manner of his coming; and face to face with her, the memory of her scorn the other night rose vividly in Herrick's mind. In the short pause which ensued, Fate seemed to draw barriers between them.

"Am I denied privacy then?" she asked.

"Had I sent to ask you to see me, you would probably have refused," said Herrick.

"Probably."

"Therefore I use the only way open to me," he answered.

"At present you are master. A prisoner complains of insult in vain."

"You are free to go where you will in the castle, mademoiselle. I thought you understood that."

"I wish to leave the castle," she answered.

"At present that is impossible," he replied. "I have too many enemies abroad as it is."

"Why not crush them while you have the opportunity?" she said. "Kill the Count, kill me. Why do you hesitate?"

"Count Felix certainly merits death," Herrick returned, "but I fear others more than I do the Count."

"Is it Maurice you fear? Your ambition hadn't fully blossomed that day in the forest, or you would not have saved him."

"You are unjust, mademoiselle."

"Do you suppose your action the other night would have been possible had you spoken the whole truth, and declared that Maurice was alive, that you were the one man who knew that he was alive?"

"I took the throne by right of birth, mademoiselle, you forget that. Why should I trouble to explain away Maurice's claim when his cousin Felix had had him buried in St. Etienne?"

"You know Maurice was not buried there?"

"But I do not know for certain that he is alive. Surely I am a better Duke than Felix?"

"You? An Englishman! A mere adventurer!"

"You used kinder language, mademoiselle, when you chose to accept my service."

"Like others I have played into your hands," she answered. "I fail to see the use in prolonging this interview."

"Mademoiselle, I came to explain certain things to you."

"You can force me to listen to you, but there is no explanation I will willingly hear."

"Trust me, there shall be no explanation that you do not willingly listen to," said Herrick. "You compel me to silence, you drive me to harsh measures. Your enmity lends strength to these nobles who refuse to submit to my rule. They await their opportunity to rebel, but alone they are powerless. Their only hope of success is to bring a foreign nation into Montvilliers to help them, and already there are rumors that such negotiations are taking place. I may fall, but with me falls the independence of Montvilliers, and the fault will lie at the door of the woman who has so loudly professed her love for her country—your door, mademoiselle."

"Montvilliers is in the hands of a foreigner now," she answered quietly.

"If you believe that, you know little of your country's history," Herrick answered; "but you do not believe it. I have a claim, and you know it, whether it is a good one in your eyes or not. If there is one man necessary to the state at the present moment, I am that man; and if there is one person who has it in her power to ruin the state, you are that person; therefore you are confined to the castle. Some day, mademoiselle, you may understand that I have given you a lesson in patriotism."

"In words you are indeed a bold man," she said.

"My deeds speak for themselves. They have saved Montvilliers from Count Felix; with your help they should save the land from invasion and conquest. Will you ask me to explain all I came to say to you to-day?"

"Is it necessary?" she asked. "You are afraid of me, I want no explanation to understand that."

"You once said that for your country's good you would marry Count Felix. Were they words merely, or did you mean it?"

"I meant it."

"And you hated him?"

"It would have been a sacrifice."

"Are you still prepared to make such a sacrifice?" Herrick asked. "It is in your power to save the country from the double peril of civil war and invasion. Will you do it?"

"Marry Felix? Now?"

"Why not, if your country demands it, or a worse than Felix if necessary. To-day Felix is nothing, he holds no power. The power is with me. Make the sacrifice, mademoiselle; trust me to fulfil my part—marry me."

"Marry you!" she said, shrinking back from him.

"That you hate me does not count, that is altogether beside the bargain. It is the country you have to consider; you make the sacrifice for your country."

"Enough. I refuse to make such a sacrifice as this," she answered.

"That I love you courts for nothing, I suppose?" said Herrick after a pause.

She did not answer at once. She saw again the man kneeling to her in the hut, and again that night when

Felix had broken in upon them. Had he kneeled to her now, she might have relented.

"Less than nothing," she said slowly after a pause.

Herrick's face hardened. In his heart was love, passionate longing, and the madness of desire, but he suppressed all outward sign of the tempest that raged within him.

"I had built much on your friendship, mademoiselle," he said quietly, "I had even dared to hope that my love had touched an answering chord in your heart. I little thought to stand alone in my love for this land of ours."

"Ours!"

"Truly its ruin cannot hurt you much since you care for it so little. Could I leave it, and all that belongs to it, I would do so, for I have learned hard lessons in it."

"You have reached your ambition," she said.

"Have I? I believed in a woman's trust, and I have awakened from a dream. I will trouble you no more. The times demand the Duke; Roger Herrick ceases to exist. The Duke lives to hold Montvilliers against her enemies. Roger Herrick was a poor fool who loved and trusted you, mademoiselle."

He turned, and left her, the door closing heavily behind him. For a moment Christine stood where she was, angry, defiant, then she sank into a chair, and sobbed. Wounded pride, disappointment, loneliness, and love were in her tears.

"If he were only Roger Herrick and no Duke," she said, "I could have loved, I would have done all that he—— But he shall suffer. I have power, and right is on my side. He has defied the law, why should not I? The people would make me Duchess. Why should I not wear the crown?"

And then she rose quickly, stepping back into the

shadows, as the door opened again. She thought Herrick was returning, and she would not have him see her tears. It was not Herrick, it was Father Bertrand.

"Did your master send you to me?" she asked.

"Mademoiselle, I have no masters but the Church and my conscience."

She laughed, dashing the last tears from her eyes.

"The Duke you have helped to make should reward you well."

"Even a priest may be mistaken, mademoiselle," Father Bertrand said slowly. "I came to talk to you about the Duke. Already they do not love him in Vayenne."

"And you, father?"

The priest went to the door, opened it quickly to surprise any listener there might be, then closed it again, and stepped to Christine's side.

"His friends were chiefly his friends because of you, mademoiselle. They thought you believed in Roger Herrick, that he had your support. At your word Vayenne would rise to-morrow."

Christine did not answer for a moment. Her power suddenly frightened her. Then she said slowly:

"I will listen attentively to all you have to say, Father Bertrand. You find me a prisoner and in the mood to be rebellious."

And the room grew dark as the priest talked, yet she did not call for lights.

CHAPTER XX

EVEN the busier streets of Vayenne were quieter now after nightfall than they were wont to be. Those who were abroad went quickly and direct to their destination, for to loiter, or appear to have no particular object in view, was to be suspected. The new Duke was ruling the city with a heavy hand, and those who passed in and out of the gates were closely questioned. A few there were who approved this caution; it was temporary only, and justified by the rumors of disturbance on the frontier; but others, and they were the majority, were discontented and sullen. Had they not helped to place a tyrant at the head of the state? Would there have been any trouble on the frontier if Count Felix had become their Duke?

Few people passed along the dimly lighted Rue St. Romain even in the daytime, and at night it was practically deserted. Those who went to visit Father Bertrand were fewer now than formerly. He was heart and soul for Duke Roger, had evidently been privy to the sudden and unexpected claim to the throne, and many began to mistrust him. They waited, expecting to hear that great honors had been showered upon him for his services. He was surely a politician seeking place and power rather than a priest.

Father Bertrand sat at his table in the well-appointed room where he had received Herrick. He was busy with his papers, some of which required careful study and deciphering, for to the casual reader they would have been meaningless. Opposite to him sat Mercier, watching him and waiting for him to speak.

"He who plots sets out on a thorny path," said the priest presently, looking suddenly at his companion.

"He turns enemies into distrustful friends, and his friends into bitter enemies. I sometimes wish I could steal quietly out of Vayenne in the night, and never return."

"Have you bad news there, father?" Mercier asked, pointing to the papers.

"No. On paper all is plausible and easy, but few know the resource of the man we have to reckon with. The Duke is a strong man, Mercier, a worthy successor to the old Duke. I thought to smooth my road when I helped to raise him to the throne; I have instead set a thousand new difficulties in the way."

"The hand that made can unmake, and surely the people——"

"Hist!" said Father Bertrand sharply, as he raised a warning finger. There were steps in the passage without, and then, after a knock and a pause, the door was thrown open, and a man and woman, closely muffled up, entered the room.

The priest rose to welcome them, and Mercier drew chairs to the table for them.

"You came through the city safely?" said Father Bertrand.

"Ay; hurrying like a couple of bourgeois bent on doing their marketing cheaply and expeditiously," said Count Felix, undoing his cloak; and turning to his companion, he helped her to loosen her wraps. It was the Countess Elisabeth.

"Since you came to the Place Beauvoisin the other

night you have been constantly in my thoughts, Father Bertrand," Felix went on. "Your reason for supporting this traitor puzzles me more and more."

"And why do you now plot against him?" said the Countess. It was clear that she distrusted the priest. It was her love for Felix which had brought her to the Rue St. Romain to-night. If treachery were intended she would be there to defend him or die with him.

The priest had not expected to see her, but he did not show his surprise in any way. He knew that the Count was everything to her, knew that she was prepared to make any sacrifice for him. There was no danger in her presence; indeed, she might prove a useful tool ready to his hand.

"Are we not here to talk of the future rather than the past?" he said. "If I must defend myself," and he turned to the Countess, "it must be remembered that I was not in Count Felix's confidence. Had I known everything, I might have acted differently."

"We will not quarrel, father," Felix returned. "The past is past for all of us, and many a man's future has served to obliterate the past from the remembrance of his generation. You shall not find us ungrateful."

"To obliterate the past we all have to make sacrifices," answered the priest.

Again there were heavy steps in the passage, and after a knock and a pause the door was opened, and Gerard de Bornais entered. He too had been closely muffled up, but had unfastened his cloak on his way to the room. It seemed certain that he knew who he was to meet there. He saluted Felix and bowed to the Countess. Father Bertrand welcomed him with cordiality, and himself drew forward a chair to the table for his guest.

"We meet again under strange circumstances," said Felix.

"We live in strange times, Count," answered de Bornais. "Shall we listen to Father Bertrand? Under certain conditions we are likely to be no longer enemies. Who is that man, father?" he asked shortly, looking at Mercier.

"One we can trust; a useful ambassador who is with us to the death." And then as the Countess shuddered a little, he added: "I speak of possibilities and probabilities, madame, but when we defy a strong and determined enemy there are always contingencies, and death is one of them."

"True; and time presses, father," said de Bornais, and there was an authority in his tone which caused Felix to set his teeth firmly together. He could not afford to speak as he would.

"Twice lately I have seen Mademoiselle de Liancourt," the priest began, leaning back in his chair, "and, as we know now, she does not recognize the claim of this Roger Herrick to the throne. In helping him we were under the impression that he had her support."

He looked at de Bornais, who nodded.

"Now Roger Herrick's claim is a valid one, since the descent of the late Duke is open to question, and that under certain conditions the heir in the female line can inherit. Mademoiselle de Liancourt maintains, however, that her uncle's claim was a just one, that having deposed an incompetent ruler, he was Duke by his birthright, besides which he ascended the throne by the people's will. Therefore his son, or, failing him, Count Felix, is the rightful heir. But Mademoiselle goes further than this. Roger Herrick, she argues, is an alien, an Englishman, and that any claim he may have is annulled by this fact. In this argument she is likely to have the ear of the people, for it is obvious, with an Englishman on the throne, England may at any time become the overlord of Montvilliers."

"If this fellow has any right, which I do not admit, Christine's argument is an excellent one," said Felix.

"It would appear, Count, that in Mademoiselle's opinion you are the heir; indeed, Maurice being dead, there can be no two opinions on this point; but the fact remains that you are not a *persona grata* with the people, and Herrick's damaging statement in the great hall that night has seriously affected your position."

"Is a man's character to be ruined by a lie?" said Felix.

"It often is," Father Bertrand answered quietly; "and Mademoiselle does not seem able to decide whether it was all a lie. How far this doubt influences her in her determination, I am unable to say, but her first thought, her only thought indeed, is her country. Do you follow me?"

"You use over-many words, it seems to me," said the Count irritably. "The position is simple. Those who deny my right to the throne are traitors. An ocean of words cannot alter that fact."

"Nor the fact that without help you are at this moment as powerless as any man in Vayenne," said de Bornais.

There was a pause, during which the Countess laid her hand gently on Felix's arm to keep him silent.

"We now come to Mademoiselle's last argument," said the priest. "That the people have shown themselves ready to admit a claim through the female line, a claim which has never been put forward until now in

15

the whole history of Montvilliers, seems to her a proof
that the claim of a woman herself will be recognized,
and under certain conditions, seeing that the country is
in jeopardy, she is determined to make that claim."

"Become Duchess!" Felix exclaimed. "I——"

"Would it not be well to hear the conditions, Count?"
said Father Bertrand.

"Pardon. I appear to be in the hands of my friends,"
Felix answered sneeringly.

"Believing that your coming to the throne would be
the cause of further difficulties and dissensions," the
priest went on, "believing also that she is beloved by
the people, Mademoiselle agrees to marry you, and
reign with you, equal to you in authority in all things.
The state shall have, in fact, two heads instead of one,
and no order or paper shall be valid without the signature of the Duchess as well as that of the Duke."

"The Duchess being the more powerful," said Countess
Eliasbeth quietly.

"Your decision must not be delayed, Count," said
de Bornais. "I would as soon Mademoiselle had taken
the throne without any reference to you, but on a point
of law she has her scruples."

"In these days you have become a maker of dukes,
de Bornais, and appear little satisfied with your own
work," said Felix.

"For what I conceive to be right I place myself a
second time in jeopardy," was the answer. "In Duke
Roger we have a strong man to contend with."

"I do not understand how it is you have so quickly
learned to hate him," said the Countess. "Such easy
friendship as you seem able to give is a dangerous thing
for any man to accept. I should refuse to be bound by
such conditions as these. Felix."

"Madame, the Count is powerless without his friends," said the priest.

"And with them he becomes a tool, liable to be thrown away at any moment and crushed underfoot. I have little faith in Mademoiselle or her advisers. There is something under this conspiracy which you do not speak of."

"The Count has until to-morrow to decide," said de Bornais. "If he will not fulfil the conditions, he sinks into insignificance in Montvilliers. By marrying Mademoiselle he will cement all parties in the state. If you are with us, Count, success is certain, but without you we have still a good hope of success. It is for you to choose."

"Wait. You have until to-morrow," whispered the Countess.

"The new Duke is strong in Vayenne," said Felix. "How do you propose to outwit him?"

"When we have had your answer you shall know more of our schemes," de Bornais answered.

"Success comes easiest through the sudden death of enemies," said the Count. "Is there no rascal about the castle who for a reward can shoot straight when he finds himself alone with the Duke?"

"We are not murderers, Count."

"Nor statesmen either, de Bornais, if you call such a thing murder. Is it to you I send my answer to-morrow, Father Bertrand?"

"Yes, Count."

Felix helped the Countess with her cloak, and then wrapped his own round him.

"I am inclined to doubt whether Montvilliers is worth all this trouble," he said.

"It is for you to judge," said de Bornais as the Count and Countess passed out.

De Bornais and Father Bertrand looked at each other as the door closed.

"We plot against a man to serve a cur," said de Bornais.

"It is Mademoiselle we serve," said the priest.

"Truly we serve her badly to help the Count to marry her," was the answer.

"But afterward." And the priest laid his hand on his shoulder. "The fight has been a long one, de Bornais, but the end is in sight. The labor of years is soon to be paid for. It will be a glorious triumph."

"Father Bertrand, all is yet to win, remember," was the answer. "Whatever his faults, whatever his ambition, this Roger Herrick is a man. You thought to make him a tool, and you find you cannot use him; now you hope to put him aside, it is possible we shall not be able to do so. He is an honest man, and if we overthrow him, in my heart I shall feel a traitor to the end of my days."

"True, quite true, but our cause acquits our conscience," said the priest.

"Do foul means justify even a good cause?" asked de Bornais.

"In this case, yes—a thousand times, yes. I speak not as a man, but as a priest. Evil must sometimes be done that good may come. It is a truth burnt into the record of all times and into the annals of every nation."

"I would there were another way than this," de Bornais returned as he fastened his cloak, "or that the work had fallen into other hands."

"But you are faithful?"

"To the death, father; and I almost hope that death may finish it."

The priest raised his hand in a silent blessing as de Bornais went out.

Father Bertrand reseated himself at the table, and Mercier put back the chairs into their places. Then he sat down on the opposite side of the table, and watched the priest, who, taking up paper after paper, seemed to do so half unconsciously, and merely to look at them, while his thoughts were elsewhere. It was Mercier who broke the silence.

"You drive a strange and unruly team, father. I do not understand it."

The priest looked at him as though he had forgotten his presence altogether until he spoke.

"True, Mercier. The goal I have struggled toward lies at the end of crooked ways, but the ways are justified. The judgment of men would condemn me, but for such judgment I care nothing." And he paused, almost as if he doubted the truth of his own statement. Then he went on hurriedly. "This you know, Mercier, that the end I strive for is the Church's good, her triumph here, and throughout the world. Long ago my superiors decided that it was not for the Church's good that Montvilliers should remain a separate state. Their reasons were many and complex, looking toward the future, and when I was chosen for the work, I had only to obey. Duke Robert's position was too strong to be assailed. I could no more than prepare the ground; but the future held great possibilities. His son was a weakling, yet strongly supported by Mademoiselle de Liancourt; Count Felix was feared, but he was strong since he was unlikely to let any obstacle stand in his way to power. Here lay all the elements of a civil war, and with such a war would come the opportunity of the neighboring nations. They were ready to strike when the word was given, are awaiting at this moment as you know, Mercier."

Mercier nodded.

"I espoused the cause of the scholar of Passey—Mademoiselle's cause. A weak man in power would inevitably have brought rebellion. In the midst of my plotting, on the night of the Duke's death, I saw Roger Herrick at the Croix Verte, and recognized that his face was strangely like the face of the picture yonder. It was not so wonderful that I should do so, for in seeking for means to bring about the desired end, I had often wondered whether a further element of discord might not be introduced through this branch of the family. You know our attempt to secure him."

"I am unlikely to forget it," Mercier answered, "and poor Pigou will go crippled to the end of his days."

"He has suffered in a good cause," said Father Bertrand. "Then came the death of Maurice. The way was open to Count Felix; all my schemes had come suddenly to the ground. This Roger Herrick was the only hope. He had a claim—a good one. The success of my scheme was only too complete. It is true rebellion smoulders in Vayenne, but it is also true that we have raised a strong man to the throne, a worthy successor to the old Duke. Left alone, he is capable of turning his enemies into friends, of strengthening Montvilliers, of annulling all my work of years. That Mademoiselle de Liancourt now plays into our hands, that de Bornais is for the Church before all else, these things constitute our last hope. Duke Roger has not had time to win the hearts of the people, but he will fight to the end. We strike without delay, Mercier; the hour is at hand."

Mercier did not answer.

"Does your silence accuse me?" said the priest, rising and standing by the table, and the inspiration of enthusiasm was in his face. "It is naught to me who rules, so that the Church triumphs. Am I seeking rewards for myself? Would not high place be mine if I threw in my lot with the Duke? It is along that road that riches and honor await me; yet I choose the other, which may lead by a quick descent to death. There is nothing of self in this—nothing, nothing."

"My silence did not accuse you," said Mercier. "I have served you, Father Bertrand, and shall serve you. If I take reward for my services that does not alter your position. I am a worldly man. After my fashion I am honest, too, for I do not pretend that self does not enter into the bargain. I only claim to keep my word to those to whom it is given. I am satisfied, father. It has paid me well."

"We have worked together so long, Mercier, that, almost unconsciously, I have been justifying my actions to you," said Father Bertrand, with a smile. "For all my boasting I suppose, like others, I do care something for what men—for what my friends think of me. Something of the world must cling to the cassock of even the saintliest priest, and Heaven knows, I claim no such exalted rank for myself. For you, Mercier, there are greater rewards in store. These papers are ready. At dawn to-morrow, Mercier, you must leave Vayenne, and make all speed for the frontier. There is no suspicion that we are not heart and soul with the Duke. There will be no difficulty at the gates. But every moment counts, Mercier. Already the Duke has cleverly appealed to the nobles who will not submit. The country is in danger of invasion, he has told them, and has urged that internal enmity should be set aside until the common foe is driven back. Afterward he has pledged himself to retain the throne only at the call of three-fourths of the nation. Oh, he is a man, a great man. I have not dared to tell de Bornais this; he is too much fascinated with him as it is. To return successful would win for Duke Roger the applause of the whole nation, so there is no time to lose. Start at dawn, Mercier, at dawn."

"I shall not fail." And as Mercier went out, Father Bertrand lay back in his chair pale and exhausted. When the dawn crept into the room it found him sleeping there.

CHAPTER XXI

THE OLD HAG

EVERY man has his weak points, even the strongest, and it will often happen that the greatest weaknesses are to be found in the strongest men. The very characteristics which make them great in one direction tend to make them contemptible in another.

It had never occurred to Roger Herrick that he was in any way a hero; he had merely played a man's part in the circumstances which had forced him into a prominent position, and so far he was a strong man; but he entirely overlooked the fact that others could not possibly judge his actions from the same standpoint as he did himself, and herein he was weak. Pride and obstinacy fastened themselves upon him. He had fully intended to give an explanation to Christine, and because she was not ready to applaud his actions, he remained silent. He loved her with the sudden strong passion of a man who has not frittered away his affections by playing at love with many women, and he obstinately resented her outspoken criticism, while pride stepped in and made him play the tyrant. He became conscious of his own strength, and would bend her to his will. She must recognize that he was right and that she was wrong. Out of her knowledge of him she must learn not to misunderstand him. The Herricks had always been proud and self-willed, and it was perhaps hardly wonderful that the family trait should forcibly show itself now.

It was unfortunate for the country that the man's self-will was opposed to an equally strong will in the woman. She, too, was proud, and since she had been kept in the dark it was only natural that she should suppose Herrick's ambition had triumphed over every other consideration. A woman loves a man for what she believes him to be, and in Christine's case the proud woman had bent to a humble though brave suitor. She was prepared to give much, but it must be pleaded for. Now it was demanded of her by a man who, having promised to serve her, had merely used her as a stepping-stone to power. She could not hate him even now, although she told herself that she did, but he must suffer, he must recognize her power, no matter what the consequences to herself might be. She found the means ready to her hand in the schemes of Father Bertrand, who, although he had not divulged to her his true and ultimate aim, had persuaded her that the actions he suggested were for the good of the country. It was an appeal which went straight to her heart, and in her present state of mind no sacrifice was too great.

The savage instinct lies latent in us all, and it was well that Herrick had little time to brood over his trouble. The pressing affairs of the state called forth all his energies, and the dangers which surrounded and threatened him brought out all that was best in his character. The fact that he was Duke absorbed him, and the individuality of Roger Herrick, the English country gentleman, was swallowed up in the wider personality of the Ruler of Montvilliers. He was a changed man, and while the dwarf missed something in the new man, Gaspard Lemasle rejoiced in the Duke he served. The captain knew that he was a fighter and a man of resource; he now understood that he was a strategist, a statesman, and a born leader of men.

The rumors from the frontier grew each day more definite. The enemy was gathered there ready for invasion. Any day news might come that the frontier had been crossed, and the Duke's actions were eagerly watched. His enemies said he was afraid to move from Vayenne, that he would not be able to get even the semblance of an army to follow him, while even his friends wondered how he could extricate himself from his difficulties.

The Dukes of Montvilliers had ever been autocrats, asking advice but seldom, and Herrick, even if he had wished to be otherwise, was forced into the same position. To none did he explain all his thoughts and actions. Only Jean knew that Piere Briant and the charcoal-burners were searching for the hag. Only Lemasle knew what steps he had taken to meet the dangers that threatened on the frontier. Only de Bornais had been his counsellor in other matters, and he had encouraged Father Bertrand to visit Christine and bring her to reason. He had not attempted to see her again himself.

Jean was alone with him when news came from Pierre Briant.

"Sir, we found her lying on a heap of dead leaves in the most solitary depths of the forest," said the soldier.

"She cursed us for not leaving her to die in peace. She was ill, of that there was no doubt, and we carried her to the charcoal-burners' hut. She is still alive, but Briant thought it would not do to bring her to Vayenne. The journey would probably kill her."

"We will come to her to-morrow," said Herrick.

"Hasten back at once, and tell Pierre Briant to treat her well, and keep her alive."

The man saluted, and went out.

"So we are not contented with the difficulties we have, friend Roger, but go quickly to raise up others," said Jean.

"We try to be honest," was the careless answer, "but it's a difficult world to be honest in."

"Ay; even our friends stand in the way," said the dwarf. "You'll have to choose between your friends and honesty some day."

"I am going to try and satisfy both." And the dwarf laughed as Herrick sent for de Bornais and Lemasle.

They entered the room together, Lemasle expecting orders that had been long waited for, de Bornais a little disturbed in his mind, as was natural to a man holding such a secret as he did.

"It is time that the threatened danger on the frontier should be brought to a definite issue," said Herrick. "Lemasle, we march to-night. De Bornais, we leave the city in your charge. We must keep what men are necessary to defend the castle and the town, but as few as possible must remain. We shall have need of all the men we can command. Arrange it with Captain Lemasle. At the first sight of riot in the city, deal firmly with it, de Bornais. The men who would plot and rise against us when their country's freedom is at stake, deserve little mercy."

"I will defend the town," said de Bornais, and perhaps he hated himself a little for the deceit he practised, for he added: "Your army must be small, my lord; is it wise to leave Vayenne?"

"Before we meet the enemy I hope it will be larger," Herrick answered. "There are some honest men amongst my enemies. In the country's need I have appealed to them to forget civil dissension for the time being, and some are inclined to listen to me. I have appointed a meeting-place, where all honest men in Montvilliers shall send me what help they can. To-morrow I expect to find a goodly array of stalwart soldiers there. The enemy at the frontier shall find that we can still bite, de Bornais, and are not such curs that we cannot drop our own quarrels when face to face with a common danger."

De Bornais bowed. Words could not come easily. Did the Duke suspect him, and was this a subtle appeal to his honor?

So at midnight, when a moonless sky was brilliant with low-hanging stars, the commotion in the court-yard woke Christine out of her first sleep, and she got up, and went to the window. The torches threw a weird, dancing light over the scene. Impatient steeds were pawing the uneven stones, men called hoarsely to one another, and at sharp commands swung themselves quickly to their saddles, and in troops passed through the open gate and across the great square, and caused other sleepers to awake and go to their windows, disturbed by the unusual noise in the streets. Vayenne had heard no rumor of this midnight march. Christine had known nothing of it. She watched the men mount and go, recognized Captain Lemasle as be superintended the departure, and presently saw him mount his own horse. Then a figure appeared on the terrace and slowly descended the steps. How different now to that night when, at the foot of those steps, she had mounted her horse, and had ridden across the court-yard to look into the face of a spy. Herrick stood for a moment at the bottom of the steps, and looked up into the starlit sky—or was the look only toward her window?—and the next moment he was settling himself in his saddle. Jean was leaning from the terrace to look at him, and Christine leaned forward to see him better. Had Herrick looked up again, he might have caught sight of the white figure at the window. But he did not turn. He bent down to say something to de Bornais, and then with the last of the soldiers rode out of the gate, which was immediately closed. Then the dwarf looked up at the window, and saw the white figure, and wondered!

The city grew silent under the night when the last of the soldiers had passed out of it and across the river, the last round was that of the horses as they passed over the bridge; and to Jean the castle seemed empty, ghost-haunted, and a place to feel fear in. He could not sleep on such a night; he climbed to the summit of the western tower, and was alone with the stars and his thoughts.

When they had been riding for about an hour, Herrick left Lemasle in command, and taking half-a-dozen men with him, turned in the direction of the forest. One of the men who knew the hut of the charcoal-burners acted as guide, and early in the morning they came to the place so full of memories to Herrick. Pierre Briant heard the horses, and came out of the hut.

"Is she still alive?" asked Herrick, swinging himself from the saddle.

"Yes, sir: but dying."

"Or shamming, think you?"

"Really dying, sir; there was a rattle in her throat in the night."

The old hag was lying in much the same spot that Herrick himself had occupied. A fire was upon the hearth, and the smell of the peat was pungent. The old woman's face looked like a skull over which yellow skin had been lightly drawn. The closed eyes, sunken, and like empty sockets, increased the likeness. The noise of Herrick's entrance disturbed her, and she looked up at him as he stood over her.

"You know me," he said sternly.

"You're a liar, curse you." And although the words were feebly spoken there was venom in them.

> "A wounded man
>   In a forest lay,
> Who the fates decree
>   Shall be Duke one day."

recited Herrick.

The sound of the doggerel brought a look of interest into the old hag's face.

"Now do you know me?" asked Herrick. "You were wrong. I was not the wounded man. I am the one you had bound to a tree, to be left to the will of fate. Fate has been kind. I am the Duke."

The hag tried to raise a skinny arm, as though to protect herself from his vengeance.

"Tell me, where was the wounded man taken? Where is he now?"

"Shall be Duke one day," mumbled the old woman.

"Where is he?"

"Ah!" she said, not sharply, but in a long drawn out sound almost like the hiss of a snake.

"Quick, or we will find means to make you speak."

"You can't, curse you."

"We'll tie her to a tree," said Herrick. "I know the method of it, and there is no need for care that the rope is loose at her throat."

Two of the men moved forward as though to seize her and carry her out.

"Curse you, let me be," she tried to scream, but the words were only a whistle. "If I tell, what then?"

"We make no bargain."

"You—you—curse you!"

"Out with her to the tree," said Herrick, and one of the men bent down, and touched her.

"I'll tell—I'll tell."

"Quickly then."

"Simon sold him to the enemy," the old woman said—"the enemy that's now on the way to make carrion of such as you. He's dead, or if he isn't he's safe in a tower by the frontier close to Larne, and you'll never get him, curse you."

"I know the place, sir," whispered one of the men. "She may be speaking the truth."

The hag had closed her eyes again, but after a few seconds she opened them, and in that short interval she seemed to have forgotten all that had gone before. She started, as though for the first time she realized that men were looking down at her, and she began to curse them in a long string of foul oaths which were truly appalling. Herrick thought she must be shamming sickness, for she suddenly raised herself almost into a sitting posture, and pointing at him with her long, skeleton hand, let loose all the vials of her vituperation upon him, promising him a hell here and damnation of the most horrible and fantastic kind hereafter.

"Duke!—Liar!" she screamed, and her voice was strong for an nstant. "Duke!—curse you—wounded man—fates—some day—curse!"

The words were in a descending scale, the last a mere whisper, and then her body heaved as if she would spring to her feet. The next moment she fell backward with a thud—dead!

Herrick turned away with a shudder. Such a death was horrible.

"The world's well rid of her," said Briant.

"Bury her presently," said Herrick to the charcoal-burners. "God knows her history, and shall judge her. Bury her out of the beaten track, and deeply, and then if you will, follow us toward Larne. Montvilliers has need of every stalwart son she has given birth to."

They were soon riding through the forest again, Pierre Briant and his men with them. Herrick rode alone a little in advance, and the old hag's doggerel was singing in his ears. Her last disjointed words were evidently an attempt to repeat the rhyme. It was well that the soldiers knew nothing of the circumstances under which it had first been spoken, or they might have been superstitious enough to look upon him as a leader foredoomed to failure.

Toward evening they came to the rendezvous, and the sight put new spirit into Herrick. The nobles had responded to his appeal in a manner far beyond his greatest hopes. Many of them had come themselves to the meeting-place bringing all the men they could, and others had sent men. Herrick found his army greatly increased.

There came forward to meet him the old noble who had spoken in the great hall that night, and Herrick dismounted to receive him.

"Sir, there was only one way of answering your appeal," said the old man. "It was worthy of a Duke. My arm is not so strong as it was, but there is still too much energy in it to stay at home when every good man is of service."

16

"I thank you," Herrick answered. "You shall find me as ready to fulfil my part of the bargain when we return in peace."

"Sir, I know you for a true man, and if I return you shall find me amongst your friends."

Not all met him in this generous fashion, but they were all willing to follow him in the defence of their country.

"With such loyalty, who can dream of failure?" said Herrick. "In Vayenne yonder, they have whispered that the nobles of Montvilliers were in league with the enemy. It was a false report. Surely there can be few in the land."

"And they may be in the city," said one.

Herrick would not believe such a thing.

"Their quarrel was with me," he said, "that is a different matter to treachery toward their country. We march at dawn. See to it, Lemasle. Not yet is Montvilliers to fall a prey to her enemies."

A great shout welcomed his words, but Herrick's heart was heavy that night in spite of all. Were there traitors in Vayenne, subtle and powerful enough to make terms with the enemy? Who were they? Felix? De Bornais? Christine? Did she hate him so much, that to punish him she would sacrifice her country? And all night he lay awake, thinking not of the task before him, but of the woman he loved.

CHAPTER XXII

JEAN'S face and manner were more sadly at variance with his gaudy attire than ever. He barely had a jest for anyone, and earned the opinion that he was a dull fool after all. He spent many lonely hours on the battlements of the West Tower, and for days he did not go outside the castle. In the body he was in Vayenne, in spirit he was with the Duke and his sturdy fighters on the frontier, and sometimes with his bauble for sword he would make savage passes at an imaginary enemy.

It was not long before rumors, conflicting and uncertain, began to find their way to Vayenne. It was whispered that many of the nobles had gone to fight side by side with the Duke, but this was not generally believed. Father Bertrand had denied it, and was it not well known that the first and best information always came to the house in the Rue St. Romain? Then came rumors of battles, of victory, and defeat. The Duke had driven the enemy back, said one report; he had been defeated with great loss, and was in full retreat, said another. Jean wondered where the truth lay, and noted that Vayenne was preparing for the worst. The gates were shut, few were permitted to pass in and out of the city, military discipline was everywhere. De Bornais was ready to resist a siege. Then for a while no news came. It was a time of anxious waiting in the city, and many there were who started at any unusual commotion in the streets or in the castle, their real hopes and fears known only to their own hearts. Suddenly came news of fierce conflict in the vicinity of Larne. The Duke had suddenly attacked a stronghold there, on the other side of the frontier; and that the men of Montvilliers had shown splendid courage, had proved themselves worthy of their forefathers, seemed certain, but the issue was not known. Some said the Duke had fallen as he led the attack, and something of regret was in the hearts of those most ready to plot against him. At any rate he was a man.

"Is it true that the Duke is dead?" asked Lucille, coming hastily into Christine's room.

"Who says so?" Christine asked, rising suddenly from her chair, the color going from her cheeks.

"They are saying so in the court-yard, mademoiselle."

"Go, Lucille, quickly, find de Bornais, and send him to me."

De Bornais came presently.

"Is it true?" she asked.

"I know nothing certainly," was the answer, "beyond the fact that there has been heavy fighting. There is no doubt of that, and Roger Herrick is not the man to stay in a place of safety."

"No. He would be in the front of it all. I am sure of that."

"Mademoiselle, may I urge that you should no longer delay the scheme we have decided upon? The people are always fickle; it is well to please them while they are in the humor."

"A few hours can make no difference, de Bornais; I will decide everything in a few hours."

"Time is of value, mademoiselle. If Roger Herrick is not dead, if he has been successful, in the flush of

victory the people will be shouting his name in Vayenne.
Our opportunity will have gone.   Why delay any longer,
mademoiselle?"

"Would not any victim delay the sacrifice if it could?"
she asked.   "See me again in a few hours, to-night; I
will decide then."

And, left alone again, Christine was in spirit with the
leader of those fighting men on the frontier, even as
Jean was, sitting alone on the battlements.   Christine
had no thought for the dwarf, but she came into all his
visions.   He did not go to her; he would not go unless
she sent for him.   He feared that he might be tempted
to break his word to friend Roger, that he might speak
of things which he had been told to keep secret.

Buried in his own thoughts, concerned for the safety
of Roger Herrick and the happiness of Christine de
Liancourt, he had little spirit to jest, and took small
notice of what was going on about him.   The city had
been left to the care of de Bornais, and it was quite
evident that he was watchful.   Vayenne was prepared,
and there had been no rioting.   In the castle there was
no slackness.   If the Duke were driven back upon his
capital, all was ready to stand a siege.   Montvilliers
could not be considered conquered while Vayenne held
out, nor was Roger Herrick beaten while he held
Vayenne.   Jean found consolation in the thought, for he
had prepared himself for the worst.   He sat for hours
upon the battlements watching for the first stragglers
of the retreat.

Late one afternoon he came down from the tower,
and was crossing the court-yard when he caught sight
of a man hastening toward the postern by the great
gate.   Jean rubbed his eyes, thinking they must be
playing him a trick.   The man was Count Felix, and

the Count was not allowed within the castle! How had he got in, and why had he come? The dwarf had taken a few hasty steps with the intention of going to inform de Bornais at once, when he stopped, and turned suddenly into the nearest doorway. Danger set his wits working, and it was well to hide until he had decided what to believe and how to act. Was it possible that de Bornais was a traitor? This was the sudden thought which had stopped the dwarf. Count Felix had just left the castle; he had made no pretence of concealing his presence there; others must have seen him, yet none had attempted to stop him. If de Bornais were a traitor, then Vayenne was not prepared as a stronghold for the Duke, but was closed against him.

"What can I do?" Jean whispered. "They know I am faithful; that will be enough to hang me if de Bornais is false. There is too much for me to do to run the risk of being hanged at present. I must get to Mademoiselle. If she proclaims herself for the Duke, the curs will get afraid and fawn upon her. I must see her now, before they stop me."

Few knew the castle as Jean did, and by many a passage in which he would be least likely to meet anyone, he made his way in the direction of Christine's rooms. The last part of his journey must be along one of the main corridors, and he waited until the way was clear, and then went forward hurriedly.

A soldier came from a recess, and laid a heavy hand on his shoulder.

"Where do you go, Master Fool, in such haste?"

Jean's hand was upon the knife underneath his gay tunic, and for an instant he debated whether it would not be wise to use it.

"I came along a passage in which there were dark shadows," he answered, "and sometimes I'm afraid of shadows."

"Well, I'm no shadow," laughed the soldier; "and why go along such passages? You are being looked for. Mademoiselle has sent for you."

"Ah, then I am happy again," said Jean. "I am all eagerness. Announce me. There are not many Mademoiselle sends for. I warrant she does not send for you, for instance."

"Think of your wonderful attractions, Jean," laughed the soldier.

"True; it's unique men like myself that the women favor. But you're a good fellow, and I am sorry for you," said the dwarf as he strutted by the side of the soldier.

Christine was seated by the window, and Jean hurried across the room, and bent his knee to her.

"You sent for me, mademoiselle."

"Did I? Oh, yes, I remember; it was because I was dull and would be amused. And there was something else; I will speak of it presently."

"I am in no humor to jest," said the dwarf.

"Why not?"

"Mademoiselle, listen. I fear the castle is in the hands of traitors."

"Since when have you feared this?"

"Not an hour since I saw Count Felix in the court-yard."

"Well, Jean?"

"He is not allowed in the castle. It was the Duke's strict command."

"Foolish Jean, to be carried away by a man's bold-ness. At present there is no Duke of Montvilliers."

"Ah, mademoiselle, listen to me," pleaded the dwarf. "I was coming to you when the soldier found me in the corridor; I was coming secretly lest they should stop me, because they know I am faithful. I am not as other men, therefore you—everyone—treats me differently. I am told secrets which I keep, and I am of such small account that no one minds me if I do overhear their words. I do not forget the night I came to you in the Place Beavoisin, nor the message you gave me to deliver."

"He has played with us all, Jean."

"No one has been so constantly near him as I have," the dwarf went on earnestly. "You have not understood him, I cannot tell you all, but you have misjudged him. You have never been out of his thoughts since the day he came to you in Passey, came to fight for you and serve you. He is beset with difficulties, but all his actions have been honest ones, and behind them all has been the thought of you."

"Did he bid you tell me so? Surely you have learned your lesson well."

"I should have run to do his bidding, but I had no command to speak to you. I have kept away, mademoiselle, lest I should say too much. All the people love you, I love you, crooked-limbed and mean as I am. Do you think I would lie to you when I speak of the Duke?"

"Call him Roger Herrick, Jean; it offends me less."

"We may call him what we will, mademoiselle, but yonder on the frontier he has shown himself a man and a leader of men. He has fought for Montvilliers, the land you love, in the forefront of the battle. There have been rumors of victory and of defeat, all vague and uncertain, but there is no uncertainty about Roger Herrick. He is a brave man, even his enemies say so, and half regret that they are his enemies."

Christine had turned from him; memory held pictures for her. They passed slowly before her, and her eyes, looking through the window, were not conscious of the castle battlements sharply defined against the growing twilight of the sky

"If de Bornais is a traitor, and since Count Felix was here, how can he be anything else? Vayenne will be shut against Roger Herrick. There is one way to make the curs afraid. Let it be known in the city that you are for Roger Herrick. If he is being driven back to the city you can save him and the country by such a proclamation. Do it now, now before it is too late, and I swear to you, mademoiselle, that in believing evil of the Duke you do him wrong."

Christine turned upon him suddenly. "Can you bear other secrets, Jean?"

"Command me, mademoiselle. I will not fail you," said the dwarf eagerly.

"I love Roger Herrick," said Christine, "but I hate the Duke. Love and hate are in the scales; I have weighed them, and am persuaded that my duty compels me to hatred rather than to love. There is no Duke of Montvilliers, and the country calls to me. I have answered that call. Count Felix came because I sent for him. I am to marry the Count at once."

"You! Then you are——"

"Yes, Jean, a traitor to the man you call Duke."

The dwarf shrank back with a little cry.

"I quarrel not with your faith," Christine went on. "You are honest, and I, a Princess in Montvilliers, a

Princess of that house which this Roger Herrick would depose, am honest too. Your faithfulness is a danger to us, so great a danger that some in the castle have suggested that the greatest safety lies in your death. That is why I sent for you. You are my prisoner, Jean, and shall be tenderly treated. When I am mistress of Montvilliers you shall have your freedom, and I will ask you for your loyalty."

"Ah, mademoiselle, that I, the poor fool, should have to call you traitor," said the dwarf as two soldiers came at Christine's summons.

"Soon I hope to hear you welcome me as Duchess, for such in my own right I shall be," she answered.

Jean stood between the two soldiers bewildered. They laid their hands gently on his shoulders. He was a prisoner.

"Let it be known that he is to be gently treated," said Christine. "The man who does not obey me implicitly in this matter shall surely suffer for it."

"I am to be petted like a spoiled child," said Jean sharply, looking up first into one soldier's face, then into the face of the other.

"Taken care of, Jean, as a foolish man," said Christine.

"I'd rather be a child. I am tired of it all, and long to be carried." And he sank to the floor, his legs doubled under him. It was so ludicrous that Christine laughed, but the next instant her laughter stopped short. Jean's movements were like lightning. With a sudden thrusting out of his foot, he had shot himself back as the soldiers stooped to lift him up, and had darted through the open door.

The corridor was empty, and the dwarf ran swiftly

along it, and turned into a narrow passage. The soldiers followed him shouting, but in the gathering twilight the shadows came early, and the soldiers did not know the castle as Jean did. He dared not hide, the chase must not be prolonged, or every man in the castle would be in his way. Probably only a few knew that he was to be arrested. The fact would serve him if he acted quickly. Jean could hear that others had already joined in the chase; there were more than two men following him now. He must reach the open—the terrace by the South Tower. As he ran across the court-yard men ran to intercept him, but not knowing the goal he was making for, they ran wide, and Jean turned sharply, and dashed across one of the smaller yards. As he ran toward the south terrace he saw there were four or five men there.

"Stop him!" shouted those behind.

Jean ran on. The men in front were evidently surprised at the commotion, but they spread across the terrace to catch him. Could his wit save him now? He shook his bauble as he ran forward.

"I've made such a fool of the big soldier yonder that he thinks he ought to have my clothes," Jean cried. "I'll let him catch me presently, and show you some fun. I'll not run farther than the end of the terrace. See how the big fellow puffs already! Who would spoil such sport?"

Not these men. They knew nothing of the dwarf's arrest, and a comrade made a fool of was always a good jest, so they let Jean through.

"Stop him! He's a prisoner!"

At the shout the men turned to catch him, but the momentary respite was Jean's opportunity. He dashed to the low wall of the terrace, and threw himself upon it. Two bullets chipped the stonework where he had been the instant before, but he was gone.

"Killed!" the men cried as they ran forward and jumped upon the wall to see where he had fallen. They were in time to see Jean let go of the rope and drop on to the dilapidated roof of the house below.

CHAPTER XXIII

WHEN Count Felix left the castle he returned to the Place Beauvoisin. Countess Elisabeth turned quickly toward him as he entered the room. She did not put her question into words, but he saw it in her eyes.

"It is the only way, Elisabeth," he answered.

She turned away from him without a word.

"Cannot you understand, dear, that I am a broken man and have no choice? Do you think I enjoy the sullen temper of de Bornais or the patronage of this priest?"

"But you love Christine."

"She must be my wife. The country demands it. She will hate me, you say; well, may there not presently lie a way of escape in that? Her power shall be nominal before we have reigned long together. A woman who hates is no wife for a Duke of Montvilliers. Do you not see the road of escape?"

She laughed.

"The nominal power will be yours, Felix."

"How little you know me," he answered.

"I know you for the tool of de Bornais and this Father Bertrand," she returned. "The other night in the Rue St. Romain it was plain that they only used you for a purpose. They tried to use this Roger Herrick for their own ends, but he has proved too strong for them. They are forced to plot with a weaker man—with you, Felix."

"For what purpose?"

"We are not in their councils," she answered, "nor, perhaps, is Christine, but their aim is not to quietly settle the crown upon you. This Herrick is a man, one who holds what he has, and will fight for it to the bitter end. This plotting you favor can only breed more dissension. It is civil war these men are bent upon."

"Herrick has made civil war already," said Felix.

"He fights upon the frontier," she answered. "The rumors are uncertain, but had he been defeated we should have heard certainly of that. Ill news ever comes quickly. He wins, Felix; that is the truth, depend upon it, and for such a leader men easily fight and die. You will wake one morning to find Roger Herrick at the gates of Vayenne, a victorious army at his back."

"Then we must fight," said the Count.

"Fight! Where are your men? The rabble of the city? Are you fool enough to trust to such reeds as de Bornais and this priest?"

"No. I trust in myself," Felix answered.

"To-day not a hundred men would raise a cheer for you in Vayenne, that is why you are to marry Christine. She has scruples in leaving you out altogether, but she will be Duchess, with all the power held at the pleasure of these two men."

"You exaggerate their abilities."

"Felix, answer me one question. How came it that the enemy were gathered on the frontier, ready, waiting? It was not the crowning of Roger Herrick which brought them. Perhaps de Bornais and Father Bertrand could tell us."

"You are fanciful, too, Elisabeth. Tell me, how would you have me act?"

"First fling this plot in the teeth of the makers of it, and then ride out, and offer your sword to the Duke."

"How absurdly the dearest of women can talk," said the count; "and afterward beg his Grace's sanction to marry the Countess Elisabeth, I suppose. Are you really serious? Would you have me bend the knee to this adventurer?"

"Better that than be the tool of de Bornais. As for marriage with me, all thought of that is over. I told you the other night that your participation in this plot separates us entirely, and for ever. The plot may fail, indeed I believe it will, but whatever happens I step out of your life."

"Elisabeth!"

"The choice has been yours. To-day you have seen Christine, you have passed your word. I have already written to Christine for permission to leave the city. See, here is the letter."

"No order is valid without the signature of both of us."

"Poor Felix, how dense you are! You are a tool. You will have to do as you are bid. The tool has no choice how it will work or what work it will do."

The Countess had taken up a definite position. Whatever the Count's faults were, he had succeeded in winning the love of this woman, a love that was ready to sacrifice itself in his interests. Elisabeth had never really considered the possibility of becoming Duchess of Montvilliers, and since it had seemed certain that Felix must be Duke, there had from the outset been a hopelessness in her love. With the coming of Roger Herrick, however, the whole aspect of affairs had changed. There may have been some unreasonableness in her love then, for she hoped that Felix would accept the inevitable. Hope, in fact, had burst into flower. But not only did the Count refuse to accept defeat, he was indefinite besides. He strove to serve two ends which were totally opposed to each other. He must fight for his rights, he was obliged to marry Christine, yet he tried to believe that the future held happiness for him in the love of Elisabeth. His whole scheme was an impossibility, and the Countess knew it. With this new plot his last chance of definite decision had come; he had made his choice, and Elisabeth had accepted the inevitable.

They were still together, although silence had fallen between them, when Father Bertrand was announced. There was eagerness in his face, and his manner had nothing of its usual calm and strength.

"You were with Mademoiselle this afternoon, Count, but I understand that nothing absolutely definite was fixed between you."

"She has not said definitely when the marriage shall take place, if that is what you mean."

"She has spoken definitely now," the priest answered. "It will be the day after to-morrow. Already the news is being spread through the city."

"Here is proof of my statement that a tool has no choice," said the Countess.

"Why this sudden haste?" asked Felix haughtily. Elisabeth's words and the priest's bearing angered him.

"Mademoiselle had the fool Jean arrested, but he escaped by means of a hidden rope from the terrace of the South Tower. They are searching for him, but he may not be found."

"He should have been killed, as I counselled," said Felix.

"The fact remains that he is free, and faithful to Roger Herrick."

"Ay, Father Bertrand; and since he had wit enough to prepare so unexpected a way of escape you may rest assured that he has wit enough to find means of communicating with his master," said the Countess. "Your bubble scheme is pricked already."

"Madame, I——"

"And you will be called upon to pay the price, father," she went on. "Words do not deceive me, and upon honest men there is ever a mark that cannot be mistaken. Women may fail to reason adroitly, but instinct carries them to the heart of the matter."

"Being a priest, I know little of women and their methods," he answered. "The day after to-morrow, Count. You will be ready?"

"Yes," was the answer, given firmly after a moment's pause. Elisabeth came slowly across the room.

"Until then use my house as you will, Felix, but it is better that we should meet no more. Your road and mine are not the same. I wish you well upon your journey; I hope that in strewing it with so many and great difficulties I may prove a false prophetess. For my own journey I have much to prepare. Good-bye!"

She held out her hand and there was a smile upon her lips. After a moment's hesitation Felix took her hand, held it an instant, and let it go. He did not believe this was a final parting. She spoke no word of farewell to the priest, but taking up the letter she had written to Christine, passed out of the room.

"She must be watched. She is a dangerous woman," said Father Bertrand.

"With her you have naught to do," said the Count,

turning to him quickly. "I shall be ready. You have delivered your message. I have answered it. You may go."

Whatever the priest's knowledge of women may have been, he understood men. He understood Count Felix. Why should he resent his tone? He would fill the part that had been allotted to him. Father Bertrand's mind was full of graver matters than paltry quarrelling. Jean's escape had brought matters to a crisis.

Vayenne was full of excitement. Some searched high and low for the dwarf, others made rapid preparation for the wedding. The rabble filled the cafés and the taverns again, and hung about the corners of the streets.

Jean was nowhere to be found. As he slid down the dilapidated roof the men who had sprung upon the wall recovered sufficiently from their consternation to fire at him. Half a dozen bullets spattered about him, and it seemed impossible that he could escape being hit; indeed, so suddenly did he drop through a hole in the roof that they believed he was wounded, if not killed. No man, however, was ready to trust himself to that swinging rope, and one of the soldiers cut it from its fastening. At least no one should enter the castle that way.

No long time elapsed before men were searching the house which clung like a limpet to the castle wall, but there was no sign of the dwarf. If he had crept into some hole to die, even as a wounded animal will, that hole was not to be found.

But Jean was not hit, and knowing how soon the hue and cry would be at his heels, he lost no time in getting as far away from the house as possible. The fast deepening twilight favored him; he knew every alley and byway in this corner of the city, and he ran lightly, dodging into doorways and waiting now and again to escape the observation of some passers-by. Not many could know of his arrest and escape yet, but he did not want anyone to see him in this part of the city. He had always come here secretly. He had no haunt in the neighborhood where men would naturally look for him. The house by the wall, which legend peopled with ghosts, had served as a secure retreat before now. Jean reached it unobserved, and waited for more than an hour.

It had grown dark then, and the dwarf climbed down the face of the wall, and was soon sending his boat with vigorous strokes to the secret landing-place on the other side of the river.

Farmer Jacques had not seen him in his motley before, and he laughed aloud as the strange figure came in at the door.

"Hist, this is no time for laughter," said Jean. "Lend me a cloak of some kind to cover myself, and a horse, farmer. I must borrow a horse to-night."

"The horses have done work enough for to-day."

"Then one of them has got to do more than enough for once," the dwarf answered.

"Art in trouble, Jean?"

"Ay; though it's not my own—it's the Duke's."

"Which Duke's?" asked Jacques. "We hear such stories of first one and then the other that Vayenne would seem to be full of them."

"The Duke's—the one fighting yonder," answered Jean. "I must ride to him to-night."

"Well, for all you're a fool, you're a friend of mine, and have done me a service before now. You shall have a cloak and a horse, and Jean, come to think of it, the beast that carries the saddle best has had a lazy day of it. You'll find plenty of pace in him. And, Jean, I heard a report this morning that the fighting was all over yonder, and that the Duke was coming back. Is that true?"

"My heart leaps at the possibility, friend Jacques," said the dwarf; "and mark, if any come asking about me, you have seen nothing of me for many a day. If the lie is distasteful, think of the good it will do your country, and find consolation."

So, while they searched for him high and low in the city, Jean galloped away into the night toward the frontier.

And that evening Mercier returned. He had no news for the men at the gate, no answers to the questions which assailed him in the streets; he went hurriedly to the Rue St. Romain. Father Bertrand rose from his chair as he entered the room.

"Well, Mercier?"

"I have been long upon the road. I have had to make my way warily to Vayenne for fear of falling into the hands of the Duke. He has many more friends in the country than we supposed. These papers will tell you, father."

"I had hoped for one word—victory," said the priest as Mercier placed the packet on the table before him.

"It is some days since I left the frontier, and I have come on foot. Even this news is old, for events are moving rapidly. Read the papers, father."

Mercier watched him as he broke the seals and read the communications hurriedly. By the priest's face it was impossible to tell whether the news were good or bad, but Mercier evidently knew something of what was written there.

"Is it bad news, father?" he asked.

"It might be better, my son."

Mercier bent down to him, and whispered:

"Father, why not leave Vayenne for a little while?"

The priest smiled.

"You must be faint, and need rest and refreshment after your trying journey, or you would never give such foolish counsel. Does a man turn aside out of the track when the race is just won? These men are not our masters." And he struck the papers sharply with sudden passion. "The commands must come from us, not from them. This Roger Herrick is a good man, and I am sorry for him, but he stands in our path, and must be swept aside even as though he were rubbish. I shall have others papers to be delivered presently. Go, rest, Mercier, and have no fear. Within the city there is safety. Vayenne is living with closed gates."

Father Bertrand still smiled as Mercier went out, but the moment he was alone he turned to the papers again, and studied them carefully. And as he did so his face became grave, and there was an anxious look in his eyes.

CHAPTER XXIV

THE moral effect of swift and determined action has won many a victory against strong and apparently overwhelming opposition. The sudden charge of a handful of desperate men has often demoralized a whole army, the reckless courage of even a single individual has constantly plucked success out of failure.

To possess the fertile lands of Montvilliers was a hereditary desire amongst the surrounding states. History recounted many a determined struggle in the past which had this end in view, but sometimes by diplomacy, sometimes by splendid and self-sacrificing courage, the attempt had always been frustrated. In later times mere force of arms was not sufficient to ensure success, the rivalry of the nations had to be taken into consideration; and so long as a strong man ruled in Montvilliers the conquest, or the partition, of the state was a difficult matter. This fact was so well understood that during the late Duke's lifetime there had been peace. If for a time his doubtful right to the throne had raised hopes that internal dissension would mean an appeal to the foreigner for help from one party or the other, the Duke had swiftly proved himself a man able to win the confidence of his people and to keep the throne which he had taken. The utter hopelessness of a successful invasion while such a man held the reins of government was apparent to all statesmen. Even such men as Father Bertrand, whose work was done in secret, could do no more than

make preparation for the future, and foster that feeling
of dissension which was certain to break out at the
Duke's death.   Pursuing the game which had been
mapped out for him, Father Bertrand had played his
cards cunningly.   He had ingratiated himself with the
old Duke, had openly espoused Felix's cause while
in secret he had urged the right of Maurice, and had,
at the same time, lent countenance to those who would
make Christine de Liancourt Duchess.   With the
Duke's death, and with all these different interests
dividing the state, the time to strike had surely come.
Secretly the enemy was gradually gathered on the
frontier, and their leaders were in constant com-
munication with the Rue St. Romain.   Many of these
differences, however, seemed likely to adjust themselves
at the critical moment, and then, to strengthen his
hands, the priest had suddenly given his support to
Roger Herrick, a stranger and a foreigner.   Almost
as soon as he had played this final card he recognized
that he had made a mistake.   True, there was plenty
of opposition to the new Duke, but he was a strong
man, equal to grappling with the difficulty, and moreover one who could keep his own counsel.

Rumor had it that some of the nobles who had
refused to recognize him and had withdrawn from
Vayenne had, nevertheless, joined the Duke's standard
on the way to the frontier; but it was only rumor, and
Father Bertrand laughed at it.   The papers which
Mercier had brought came as an unexpected blow.
They confirmed the rumor, and told him much more
besides.   All the plans and schemes so carefully
prepared during the last few years were in danger of
ruin at the eleventh hour.

The enemy on the frontier, awaiting the final word

from the Rue St. Romain, had come to consider the
task before them an easy one. A few desperate men
might dispute the invasion, but the support of the
country would not be behind them. They would be
a mere handful, seduced by the glamor of the adventurer who led them, while the great mass of the
people was only too anxious for foreign intervention.
Such was the story told by Father Bertrand, and fully
believed; and a small body of the invaders had already
crossed the frontier when the Duke and his army
arrived. Compared with the resources of the enemy,
Herrick's followers might be considered a handful of
men, but the force was far larger than had been antici-
pated, and the skirmish which quickly occurred proved
that this adventurer was a leader of no mean skill.
The enemy was repulsed with serious loss, and the
first shouts of victory rang from the ranks of the men
of Montvilliers.

A narrow stream, swift and deep, formed the frontier
line here, and for a few days Herrick maintained his
position, and prepared to attack in force. This ag-
gressive policy was totally unexpected, and the enemy,
who were weak at this particular spot, sent hastily for
reinforcements. Certain of the nobles urged an engage-
ment before these reinforcements could arrive, but
Herrick did not move, and although his reasons for
delay were not understood, there was no murmuring,
for he had already succeeded in inspiring confidence.

One evening, just as darkness fell, the leaders were
summoned to his tent, and Herrick explained his plans.

"Comrades, the odds are against us," he said. "With
dissension in the country behind us we cannot hope to
sustain a long campaign. A sudden and quick issue
will serve us better. We have succeeded by the

exhibition of great activity in drawing the enemy into force before us, but we do not fight here. There is another battle-ground awaiting us. You know the castle by Larne; to-night we march thither, and the wood behind us will screen our departure. We ought to be well upon our way before the enemy discover that we have gone. Now I want a few brave hearts to remain behind to keep the watchfires burning and to multiply themselves in the shadows so that our secret may be kept until morning. Those who remain must expect a hard reckoning with the daylight."

The certainty of the swift vengeance sure to follow gave fear to none. Every man present was ready to stay, indeed pleaded for the honor.

"I expected no less from such gallant friends," said Herrick, "but at Larne there will be desperate fighting too. Our real effort must be made there."

"Sir, I claim the right to stay," said the old noble who had been so swift to answer Herrick's message bidding all patriots to the meeting-place. "My age, if not my birth, gives me precedence of all here, and my age also tells me that in the midst of a fierce fight my blows may not be so effective as those of younger men. I pray therefore that you will grant me this place of trust. Give me a few stout fellows, and I warrant we will make fires enough, and shadows enough, for a whole army."

"The trust is yours, and I thank you," Herrick answered. "At dawn, as soon as the enemy understand the strategem, to horse at once, and follow us. You shall see our flag floating over Larne, or you shall be in time to help us place it there."

Within an hour men were withdrawing silently through the wood and hurrying toward Larne. There was no moon to betray them, and one of the charcoal-burners, who had joined the army, knew how to avoid the windings of the stream and shorten the journey. But the camp fires blazed all night, and the men who tended them moved rapidly from place to place so that no watchful sentry might have any suspicion of what had happened.

Herrick had hoped to find the garrison at Larne unprepared, but as they approached the castle soon after daylight he found that in this respect he had been too sanguine. The castle stood upon the other side of the stream, and consisted of a great donjon tower and one massive wing in good preservation; the remainder was falling into ruins, or lay in heaps of débris. For a mile or more to left and right the river broadened out, but close by the tower there was a ford, impassable in the winter-time, but comparatively easy to cross at this season of the year. This ford was well defended. Across it the enemy had intended to enter Montvilliers presently, and until the call for reinforcements had come, it was fully expected that whatever opposition was made would be made here. Although Herrick's strategem had had the effect of weakening the defence, it was soon evident that if victory were to come it would have to be dearly bought.

"The castle must be ours," said Herrick as he gave his commands; "the salvation of Montvilliers depends upon it."

"It shall be!" was the shout as Gaspard Lemasle led his men to the attack.

That fight for the ford by Larne will live long in history. With the first dash into the swiftly running stream the tower belched forth fire, and the clear waters were quickly stained with blood. Corpses were

swirled away savagely as though the waters themselves
took part in the struggle, or slithered along by the
banks with the other rubbish which the stream brought
down. Some there were who, sorely wounded, managed
to reach the bank, and others with a cry slowly sank,
and were drowned. Lemasle and his men were
presently sent reeling back, and the enemy attacking
fiercely were driven back in their turn. Rush after
rush was made, now from one side, now from the other,
and each time a deadly struggle ensued for a few
minutes in the midst of the waters, friend and foe so
intermingled that the fire from the tower was forced to
cease, and the struggle became a hand-to-hand one.
Blades flashed above the seething mass as though
lightning played there, and the air was full of panting
endeavor, of rough, loud oaths, and shrieks and groans
of pain. Ever the stream ran mcre deeply red and
carried down its human rubbish. For two hours or
more the equal fight went on, and to neither side was
there any advantage. Herrick had ridden this way and
that to find another crossing out cf the range of the
fire from the tower, but in vain; the stream was too
deep and wide to cross except at the ford. Time
became of increasing value. Long before this the
enemy farther up the stream must have discovered the
deception which had been practised upon them; in a
little while they would be hastening back, and then all
hope of success must vanish. The ford must be won,
and that quickly.

"Charge once more, Lemasle, hold them for a few
moments, and when I shout break to either side, and
let us through. We must win now, or we shall be too late."

Again the waters were churned and blood-stained by
a fiercely fighting crowd, and then, at a shout, the

attacking party broke suddenly, many of the men plunging into the deep waters on either side and swimming back to the bank. At the head of a strong and chosen band Herrick dashed into the gap. The sudden and unexpected relaxation of the pressure had thrown the enemy forward in some confusion, and they were unprepared to stand against the swift and compact mass hurled against them. With irresistible force they were swept back across the ford, and Herrick and his followers stormed the opposite bank.

"It is now or never!" he cried, and the foremost ranks were carried forward by those who rushed across the stream behind them. Nothing was able to stop this supreme effort, and the stormers swept up the bank as a great wave rushes up a low beach of shingle.

Whether they lacked leaders, or whether the heart was out of them, the enemy quickly became a struggling crowd rather than a compact fighting force, and Herrick was prompt to seize the advantage gained. With sharp commands, rapidly repeated on all sides, he kept his men together, and almost before the enemy were fully conscious that they had lost the ford, they were being attacked and driven from the gates which gave entrance to the tower. It was soon evident that every available man had been used for the stream's defence, and, the ford lost, the winning of the castle was an easy matter. No determined voice or action arrested the sudden panic. Men threw down their arms, the guns were silent, and in a very little while Herrick was issuing quick commands for the castle's occupation.

"Turn the guns to face the enemy, who must soon be upon us," he said. "See to it, Briant. Post sentries, and then rest, comrades, while you may. Before nightfall we shall be in the thick of it again."

For Herrick there was no rest yet. He was busy
looking to every point of defence and giving brief words
of praise to every man.   The victory was even more complete than he had hoped for, because the castle had been
used as a base of operations, and a large quantity of stores
had consequently fallen into his hand.

The cheers which greeted him as he passed from point
to point were pleasant to his ears, as they always must be
to the man who has set heavy odds at naught and
triumphed.   Only a little while since many of those who
now shouted the loudest had left the great hall at
Vayenne in silence—his enemies.   It would have been
strange, beyond all human nature, if for a time some sense
of self-satisfaction had not dominated his thoughts.
For a little he enjoyed the shouting, and then turned to
Lemasle.

"That is a good sound, but the struggle is not yet
over."

"Perhaps not, but we have the tower, sir."   And the
captain's face, grimy and blood-stained, broke into a wide
smile of complacency.

"True, and that counts for much," Herrick answered,
and as he hurried away all thought of self was forgotten.
He went to one of the guard-rooms, where some of the
prisoners had been gathered, and after looking at them
he selected one man, and commanded him to follow him.
Once in the passage outside he put his hand firmly on
the man's shoulder.

"In which part of the castle is the prisoner confined?"
he asked.

"The prisoner!   What prisoner?" said the man, turning toward him to find himself looking into the barrel
of a revolver.

"I could find him, but I have no time to waste in

searching," Herrick returned, "therefore, my friend, choose quickly. If you prefer death, one of your companions yonder is likely to prefer life under the same persuasion."

The man hesitated for a moment, and then went forward, turning presently to mount a spiral stone stairway set in the tower. Before a small door on an upper landing he stopped.

"He is in there."

"Good. Now you shall show me where I can find the key of this prison."

"Indeed, sir, I was not his jailer."

"Still you may find the key. There is little secrecy about the jailer's office. You must go quickly, for this is not the sort of day on which a man has much patience to spare."

The key was found in the jailer's empty room, and when Herrick had taken the man back to the guardroom he mounted the spiral staircase alone. He paused for an instant before putting the key into the lock, and it was evident that his thoughts had suddenly wandered.

"At least one task I have set myself is accomplished," he murmured as he opened the heavy door.

There presently galloped across the ford the old noble and those who had remained to cover the secret night march of the army. They had not escaped unscathed, for in the early morning they had been fired at, and half a dozen men had fallen by the watchfires they had tended. No opposition met the little band at the water's edge, for the flag was already flying from the tower at Larne. Their coming, however, heralded the speedy return of the main body of the enemy, and before nightfall the guns were speaking again.

The struggle was not at an end. With the greater

part of their stores lost, the foe were in a precarious position, and desperate attempts were made to recapture the castle. Time had become of consequence to them. Herrick recognized that the castle was not strong enough to stand a siege, and his first care was to prevent the besiegers taking up any strong position. Sorties were constantly made, and there were skirmishes which were almost of sufficient importance to be called battles. In these, ever fighting by his side, was the prisoner Herrick had released from the tower. When he was not fighting he kept himself in the background, and few knew, or cared, who he was. Each man's time was too fully occupied to indulge in idle speculation.

In these skirmishes Fortune's favors were distributed fairly equally. Often, Herrick did not accomplish all he meant to do, but he had one real advantage: the chief success of the struggle was his, and his enemies were disheartened. Dissensions, too, had grown up in their ranks, and many declared that they had been deceived by the information sent them from Vayenne. Instead of the easy task they had been led to expect, they had been vigorously attacked, and all the fighting had taken place on their side of the frontier. They began to talk of peace, and the first flag of truce had been raised before Mercier had left for Vayenne. The papers he brought to Father Bertrand declared that peace was imminent, and indeed terms had been agreed upon by the time the papers came into the priest's hands, and Herrick was leading the larger portion of his victorious army back to Vayenne.

The camp had been pitched for the night at the juncture of the Passey road with the high road from Larne. No messengers had been sent forward to the city. Herrick intended to return witnout warning, and if treachery were within the gates he could easily crush it now. Some of the nobles had left him, returning to their own estates, but it was with a promise to come to Vayenne within a week. They understood the Duke much better than they had done, and Herrick's popularity was established beyond all question.

With early morning came another parting. A small body of men separated from the rest and went slowly along the Passey road. The man who had been released from the tower at Larne lingered beside Herrick for a few moments, talking earnestly, then he saluted, and rode after his companions.

"Forward, comrades!" Herrick said when he had gone. "They must be eagerly awaiting our news in Vayenne."

Some hours later a solitary and queer-looking horseman met them. The animal had been ridden hard, the man was bare-headed and unkempt, and green and scarlet showed from under his disordered and dusty cloak. There was a strange, low jingling of bells as he came.

"Where is the Duke?" he cried as he met the foremost ranks.

"Jean! What is it? What is the news?"

"Ay, Jean it is. Where is the Duke?"

"Yonder. What has happened?"

But the dwarf stayed to answer no questions. He pressed forward to Herrick.

"Jean! What is it?"

"Treachery and rebellion in the city. The gates are closed against you, and Mademoiselle is to be Duchess, and marries Count Felix."

"When?"

The sharp question had a note of agony in it.

"At once; but we may yet be in time. No one knows of the landing-place you and I used that night. I can tell you everything as we go."

"Lemasle! Lemasle!" cried Herrick, and he hastened to meet the captain as he came hurriedly at the call. For a few moments he poured a torrent of eager orders into his ears. "I will ride forward with a score of men, Lemasle. I know a way into the city that they do not dream of. You shall find the gates open to-morrow, or there will be need for another Duke of Montvilliers. Give Jean another horse. That poor brute is done, and will never do the journey in time. A score of men, Lemasle! Quickly! There are vipers in Vayenne, comrades, that must be crushed. We go to crush them. Come, Jean! Forward! Gallop! The next few hours hold more than life for me."

"Long live the Duke!" they cried as they galloped forward, and the same shout rang out lustily from the ranks of those they left behind them.

That night Jean's boat crossed the river several times, and Herrick and his men scaled the wall by the haunted house, and entered Vayenne.

18

CHAPTER XXV

DURING many generations of men the spire of St. Etienne, like a silent witness day and night, had pointed upward to the great beyond, to the immeasurable depths of stars, away from this world of struggle, passion, and human desire. Men had fought, schemed, died, and been forgotten since the rising sun first turned its fane to golden fire; yet still it silently showed the small worth of earthly matters and the limitless possibilities of the future. Jean had understood the message ever since the first night he had crept into the great church to sleep.

And through the fleeting hours day and night the carillon had rung out its happy, irresponsible music, now a laughing cadence which echoed in the night air, now a low whisper like the inspiration of a child's prayer. There was a wail of sadness in its music sometimes, but ever was it suddenly turned into a little burst of gladness. There might be pain in the city, care, and toil, and breaking hearts; but only for a time, laughed the music night and day, and Time is a little thing, and passes as a dream. The sound had floated into many a sick-room, an angel's whisper to many a wearied soul. Jean had understood the message of the carillon ever since he had walked in this beautiful House of God.

The last evening prayer had been said long since, the great west doors were shut, the great church was silent and empty. Darkness was in its vaulted roof, darkness about its forest of pillars, darkness along its aisles. There was no moon to-night to send a delicate finger of light through the painted windows, or to touch with mystery the great rose jewel high in the transept; only one dim mystic flame floated before an altar, as though a spirit hovered there keeping watch through the silent hours. Yet Jean might have seen visions to-night, thin shapes near the tombs of the Dukes of Montvilliers and by the stone effigies, might have heard voices out of the silence.

Listen! Nothing. Only a chair which slips being insecurely set against another, or perhaps a bird fluttering in the roof. All is silent, silent as the grave. Listen! That is not a chair, birds' fluttering wings give no such sound as that. That is the stealthy lifting of a heavy latch, a sharp and certain sound, for the silence after it seems so dead; and surely that is the rough grating of a slowly opened door somewhere in the north aisle, a small door, and one not often used, for the hinges are rusty. Then comes a long pause, one of fear it may be at finding the great church in darkness, or is it one of caution, of keen listening to make certain that no one is about?

"Empty!" The word is spoken in a whisper, but it sounds clearly in the silence. The rusty hinges grate again, and then there are footfalls on the stone flags, steps that endeavor to tread softly and only partially succeed.

"Quite empty!" comes the whisper again. "No need for a light. Touch me, so; keep close. I will lead the way."

The door closes again, and the heavy latch stealthily falls into its place. One, two, three, four—how many footsteps are there, clearly heard although they go on tiptoe? Then a sharp ringing sound that seems to strike upward through the darkness to the very roof. The end of a scabbard unwittingly let fall upon the stone floor! Silence for a moment, then again the careful opening of a door, but no rusty hinges this time.

"Twenty-four steps!" says a low voice, "and we may find a lantern below."

"They will be slow hours to morning," comes the answer.

"But we are in time. Here, close to the right, are the west doors. They will enter that way."

Then steps descending—one, two, three, four, and they grow confused; it is impossible to count them. Another pause, then again the closing of a door, so quietly that the sound might pass for fancy. Then comes the faint music of the carillon laughing in the night. Time passes, and the schemes of men succeed or come to naught, and new life stirs upon the earth, and Death touches all in turn. Time passeth into eternity, laughs the music.

The voice of the carillon floated at intervals into Christine's chamber, but for her there was little laughter in it. It brought sadness, and regret, and uncertainty to her sleepless hours. She had made her decision, and one side of her nature applauded her; but there was another side which shrank away from it, and whispered warnings. How many in the world before her had mistaken the false for the true, had found disaster where they had hoped to lay hold upon salvation? Christine knew Felix, but did she really understand Roger Herrick? Herrick passed in and out of her waking dreams, tormenting her. She dreaded the coming day and what she was to do in it. Love at this eleventh hour took forcible possession of her. Was there anything in life worth setting in opposition to it? No, a thousand times no, came the answer, and then again a strong purpose urged: "Yes; your country." They are not the only martyrs who die for their convictions; some there are who live, having bartered all they hold most dear. So for Christine the hours crept all too quickly toward the new day. Out of the darkness the towers and battlements of the castle began to take gray shape in the early glimmer of the dawn. Even in the crypt of St. Etienne black nothingness began to take ghostly form, ay, and vibrate with movement too.

All night the waters of the river had lapped about the piers of the old stone bridge, and no light showed from the closed gateway of the city. Men slept secure within while the sentry paced above, and never a sound across the river alarmed him. Stars for a while were quiveringly reflected in the running water, but the sentry could distinguish no moving shadows on the opposite bank; and when the dawn came there was no sign of threatening danger. The city was shut up, few went in or out; the sentry did not expect to see any one come slowly over the bridge in these early hours; and beyond, the woods were empty and silent, growing slowly out of the night, just as he had seen them do many a time before. So he paced his round, waiting for the relief, and men began to stir in the guard-room below.

In a narrow street not far from the city gate was a low little tavern of somewhat evil repute. It dozed in the morning hours, stale and half conscious as a man who has drunk heavily overnight. A sleepy youth might unbar its doors early enough, but they might as well have remained shut, for scarce a man passed in before noon, and few until night had fallen. It was after dark that it awoke to life and was filled with drinkers loud in quarrel and coarse oaths. Its frequenters had stumbled and cursed their way homeward last night, and the landlord, no better than his guests, had fallen quickly into his drunken sleep. The narrow street had become quiet, and had remained so for some hours. But a little before dawn there were creeping shadows in it, which stole into door-ways and alleys, and waited. About the time that relief came to the sentry over the gate the bars of the tavern door were unfastened, and immediately the sleepy youth was surrounded by men threatening his life if he uttered a sound. His worthless existence was valuable to him, and he remained silent. So was it with the landlord, who was too muddled rightly to understand what had happened to him.

"See that no one enters," said the leader. "This retreat will hide us for an hour or two until it is time to strike. There is a wedding to-day, at what hour does it take place?" he asked, turning to the youth.

"Early; before noon," was the answer.

The man nodded, and was satisfied, and gave instructions to one of his companions that when they left the tavern presently, he was to remain and shoot any one in the house who attempted to escape or utter a sound which might betray them.

Vayenne woke from its sleep early to-day. There would be crowds in the streets by the castle and St. Etienne, and those who came late would see little. Quite early little groups began to take their way to the upper part of the city. Few besides the sick and the

infirm remained in the neighborhood of the gate, and
the narrow street in which the low tavern stood was
soon deserted.

There were not many soldiers in the guard-rooms at
the gate. All who could be spared had gone on duty
near the castle and the great church; and most of them
could be spared. There was no danger outside the city,
and if danger should come, was not the gate strong
enough to be easily defended until help could be ob-
tained? The Captain of the Guard had no misgiv-
ings, and his men grumbled that it had fallen to their
lot to stay there where there was nothing to do.

The captain was a young man, new to his dignity,
and proud of it, or rather of himself. Perhaps never
had quite so worthy a man worn the uniform so fit-
tingly, he argued. He sat in the lower chamber of one
of the towers, and seemed lost in admiration of the
shapely leg he stretched out, tightly clothed and well
booted and spurred. Through the open door was a
glimpse of the cobbled space before the gate and the
street which led down to it; and outside the door a
sentry paced, passing it at regular intervals. The
captain looked up as he passed; the presence of the
sentry pleasingly emphasized the dignity of his own
position, and he wondered what further reward he
should attain to when this new Duke and Duchess
were firmly seated on the throne. It would be strange
indeed if he could not find means to force himself upon
their notice, and his own advancement was their chief
utility so far as he was concerned.

"A good man, if he has wisdom in him, must always
rise like a cork to the top of the water," he mused.

Then he started hastily to his feet. There was the
dull thud of a heavy blow, the beginning of a groan

which was immediately smothered, and as the captain rushed to the door men met him on the threshold, and forced him back.

"A sound means death!" one man said hoarsely, "If you are wise you will keep what bravery you have for a better cause."

"Pierre Briant!" exclaimed the prisoner.

"The same—a captain in the forces of Duke Roger. The gate is ours, the city will be ours presently. Up, men, see that none escape or give the alarm, but treat them kindly if they will let you."

The self-satisfied young officer sank back into his chair with a groan.

"Hearten up, man," said Briant. "You have failed in a bad cause, you may live to succeed in a good one. You're over-young to be a captain."

The man was quiet for a moment, and then he sprang from his chair.

"Don't be a fool!" said Pierre Briant, and the young captain shrank back from the gleaming revolver barrel.

The capture was accomplished in silence and without bloodshed; even the sentry over the gate had been seized and gagged before he had time to utter a cry. He had heard men ascending the winding stairs, but had only thought of the relief coming earlier than he had expected.

The soldiers of the guard were gathered together in one room with their captain, and Briant explained the situation, after disarming them.

"My men have orders to fire upon the first who cries out or tries to escape," he said. "They are all men fresh from fighting on the frontier, where they have learned to obey orders without question."

So Pierre Briant carried out the instructions which

Herrick had given him a few hours since in the house by the wall. The gate had been secured silently, and a messenger was sent across the bridge to the woods, where Lemasle lay with a strong force.

"Tell him the gate is ours and the wedding is before noon," said Briant.

Lemasle and many of his men had entered the city, and crowded into the guard-rooms at the gate, or stood close in side streets so as not to attract the attention of any one who might be loitering in the neighborhood, when a carriage came down the street and toward the gate. It was stopped by the sentires placed there by Lemasle.

The Countess Elisabeth, who was the only occupant, produced an order permitting her to leave Vayenne. It was signed by Christine de Liancourt and Count Felix.

"Madame, you cannot pass."

"But there is the order."

Lemasle came forward, and looked at the paper.

"Only the Duke's signature is of any value, madame."

"But Count Felix has——"

"I speak of Duke Roger, madame," said Lemasle, "and he has given orders that none shall pass out of the gates to-day."

"But Duke Roger——"

"Is in Vayenne," said the captain.

A sharp exclamation burst from her lips, and then the Countess was thoughtful for a moment. As she leaned forward to give a direction to the coachman, Lemasle interrupted her.

"Pardon, madame, but I must detain you. It is not yet generally known that the Duke has entered the city, and secrecy is still necessary. You shall be made as comfortable as possible in one of the guard-rooms here until we know the Duke's will."

The carriage was drawn into a side street, the coachman and footman were warned and added to the prisoners in the lower guard-room, while the Countess was shut in a little room in the tower of the gateway. She was powerless to help Felix any more.

Long before noon the streets about the castle and St. Etienne were crowded. Even with the soldiers at the castle there were not very many in the city, and in some places the crowd grew disorderly. Ugly little rushes were made for more commanding positions, or out of pure wantonness; little control could be exercised, and the Count's carriage had threaded its way to the great west doors of St. Etienne with difficulty. A few cheers had greeted him as he passed, but the crowd seemed chiefly enthusiastic about its own pleasure.

The great church was full. Lights burned upon and before the high altar. Music, now tremulous, now deeply thundering, rolled along the aisles. Priests and choir waited in the chancel, and alone, a striking figure, stood Father Bertrand.

In the porch by the great doors stood Felix, waiting for the new Duchess, his bride. Ceremonial demanded that he should meet her there, that together they should pass to the altar. Near him stood de Bornais, and one or two others of importance in Vayenne. It was plain that both the Count and de Bornais were ill at ease. Christine was long in coming, and they fretted at the delay.

Behind them was a small, fast-shut door. Perhaps neither of them knew that it opened upon the steps leading down to the crypt.

Lucille sat opposite to Christine in the carriage,

which slowly made its way through the crowd. The shouting now was loud enough, for the people of Vayenne, high and low, had always loved Christine de Liancourt. Very beautiful she looked, but very pale, and never a smile played about her lips as she bowed to this side and to that. It was no happy bride who slowly passed on to St. Etienne.

"She is coming," whispered Felix.

Father Bertrand moved slowly toward the altar, the music crashed out, and the cheers from without rose louder and louder, sounding even to the crypt below.

The carriage with its guard, chiefly de Bornais' men, halted, and as Christine descended Felix went forward to meet her, followed by those who had stood beside him. For a moment the porch was empty, and then the crypt door burst open. A strange figure in scarlet and green rushed out, a dozen men following close behind him.

"Long live the Duke!" he cried.

Felix turned sharply, and Christine looked up to meet the steady eyes of Roger Herrick. There was the sharp ring of steel. The men behind him stood with drawn swords in their hands.

"So we return to find treason," said Herrick. "Mademoiselle, you are my prisoner, and will return to the castle. Arrest Count Felix and de Bornais." And then raising his voice he cried: "Let him who dares dispute the will of the Duke!"

CHAPTER XXVI

By the carriage there was silence for a moment, but the more distant part of the crowd was still shouting, and the music had not ceased to roll along the aisles of the great church.

A laugh broke the silence.

"A dozen men!" exclaimed Felix, "and we stand like fools. Quick, de Bornais, shout a command! The delay need be only for a moment."

But no word came from de Bornais, and without it his men did not move.

"Are you afraid?" Felix cried. "Ho! men of Vayenne, to the rescue of your Duchess!"

He tried to spring forward to lead the attack, but two of Herrick's companions seized him, and held him fast.

But his words had their effect. Unarmed as it was, the crowd surged toward the carriage, sullen determination in its face, angry threatening in its throat.

"Curse you, de Bornais! Shout!" raged the Count, struggling to free himself.

Had de Bornais obeyed the command, it had gone hard with the little band of men that surrounded Herrick. As it was, the sword points barely kept the crowd in check. But no word came from de Bornais, yet it was difficult to believe that fear was behind that set face, that there was no daring in the man whose limbs showed no sign of trembling. As repentance may come late to a man, so it seemed to come to de Bornais. Every thought that had driven him forward in this scheme, every word Father Bertrand had drummed into his ears, all were forgotten in his admiration of the man before him. Treachery against him was of no avail. Right and Justice seemed to keep watch and ward beside him. Better to stop here and now upon the path that conscience told him he ought never to have walked in.

Christine had not moved, the folds of her train still hung over the carriage step just as the page in his sudden bewilderment had dropped them. She had not taken her eyes from Herrick's face. She had spoken no word when he had said she was his prisoner. She was almost conscious of waiting for his next order, and knew that she would obey it. This hateful marriage was not to be. The power to choose had been suddenly wrested from her, and her heart beat out its gladness. She had forgotten the surging crowd behind her, but Felix's cry to de Bornais had a meaning for her. She waited for de Bornais' quick command, knowing that, if it came, some impulse which she would not be able to control would force her to Herrick's side. It did not come. De Bornais stood still and silent, his head bowed, his arms loose-hanging by his side. There was danger; Christine saw it in the grim-set faces of the men about Herrick. They showed that they were men holding their lives in their hands, ready to lose them in the defence of thir leader, to barter them freely for the lives of their enemies.

The tension was at the breaking pitch, there wanted but a man in the crowd to throw a stick or a stone, and the little band would have been overwhelmed, when from the distance came the shouts of "Long live the

Duke!" The crowd heard them, wavered for a moment, and then turned, and began to struggle backward.

"Mademoiselle, let me help you to your carriage," said Herrick. "Yonder come the men who have fought with me upon the frontier. They shall make free passage for you to the castle."

Her hand rested in his for a moment as she stepped into the carriage. He set free the folds of her dress carefully, and closed the door. She did not speak to thank him, but she lowered her head, and a tear fell suddenly into her lap. Lucille saw it, and her hand went out to touch Christine's in silent sympathy; but it fell unnoticed by Herrick, who had turned suddenly to Felix.

The Count had made a last effort, and had shouted to stay the struggling retreat of the crowd.

"Would you leave your Duchess to her death? Strike, curs, strike!"

"Silence, fool!" said Herrick. "Only very hardly shall I save you from the swift vengeance of these men who come. To cry against me will be your death. Look! Are such men to be played with, think you?"

On they came, forcing their way wedge-like through the crowd, which burst aside from them to right and left, blows helping the pace of any who were slow to move.

"Lemasle, Mademoiselle returns to the castle," said Herrick. "See to it. A prisoner in her own rooms; none to have speech with her but her companion who is in the carriage."

There were a few swift orders from the captain, instantly obeyed, and then, surrounded by soldiers, Christine's carriage moved slowly away.

"Briant, the Count and de Bornais are prisoners. Find safe ward for them in the castle."

"Traitors!" And there was no mistaking the temper of the soldiers who surrounded them.

"I said safe ward," Herrick commanded. "Safe ward in the castle. Pierre Briant, I hold you responsible for their safety."

Briant saluted.

"Be silent if you value life," Herrick said to the Count. "And you, de Bornais, I trusted you."

"I have betrayed the trust, sir."

"And your men?"

"Are now without a leader, sir."

"They shall stay with me," Herrick returned, "and prove what honor is in them."

Another sharp command, and the Count and de Bornais were marched quickly away.

"Your horse," said Herrick to one of de Bornais' men, who immediately dismounted; and springing to the saddle Herrick gave orders that the crowd should be dispersed in every quarter of the city. The men were to march in different directions, but no violence was to be used unless it was absolutely necessary.

"The rabble will easily shout for us again now we have returned to Vayenne." And with part of his force, Herrick started to ride through the city.

"You have forgotten me, friend Roger," said Jean, who had slipped his knife into its hiding-place beneath his tunic and now had his bauble in his hand.

"Another horse, there! Mount, friend Jean. If they shout for the Duke, they shall also shout for him who has helped the Duke to know that life is still worth the living. Forward!" And there was a joy in Herrick's voice that would seem to argue he had read in Christine's eyes something of what was in her heart.

The mob, leaderless and without definite purpose, scattered in all directions. Some there were who hastened to reach their homes as speedily as possible. Some, hurrying away in gangs, and finding themselves in some quiet quarter, safe from pursuit apparently, took to plundering. The sight of a half-closed shop inflamed their desire to reap some profit for themselves before they dispersed, and they were quick to follow any man who had the daring to lead the way. The cries of those who were robbed, and the incapability of the rioters to keep from quarrelling and shouting, soon attracted some of the soldiers who were parading the city to restore order. Many of the soldiers were in no humor to be lenient, and the slightest resistance met with immediate retribution. Then were ugly blows struck, wounds given which would not heal for many a day; and here and there some persistent rioter paid for his temerity with his life. It was a case in which violence was necessary, the soldiers argued, and they had merely fulfilled the Duke's commands.

A section of the mob showed a different spirit. They had shouted Herrick's name as he rode through the streets, and his lip had curved scornfully at the fickleness of the rabble. Not an hour since the shouts had been for his enemies. Fickle they were, but perhaps with more reason than appeared on the surface. Herrick's, presence, and the sight of the soldiers in the streets brought to sudden remembrance what had been accomplished upon the frontier. There might be a doubt who lawfully should rule in Montvilliers, but this man had saved the country from invasion. So they shouted for him, and for the soldiers who had returned victorious.

It was easy for them to imagine themselves on the side of order; they became anxious to help the soldiers, and were loud in their praises of them. To some of the soldiers such praise was not displeasing; besides, many of them had friends in the crowd, relations some of them. There were no rioters to disperse here, only a friendly and loyal crowd surrounded them. Here and there an open tavern door was suggestive, and the health of the brave heroes was drunk. So it chanced that certain of the soldiers became absorbed by the crowd, became virtually their leaders. Such men, loud in their praises of the Duke, set the crowd about them thinking of the Duke's enemies. The traitors ought to suffer. Why not since they were enemies? But Count Felix and de Bornais were safe within the walls of the castle, and where was there an enemy of whom an example might be made?

Who first mentioned the Rue St. Romain no one knew, but in a moment the name of Father Bertrand was being repeated with eager excitement. He had crowned Duke Roger, and even then he must have been a traitor in his heart. Some discovered suddenly that he had been a plague to the city for years. One man, whether speaking out of his imagination, or because some chance word had reached his ears, declared that the priest would have sold the country to her enemies had he been able to do so. At this there was a hiss of rage, and a purpose seemed to come into the heart of every man.

"Ay, Duke Roger said there were vipers in Vayenne, and we had come to crush them," a soldier cried, and his words stirred the smouldering fire into flame.

"The Rue St. Romain!" was the quick answer. "Down with the priest!"

Into the quiet street poured the crowd. Justice was

19

theirs, they argued, the Duke's will was their mandate, yet they went quietly, lest they might be robbed of their prey.

One knocked at the door, but there was no answer. No cassocked figure opened it. A dozen men hammered at it. Still no answer.

"Open it, or we break it down!" was the cry.

The man in the cassock rushed up the stairs calling "Mercier! Mercier!"

"What is it?"

"A crowd is at the door angrily demanding admittance. There is murder in their eyes."

For a moment Mercier stood irresolute at the top of the stairs, while hammering again sounded on the door. He knew nothing of what had happened. He had heard the distant shoutings, but had attributed them to another cause.

"In the name of the Duke, open!" came the shout from the crowd without.

"He has come back!" Mercier exclaimed, and then turning to his companion he went on: "Quick! we can leave by the back way. Few know of it. The Duke is in Vayenne. Find him. Tell him what the crowd is doing. They use his name, but I dare swear he set them to no such task as this. Come! They are breaking the door. Run quickly and inquire as you go. Hundreds will surely know where the Duke is to be found."

As Mercier slipped out of this back entrance which opened into an alley and so into a street beyond, the crowd broke open the door, and rushed into the house.

"Down with the priest!" they shouted. Some burst into this room, some into that, their passion let loose as the waters from a dam. At first they did not stay to plunder and break, they were too intent on finding the priest; but when every room had been entered and found empty, their rage found vent in spoliation. Some of them had known the room on the ground floor with its ascetic simplicity. Had they not often said that the priest lived no better, in no more comfort, than the poorest among them? The room on the first floor was a revelation to them. Was it not a further proof of the villainy of the priest?

"Curse him!" cried a man as he sent his stick through one of the pictures. In a moment they had taken the action as an example, and the room was wrecked. The whole house was wrecked from roof to cellar, windows smashed, doors torn from their hinges, the stairs broken, even part of the walls and floors and ceilings were hacked to pieces. Might there not be some hiding hole, behind the walls or under the floors, where the priest had crept?

"Where is he?" asked one. There had come a pause, for the wreckage was complete.

"The church! St. Etienne!" came the answer.

"Is he to find sanctuary there?"

The question was asked fiercely, and none answered it, but one idea seemed to impel each one of them to reach the street as soon as possible, and immediately they were struggling toward the door.

Meanwhile a man ran quickly through the city, and ever and anon he paused to ask: "Where is the Duke?" Some answered him by questions, some pointed to the way they had seen the Duke take only a little while ago, some shouted out directions after him. He found Herrick after a long search returning from the Place Beauvoisin. Herrick had heard that Countess Elisabeth was confined in the gate tower, and he had at once had the horses put to her carriage and seen that she was safely conveyed home again.

The man in the cassock ran panting to his side, and in a few words told his story.

"They broke in as I left, sir."

Herrick stayed to hear no more. Part of the crowd were using his name as an excuse for plunder, for murder perhaps; and in another moment he was leading his men quickly in the direction of the Rue St. Romain.

There had been consternation in St. Etienne at the sudden interruption of the wedding, but the real cause was not known at first. As the whisper that the Duke had returned and had arrested both Mademoiselle de Liancourt and the Count became a certainty, the congregation left quickly.

Father Bertrand stood motionless by the altar. He stood alone there for a few moments after the last person had gone. Then he returned slowly to the sacristy, unrobed, and gave orders that all the doors of the church should be shut. It was the church he thought of, there was no thought of his personal safety. Nor was it fear that made him remain in the sacristy. The Countess Elisabeth had said that he did not bear upon him the mark of an honest man, but she had only seen part of the schemer, she knew nothing of the priest. His ways may have been narrow, cramped by the very work he had been called upon to accomplish, but according to the light that was in him, he was an honest man and a brave one. He had been called to fight in one particular direction for the church he loved, and he had allowed nothing to turn him from the thing he had set out to perform. Were many men as honest as this? for, truly had Father Bertrand said that personal honor lay along a different road. Now all his schemes were ruined. His work in Vayenne was over, the end not attained. He had failed. It was a broken man who sat leaning slightly forward in his chair in the sacristy.

The sacristy opened into a cloister, and so into a street at the east end of the church. This way came Mercier.

"Fly, father, fly. There is yet time," he said.

"Whither, my son?"

"They are seeking you," panted Mercier. "They have broken into your house. They will wreck it, and not finding you, will come here, father."

"I do not hide. When they come they shall find me."

"It means death," Mercier said in a hoarse whisper. "Hide for a little while. I have already sent to find the Duke. Surely this is not done by his command?"

"Failure to the man who plays for high stakes often means death, Mercier," the priest answered. "We have failed, and I do not shirk the penalty. Indeed, is there anything left but death for me?"

"The Duke will be merciful," pleaded Mercier.

"I look for no man's mercy. My conscience is clear. But for you, Mercier, there is danger, too; we must not forget that. Hasten. Make your peace quickly with the Duke. You were but a tool. They will not seek to break the tool, once they have crushed the hand that held it."

"Come, father, there is yet time."

"Go quickly, Mercier. Listen! They are shouting in the street. Go, I say. I would be alone." And he put his hands on Mercier's shoulders, and gently pushed him from the sacristy. "Go, and peace be with you."

The crowd were not at the door of the sacristy, but at one of the larger doors which opened into the Rue St. Romain: Father Bertrand passed into the church. For a few moments he knelt before the altar in a side chapel, and then he went with firm steps toward this door.

Long ago the crowd had lost all self-control. The spoliation of the priest's house had but inflamed their appetite for further violence. The door of the house had been locked against them, and they had broken it down and done their will; was the closed door of the church to stop them from wreaking their vengeance upon the priest? So they hammered upon the door, crying aloud for their prey.

"Break it down!" shouted those behind, some of the men who were superstitious in their sober state, and had a reverence for sacred things. All reverence, all superstition was forgotten. They would kill the priest, but they were unlikely to stop at this. All control was gone, every restraint loosened. To wreck and spoil had become fierce joy. What mad delight it would be to wreck St. Etienne!

Suddenly the door was flung open from within, and Father Bertrand with arms outstretched stood upon the step.

"Who are they that thus insult the House of God?" he cried in a loud voice.

For an instant the crowd fell back before the commanding figure. But behind, the crowd surged and shouted, as though they struggled to get to the front.

"False priest! Betrayer of his country! Traitor."

The cries were sharp and fierce, and then one man, a soldier, sprang forward, and struck twice at the priest's breast. For an instant he swayed, his arms flung upward, the fingers wide outspread, and then he fell prone across the threshold. But there was no forward rush into the church. The body of the murdered priest guarded it. That was a barrier they dared not pass.

Nor was it those at the back of the crowd seeking to press forward to the front which caused the surging and shouting there; it was Herrick and his men fighting their way to the priest's rescue. Even as the man stepped back after striking the second blow, Herrick was upon him, and cut him down.

Silence fell suddenly upon the crowd, and then another soldier who had been leading the mob pointed to his dead comrade; and said:

"Sir, is that justice? Did you not say that there were vipers in Vayenne that must be crushed?"

CHAPTER XXVII

ROGER HERRICK signed the last of the papers upon his table, and leaning back in his chair looked at Lemasle, who had entered the room a few moments before. Jean squatted in his favorite attitude on the floor beside Herrick's chair.

"Yes, yes, Lemasle, all you say is true. While they live, some men will plot and scheme, but to me this seems no reason why I should kill them."

"Sir, once before I said you were too lenient; was I wrong?"

"No; you were right, yet I would be lenient again. Do I disappoint you, Lemasle?"

"Only in this, sir. Justice and expediency demand that traitors should pay the penalty of their treachery."

"There must be something wanting in my nature to make me an ideal Duke."

"Sir, Montvilliers is proud of her Duke, and every day, every hour, the people grow to love you better."

"Surely then we can afford to be lenient," said Herrick.

"Not to traitors," Lemasle answered promptly. "Count Felix despised your leniency. De Bornais, whom you trusted, rebelled, and would have sold his country."

"And Mademoiselle de Liancourt?" asked Herrick quietly.

"She is a woman, sir."

"And is a woman never a traitor?" asked Herrick.

"At least Mademoiselle loves her country, and perhaps——" The captain paused, and looked at Herrick.

"Well, Lemasle?"

"The sentence is best left unfinished, but women's love finds strange ways of revenging itself if it is scorned," said the Captain.

Herrick did not answer, but Jean, either of set purpose or by accident, made his bells jingle for a moment.

"I would once more urge stringent measures, sir," Lemasle went on after a pause. "The people expect it. They look for such measures to bring peace to the country. You are reluctant to let justice take its course, and it may be that I understand something of your mind in this, but, if I may advise, why not postpone judgment? In a few days the nobles will be assembled in Vayenne, let them decide against the Count and de Bornais as they will. Have they not often in times past been summoned to give decision in such a case? Why should you give judgment to-day?"

"Because, Lemasle, I fear the justice of the nobles," Herrick answered. "My orders must stand. See that the prisoners are brought into the hall. And, captain, think presently of some honor you covet, and it shall be yours. If we are slow to condemn, we would be quick in our rewards."

"Sir, your trust, your friendship almost, leaves me covetous of little else."

"Yet think, Lemasle. Dukes die, or are deposed, it is well to take something off them while they have the power to give. We will talk of this again."

Lemasle saluted, and withdrew.

"What would that good soldier say if he knew?" mused Herrick.

"I wonder," said Jean.

"I had forgotten you," said Herrick, with a start. "Did I put my thought into words?"

"You spoke, friend Roger, and have still some secrets, it would seem."

"Many, Jean. I will tell you one. I am not fitted to be a Duke."

"In that matter, at least, I should leave others to be the judges," said the dwarf.

"None can judge a man so well as he can judge himself if he will only be honest," Herrick returned. "I spoke inadvisedly, Jean, the other day, and it has quickly resulted in tragedy. Would I had been in time to save Father Bertrand."

"You avenged him," said Jean.

"And for my action stood reproved by one of my own soldiers. My own words were quoted against me."

"Yet the priest was a rebel," said the dwarf slowly. "There is much in what Captain Lemasle says."

"True, but there are always other points of view besides our own. Even dukes have no monopoly in such a thing as truth. I have tried to do a great deal, Jean, and I have succeeded in discovering how much better I might have done."

"That's a complaint common to all honest men, friend Roger, and as a wise man you will be thankful that you have done no worse. Have you not saved this land from herself and from her enemies? Are not your foes easily learning to become your friends? And love itself stands without, only waiting for the opening of the door."

"Open it, Jean."

"That I cannot do," answered the dwarf. "You alone can do that, but I can show you the way."

"Speak, my wise philosopher."

"Oh, it's no work for a philosopher. Even a fool finds it easy. You have but to learn wisdom out of your own mouth, and remember that there are other points of view beside your own, and that a woman usually sees these points better than any one else. Would it surprise you to learn that in you pride and self-will somewhat mar an otherwise excellent man."

"Or come in to make my true character, my real self," said Herrick.

"Put it so if you will; mine was a gentler way," said Jean. "I would save you from yourself."

Herrick remained thoughtful for some considerable time, and Jean did not interrupt his reverie.

"I have staked out my course, Jean; I must run to the finish of it," he said, suddenly standing up, and giving the impression that he shook himself free from his thoughts as a dog shakes the water from him when he scrambles upon the bank after his swim.

"It may be a good course," said the dwarf, rising from his cross-legged position.

"And if not?"

"Disaster perhaps, but whatever comes I shall always love you."

"Love me, Jean?"

"Why not? Love's a big word, I know, but it is the right one. Trust came when I sent my knife skimming across the stone floor to your feet that night in the South Tower. We've travelled far since then, friend Roger. There has been friendship between us, different though we are, and on your side a little pity perhaps

for these twisted limbs of mine. I have gone a step
farther. Yes, love is the right word."

"I think it is, Jean," said Herrick, putting his hand
on the dwarf's shoulder.

The next moment Jean had caught Herrick's hand,
and kissed it as he fell upon his knee.

"Sir, I thank you for the greatest honor it is even
in your power to bestow."

"And, Jean, I do not like the fool's motley for you,"
said Herrick, bending over him. "You shall change
it presently."

"As you will," said the dwarf, rising, "yet it seems
to fit this queer body of mine."

"And outrages the great heart that it holds. Come.
These prisoners must be judged."

"For the present I still sport the scarlet and green,"
said Jean, making his bells jingle. "We are both
public characters. The Duke and his fool. Bother
gossips."

Three days had passed since Herrick returned to
Vayenne, and in this time order had been restored in
the city, and the Duke was a popular hero. With the
return of the soldiers, definite news of what had taken
place upon the frontier began to be known. The
people were proud of their Duke, and were ready to
cry confusion to all his enemies. Father Bertrand had
paid the penalty of his treachery, and they were glad
of it. They fully expected that a like justice would
be meted out to both Count Felix and de Bornais, but
they were in no mood to dispute the Duke's-will. He
could do no wrong.

There was no uncertain sound in the cheers which
greeted Herrick as he entered the hall with the dwarf.
A few of the nobles had already come to the city, and

were near the dais. Many officials about the castle
and in the city were in the hall, and a strong force of
soldiers. Count Felix and de Bornais stood at a little
distance from the dais, and near them sat Christine
de Liancourt. Only the fact that Lemasle and the
guard were with drawn swords showed that they were
prisoners. As Herrick seated himself upon the dais,
Jean sank cross-legged on the lowest step, his bauble
lying across his knees.

"There has been bloodshed upon the frontier, there
has been bloodshed in the city," said Herrick, breaking the silence which had fallen upon the assembly.
"The responsibility rests in varying degree with the
prisoners, and with Father Bertrand, who has already
been slain by the people. I say the responsibility is
in varying degree because I have learned the truth from
one Mercier, a tool of Father Bertrand's and himself
a schemer. Montvilliers is not his native land, however, and therefore the basest of treachery is not his
crime. It was not his own country he betrayed, therefore he has his freedom. Nor would we omit the fact
that our presence in Vayenne has fallen hardly upon
two of the prisoners. We have sought to weigh every
circumstance in arriving at our judgment."

There was a pause, and not a sound stirred in the
hall.

"Christine de Liancourt."

As Herrick spoke her name she stood up almost
involuntarily, and looked fixedly at him. Her head
was held erect, but the defiance that had so often been
in her bearing was not there to-day. Perhaps it was
Roger Herrick she saw rather than the Duke.

"Mademoiselle de Liancourt, you have had the
opportunity of knowing most of the circumstances

which led to our ascending this throne. You have misjudged those actions from the first, and have proclaimed yourself our enemy. You warned us that those who plotted should find an easy tool in you, and they have. You were to marry Count Felix, you were to reign with him as Duchess, equal to him in power. Your country's good may have been in your mind, but it was a less incentive perhaps than your hatred to us. But when Father Bertrand schemed with you he had other ends in view. This Mercier was dispatched to the frontier, where long since the enemy have been waiting to strike at this country. A religious fanatic, this priest was selling Montvilliers to her enemies, and using your marriage, your coronation, to stir up further civil strife, and thus render the project easier of accomplishment. This has been his scheming for years. The weaker the power of the Duke, the less resistance to the enemy."

Both Christine and Felix had started at the mention of Father Bertrand's schemes.

"It is evident that you were innocent of all knowledge of such a betrayal," Herrick went on, "but the state must guard against the danger of such unconsidered actions as yours. Three days hence you will depart under escort to the Château of Passey, there to remain until it is our pleasure that you return to Vayenne. Those in Passey have our orders to see to your welfare and safe keeping."

Christine bowed her head, and spoke no word. Retirement to the Château of Passey was no great punishment, but there was bitterness in her heart that she had played into the hands of her country's enemies. In thwarting her this man had saved Montvilliers. Surely he was a worthy Duke, and he was Roger Herrick.

"Count Felix, to you also the news of this scheming comes as a surprise," said Herrick, "and truly for plotting against us you have much excuse. The plot against your cousin was of another kind, and were you justly heir to this throne, your own subjects have decided against you. You possess an estate in the south of Montvilliers. To that estate you are confined. You may win ultimate pardon, but I warn you that any attempt to escape will mean death."

The Count did not speak. Neither by look nor gesture did he show that he had heard what had been said to him.

"You, de Bornais, have been guilty of a greater crime—treachery to your country," Herrick went on, and a low murmur like a sullen growl sounded through the hall. "How far religious fervor prompted you, I cannot judge, but this I am sure of, that no religion can serve as excuse for betrayal of country."

The growl became articulate.

"Down with de Bornais! Death to him!"

"Yet we cannot forget that even in the middle of your plotting you hated the part you felt called upon to play." And Herrick raised his voice almost as if he were pleading the prisoner's cause to those who had shouted for his death. "This also has Mercier told us; and more, we do not forget that the other day before St. Etienne you refused to speak the word that would have meant almost certain death to us."

"Long, long live the Duke!" was the enthusiastic cry. "Repentance had come to you, and pardon ever runs at the heels of repentance. Yet cannot the crime be forgotten or go unpunished. Within three days you must cross the frontier and never return. The whole world is free to you save only this State of Montvilliers."

"Sir, I am leniently dealt with," de Bornais answered. "My life will be one long regret."

It was over. Judgment had been given. The tension was relaxed. It was the moment one man had waited for. Herrick had descended two steps of the dais, when Count Felix sprang from his guards.

"Death rather than submission to this adventurer!" he cried, and with one bound had rushed upon Herrick. The dagger he had concealed was in his hand. The attack was so sudden and unexpected that Herrick slipped upon the steps. The dagger flashed down, but there rose to meet it a mass of scarlet and green, a mass that hurled itself upward at the weapon, and there was a jingling sound of bells.

The next moment Felix was dragged backward and thrown to the floor. A dozen sword points were at his throat, and even at Herrick's quick command, were scarcely stayed.

"Jean!" cried Christine, throwing herself on her knees beside the dwarf.

"Mademoiselle!" came the answer, and how faint it was. The dagger had done its work only too well.

Herrick was kneeling beside him too, and the heads of the man and woman almost touched over the dwarf. "Love," Jean said faintly. "It was the right word, friend Roger." And then he sighed, and lay quite still.

"Oh, he's dead," whispered Christine, "and to save you!"

The crowd were pressing round the dais now. The Duke was alive. They had seen him fall, had feared the worst, and a great wave of relief came as they knew the truth. The shout went up and echoed along the corridors, gladness in it, for the Duke was alive.

"Thank God! It's only the fool!"

CHAPTER XXVIII

THEY buried Jean in the great Church of St. Etienne, as was fitting, and a whole city mourned him. He had passed in and out amongst them, there was hardly a man, woman, or child in Vayenne who had not known him, now his place was suddenly empty. Some had laughed at him, some with him; some had pitied him; and a few, understanding him better, had loved him. To-day the whole city mourned and honored him, and a great silent crowd was in the streets as he passed to his last resting place, to sleep for ever in that beautiful House of God where he had so often crept in to sleep at night. Soldiers saluted as he passed, and men remembered what he had done for the city that he loved, crowning his good work by giving his life for the Duke's. "It's only the fool!" they had cried in their first gladness that the Duke had not been struck down, but now there was a sense of regret almost that they had expressed their gladness in such words, words which seemed to mark the loss as a trivial one. They recognized that the loss was a great one, that Vayenne would be the poorer without that strange misshapen figure in its streets.

And chief among the mourners stood the Duke himself, and those about him saw that the strong man who seemed to know no fear, to whom, as they believed, all sentiment and love were unknown, wept. They spoke

20

no more of the Duke's fool, but of the Duke's friend. They understood Jean better now, and perhaps they understood the Duke better, too, as they returned homeward.

A solemn city to-day, yet over it the carillon laughed its constant message. Time passeth into Eternity, and Time is a little matter. Always Jean had understood something of the meaning of the message. He had a fuller understanding now.

Jean's death had one marked effect upon the people's mind. Three days since they had accepted the Duke's judgment upon the prisoners without a murmur, and, if they were inclined to think it too lenient, they realized that mercy has its part in justice, and were content. They were still content to exonerate Mademoiselle de Liancourt from any part in deep-seated treachery, but they were loud in their demands that Count Felix should die the death of a traitor, nor was their fury against de Bornais much less. The Duke remained firm in his purpose with regard to de Bornais, who had left the city two days ago to the accompaniment of hisses and execrations from the assembled multitude. Only a strong force of soldiers had procured his safe passage through the streets. Now Jean's funeral had further inflamed the people's anger against the Count, who remained a close prisoner in the semi-circular cell in the South Tower. There was no loose bar in the window high up in the wall any longer, there was no Jean to come to his deliverance. Indeed, it was the safest refuge the Count could have, for in their present mood the populace would have torn down any less well defended prison to get at him.

Very sad at heart Herrick had returned to the castle after Jean's funeral. He had been met on all sides with loud demands for the Count's death. It seemed suddenly to have become the one question of importance. Many more of the nobles had come to Vayenne, and they, too, advised his speedy execution. He had added murder to treachery. No further mercy ought to be shown him.

Herrick sat alone thinking of Jean. Something had gone out of his life with the quaint figure with which he had become so familiar. He had never liked the motley, yet, as Jean had said, it seemed to suit somehow his outward appearance. Herrick would have given much to see the door open quietly and to hear the jingle of the bells. Clad in that gaudy green and scarlet, Jean had been a very wise counsellor, and Herrick missed his wisdom and advice every hour.

"I had not been so good a Duke as I am had it not been for Jean," he murmured.

The door did open presently, quietly too, but it was Lemasle who entered.

"You have not forgotten that Mademoiselle de Liancourt rides to Passey this afternoon, sir."

"No, captain. You will take a strong force. There may still be robbers on the Passey road, but not of the kind you and I have had experience of."

"Am I to return with my men from Passey at once?" asked Lemasle.

Herrick was thoughtful for a few moments.

"No," he said slowly. "Viscount Dupré has certain instructions concerning the—the prisoner, and will decide when it is advisable for you to return. Be guided entirely by him, Lemasle."

The captain regarded him curiously for a moment.

"Sir, you surely do not intend——" Then he stopped, partly because of the absurdity of the idea that had suddenly come into his mind, partly because of the expression in the Duke's face.

"I do nothing without careful consideration, Lemasle," said Herrick. "Though I seek to serve the state, I am despot enough to do it in my own fashion."

"Pardon, sir; instead of simply obeying orders, I was presuming to try and understand."

"To understand what, captain?"

"Your purpose regarding Mademoiselle."

"She is a prisoner sent to the Château of Passey," Herrick answered. "Is it too lenient a punishment? It is a dull place, Passey, likely to break the high spirits and proud defiance of any woman. Is there not some vindictiveness in my action in this matter?"

"And afterward, sir?"

"Ah, my good friend, so you would look through the Duke into the heart of the man," said Herrick, with a smile. "The passing hours must bring the afterward as they will; but this much of my heart you may know: I send Mademoiselle to Passey guarded by the man, the one man I trust as I would trust myself —Gaspard Lemasle; yet even he would be a fool to enter Vayenne again should harm befall Christine de Liancourt. She is dear to me, dear as my own soul; know, therefore, Lemasle, how I trust you."

"Your words prophesy summer weather for this land of Montvilliers," said the captain quickly. "If only——"

Herrick looked at him as he paused.

"I would to heaven my sword had been thrust deeply into the Count's throat the other day before your sharp command had had time to hold it back," the captain burst out.

"Truly he is a great difficulty," said Herrick.

"Let him die, sir. No man ever merited death more. The whole city demands it."

What would Jean have said? Herrick found himself glancing down at the floor beside his chair, caught himself listening for the jingle of bells. There was no sound, there was no quaint little figure seated beside him.

"For a few days longer he must live," he said suddenly. "He is a pawn in the game, and must keep his place on the board. He shall be judged, Lemasle. Rest assured, he shall be judged. Has not a man, because of him, died for me?"

The captain had turned to go, fully satisfied that the Count's fate was sealed, when the door opened, and a messenger entered.

"Sir, Mademoiselle de Liancourt prays that she may see you before she leaves the castle."

"I will come to her at once," Herrick answered, and the messenger withdrew.

The prompt answer, the sudden change in Herrick's face, the alertness of his movements as he rose from his chair, were not lost upon Lemasle. The least observant of men could not help but be conscious of them.

"Is it possible that, after all, Mademoiselle will not leave the castle?" he asked.

"Nothing will prevent her going to Passey, Lemasle, I trust you to see that she goes in safety." And then as Herrick reached the door he turned back. "You must take a strong force. The rabble is fickle, and may think to please me by jeering at her. Should any cur fling so much as a sneering word at her, drag him to his knees, captain, make him kiss the dust before her, humble himself, and crave her pardon. If, as you let him go, you so far forget yourself as to give him a sound cuff to help him to better manners in the future,

no great harm will be done. There is more vindictiveness in me than you supposed."

With the stripping off of her wedding garments a
gladness had come into Christine's heart, a feeling that
in casting them aside she had escaped some great
disaster. Herrick was hardly absent from her thoughts
for a moment. She had credited him with an overween-
ing ambition; had judged all his actions in this light.
She could no longer believe that he was prompted by
mere ambition. He had fought for, and saved Montvilliers. He had returned to save her from a disastrous
wedding. She knew now that others about her had
schemed and plotted for their own ends, and that, whatever motive lay under Roger Herrick's actions, the love
of this land was deep rooted in his heart. He had
indeed taught her a lesson in patriotism. She did not
understand him, how could she? but the outlines of the
man, as it were, began to take a different and a larger
shape. They were indefinite still, she could not fit the
Roger Herrick who had knelt to her offering his service
with the Duke who seemed desirous of bending everyone and everything to his will. His splendid courage
before the Church of St. Etienne had fascinated her.
The man she had come to marry, all the men about her,
seemed to sink into insignificance beside this one commanding figure; she felt that he must be obeyed, and
forgot to be resentful. The words he had spoken to
her were stern ones, yet there was a look in his eyes,
something in the touch of his hand as he helped her
into the carriage, which had thrilled her. Then had
come that day in the hall. Surely he had excuse
enough to avenge himself, not upon herself, she had not
expected him to do that, but upon Felix and de Bornais.
She had to confess that his judgments upon them

were more lenient than probably her own would have
been. Too lenient, surely, for the swift tragedy of
Jean's death had followed. As surely as the downward
stroke of that cruel dagger had taken the dwarf's life,
so surely had it shown to Christine, in an instant of
time, what this man Roger Herrick really was to her.
Real grief had cast her upon her knees beside Jean, but
there was wild joy in her heart that it was not Herrick
who lay there.

They had hurried Felix roughly from the hall, and
she had left Herrick bending over the body of the man
who had died to save him. He had not spoken to her,
he had not replied to the words she had whispered
as Jean died; their eyes had met for a moment, and
she had not seen him since. Lucille, her only companion, was as close a prisoner as herself, so nothing of
the gossip of the castle was brought to Christine. One
of those who watched and waited upon her told her
that the Count was confined in the South Tower, and
gradually Felix began to come into her thoughts. For
prisoners ere had ever been a sinister meaning in
that semi-circular cell in the South Tower. Death had
so often been the only road to freedom from it. Felix
deserved death. It was almost certain that the Duke
had decided upon his death. It was just, and yet
Christine shrank from the contemplation of it. By
reason of Roger Herrick's coming, Felix had suffered
terrible humiliation; there was surely some excuse for
him. There was, Herrick himself had admitted it, but
that, of course, was before Jean had been murdered.
Yes, it was just that Felix should die, and yet he was
her cousin, the man whom a few days ago she had been
willing to marry. Was she not in some measure responsible for what had happened? The thought that

in an hour or two she would have left Vayenne, would be powerless to plead for mercy, made her send impulsively to Herrick and pray for an audience.

She had sent Lucille into another room, and was standing by the window clad in her riding habit ready for her journey to Passey when the door opened, and a soldier, saluting, announced the Duke.

Christine remembered that last time he had come unannounced.

For a moment Herrick paused upon the threshold. She had been dressed as she was now when he had first seen her. She had looked like this when he had first offered her his service. Nothing could suit the pretty head so well as that astrakhan cap. It was with an effort that he advanced slowly toward her; he would like to have caught her in his arms, and stopped all remonstrance with his kisses on her lips.

"You sent for me, mademoiselle."

Now he had come Christine hardly knew what to say to him, or how best to say it. Could she move him to mercy if she were humble enough?

"I wanted to thank you," she said, "for your leniency to me and—and to others. You might have chosen a harder prison for me than the Château of Passey. It has its associations for me. You thought of that when you chose it."

"Naturally I had reasons for choosing it," he answered.

"My lord, Count Felix is——"

"Mademoiselle, for these three days past the Count's name has been ringing in my ears. Spare me more of it. They shout in the streets at me for his death. In the castle they are insistent that he should die. I cannot forget that Jean's love for me saved my life, and Jean is dead."

"Neither do I forget it; still, I would plead for the Count."

"Surely he merits death?"

"Yes; still, I would plead for him," said Christine earnestly. "You know—you said—you have admitted that for his plotting, at least, there was some excuse. He was mad with the uncontrollable madness of a desperate man."

"It was murder, mademoiselle, no more, no less; that the victim was not the one he hoped for makes little difference."

"Yet I plead for him," she persisted. "You have already shown great generosity; show it once more, if not to him, to me. Felix is my own flesh and blood. How far I may be responsible for his madness I do not know. He had lost everything, his kingdom, his honor, the woman he has always desired to marry. In his own fashion he may have loved me. I had plotted with him against you. Truly in a large degree I am responsible, and I pray you have mercy. Make my punishment greater if you will, so that you save Felix. Banish him, anything, but do not kill him."

"You forget that the state has laws, and that the Duke but serves the state," he said quietly.

"You are all-powerful, and you know it. On my knees I beg this thing." And she suddenly dropped at his feet. "I beg it of the Duke, the Duke I promise to serve should it presently please him to give me freedom. You have taught me patriotism. I would I had the power I once had to make my service a worthy gift."

"Mademoiselle, I doubt not the people still love you," said Herrick, putting out his hand to raise her; but she would not see it.

"You believe that? You believe that I might still be a danger?"

"Am I not sending you to the Château of Passey? If you were of small account in Vayenne, why should I banish you from the city?"

There was a moment's pause, then she said quietly. "Not long ago in this room you asked me to make a sacrifice, it was your own word, and I refused. I have learned much since then. I will do anything to serve the Duke and my country."

Herrick remembered the manner in which he had asked her to marry him. For an instant now he nearly lost control of himself, almost bent down and caught her up in his arms to tell her all that was in his heart, but he quickly had himself in hand again.

"Mademoiselle," he said, gently raising her, "I do not like to have you kneeling to me, and I will not bargain with you in this fashion. For the present Felix must remain where he is, but this I promise, you shall have speech with me again before he is condemned."

"Thank you," she said. "Before he is condemned; you mean before——"

"There is no juggling in the words," Herrick answered. "Is it too much to ask you to trust me?"

"I trust the word of the Duke," she said.

"I will leave you, mademoiselle. I hear your escort assembling in the court-yard. You may find the Château of Passey a less dreary prison than you imagine."

A little later Christine and Lucille rode out of the great gates with Gaspard Lemasle and a large escort, and from a corner of the terrace Roger Herrick watched them go. His world had moved since the night he had seen her ride out upon the same journey when she went to bring the pale scholar of Passey to Vayenne.

CHAPTER XXIX

HERRICK'S parting words remained with Christine. At first she had paid small heed to them. They were a mere conventional phrase, spoken to do away with any abruptness there might be in his leaving her, a slight courtesy in the place of a farewell which could have little meaning since she was a prisoner. But the words would not be forgotten, and there were circumstances which accounted in some measure for their insistency. A guard was drawn up at the castle gate, and at the sharp word of command saluted her as she passed through. Again at the city gate it was the same. She had not expected this as a prisoner. There had been no crowd in the streets of the city, but all who recognized her raised their hats. She had their sympathy if not their love. She was prepared to hear some hisses as she passed, for not every one could believe that she was innocent of any part in the plot to betray the country since she had schemed with those who had this end in view; yet no sound of anger had reached her. It seemed evident, too, that Captain Lemasle had not felt certain of the temper of the people, for as they went through the city, he was watchful, and the soldiers rode close about her and Lucille. Once across the river, however, Lemasle divided his men more, and Christine and Lucille rode alone side by side, soldiers before and behind them.

It was then that Herrick's words began to drum in

Christine's ears as though to impress upon her that there was a meaning in them. Why should she find the Château of Passey a less dreary prison than she imagined? True, it had been Maurice's home for many years, and had associations for her for this reason, but they had spoken of that before, and she had thanked him for choosing such a prison. Why should he refer to it again? Or was it that the Duke had in some way brightened the château for her reception? But this was an absurd idea. It did not belong to the Duke but to the Viscount Dupré, and besides, there had been no time to make much preparation for her. She knew that her appeal for Felix had not been altogether in vain. The Duke had been touched, he had treated her very gently, not at all as a prisoner, and he had left her with these words. What was the meaning that they held? What was the Duke's real purpose concerning her? It was strange how persistently she thought of him as the Duke.

"You are sad, mademoiselle."

Lucille broke the long silence so suddenly that Christine started.

"Not so sad as the circumstances might well make me," was the answer.

"Then you will smile again, laugh even, and there will be quiet, peaceful days at Passey."

"Quiet enough," said Christine, smiling at once, "and such peace that we are likely to grow dull and gloomy with so much of it. It was selfish of me to let you come."

"I shall not be unhappy with you," said the girl.

"And presently you can return to Vayenne," said Christine, "you are not a prisoner, and for a time the ruined old place will amuse you."

"Ruined, mademoiselle?"

"Oh, there is plenty of room to live in it decently if they will let us do so," was the answer; "but it is no longer a castle that could defend itself against an enemy. Grass peeps between the stones in its courtyard, and the moss and lichen find rootage in its broken walls. No sentry paces through the day and night, and the corridors give forth an empty sound as one walks along them."

"What a strange place for a prison," said Lucille.

"It is pretty, and for a time will while away your hours, and you can always return to Vayenne. What kind of treatment we are to receive I do not know. There may be deep-dug dungeons which decay has left untouched."

"Ah, now you would try to frighten me, mademoiselle."

"No, I do not think they will put us there," said Christine. "We shall probably be allowed to wander about the château as we will, but you will soon tire of it, child. It is an unlikely place for a prince to come who, passing all others, shall kneel before you."

"You will not let me forget my dream," said the girl, with a flush in her face; "yet, mademoiselle, think, if he came the broken walls could not keep him out, and there would be no challenge from the sentry."

"No, and no other woman to pass before he came and knelt to you. In Passey you will have no rival if the prince should come," Christine returned.

"Yes, mademoiselle, one—you."

Christine laughed, and her thoughts flew back to Vayenne and to Roger Herrick. Full well she knew that her prince had come long ago. It seemed almost as though the strong walls of circumstance and the sentries which keep vigilant watch over the affairs of men had shut him out.

The twilight was deepening into night as they drew near to Passey. The château stood gaunt against the fading light in the western horizon, and Lucille shivered, while even Christine's fingers tightened on the reins. Perched on its hill, grim and alone, the château looked uninviting to-night. A feeble light glimmered here and there in the village, but no light shone from the summit of the hill. Ghosts might well be the only inhabitants of those ghostly walls, and as they rode forward the light in the west and the château vanished in the night as though it had been the mere outline of a dream.

A few doors were opened at the unwonted clatter as they went through the village street, and then they rode into the court-yard. There was a sentry by the gateway, and one of the ruined guard-rooms seemed to have been repaired. There was a light there, and Christine saw the shadowy figures of two or three soldiers. Some change had been made, and then she remembered that this was to be her prison, and that, of necessity, there must be men to guard it. Lemasle assisted her to dismount, and, silhouetted against the light within, the figure of the old Viscount stood on the threshold to receive her.

"Welcome, mademoiselle, to the Château of Passey," he said.

"I am grateful at having so courteous a jailer," she answered. "This child loves me enough to share my banishment for a time."

The old man bowed to Lucille.

"I hope you will consider me your host," he said to Christine, "and not think of me as a jailer. There is no great severity here. I will take you to the rooms which have been prepared for you."

He led the way across the wide hall and up the stairs. At the top he paused, and, opening a door, turned to Lucille.

"Will you wait here for a few moments? Mademoiselle de Liancourt shall first see whether she approves of the arrangements which have been made, and will return to you."

Without a word Christine followed the Viscount along a corridor, and then as they approached the end of it she stopped.

"Is one of my rooms to be that which Maurice used to have?"

"Yes, mademoiselle. The Duke thought you would like to have it."

"It was a kind thought," Christine said.

"The people of Montvilliers have much to learn concerning Duke Roger," said the Viscount. "For once we are ahead of the times in Passey, and love him already."

"Perhaps I shall learn the lesson easily in Passey," Christine answered.

"I hope so, mademoiselle. You will find this room little changed." And the Viscount stood aside to let her enter. He did not follow her in, but, closing the door, walked back along the corridor.

Lighted candles were upon a table at the far end of the room, and a man rose from a deep chair, and came toward her.

"I have been expecting you, Christine."

"Maurice!"

Even as she spoke his name, tears of joy and excitement at this sudden and unexpected revelation in her

eyes, her thoughts flew to Roger Herrick. She understood the meaning of his parting words now. And
as Maurice told her of his slow recovery; his waking
to consciousness to find that he was in the hands of his
enemies; his refusal to purchase his freedom by accept-
ing their help to regain his kingdom and to hold it
as a tributary state; his close confinement in the tower
by Larne; the sudden coming of Roger Herrick, and
all that he had achieved upon the frontier; Christine
began to understand the character of the Duke better.

"And what is the Duke's purpose with regard to you
now?" she asked at length.

"I hardly know," Maurice answered. "He would
send for me presently to come to Vayenne, he said,
but for a little while I was to return to Passey. I was
glad to be back in the dear old place, to have my books
about me again, but somehow, Christine, they had lost
part of their charm for me. The scholar of Passey has
changed. Side by side with Roger Herrick I had
struck a good blow that day at the clearing in the
forest, and after my rescue from the tower at Larne
I rode by his side again, fighting, and a different man.
I wanted to prove to him that I was a man, and a
fighter, something more than a pale student. In his
presence I felt all the spirit of my fathers rise in me,
bubbling up joyously like water from a newly tapped
spring. No one else's opinion counted to me but his.
There were few who knew even who I was. I have
not been a prominent person in Vayenne."

"And now, Maurice?" questioned Christine.

"Do I look only a scholar now?" said Maurice,
drawing himself up, and standing before her. "I shall
have some place about the Duke, high place, I doubt
not, since I intend to make myself worthy of it."

"And the last time I came to Passey it was to persuade you to go to Vayenne to be crowned," mused Christine.

"I have no quarrel with Duke Roger," laughed Maurice. "I recognize his claim, and I know that Montvilliers is ruled by the right man, the man who will make history for her."

"Yes; I feel that too," said Christine.

"So again you come to Passey on an important mission," Maurice went on. "You come to summon me to Vayenne to prove myself a man."

"What are you saying, Maurice? You have been misled. You are wrong, indeed; you are wrong. I come to Passey a prisoner."

"A prisoner! You!"

"To the Duke I have been a traitor. This castle is to be my prison during his pleasure."

"I do not believe it. The Duke said—ah! he would make no false promise. I would trust his word against the sworn oath of other men. I do not believe it." And Maurice went to the door, and shouted loudly for the Viscount.

The old man came hastily along the corridor.

"Viscount, is it true that mademoiselle has come here as a prisoner?"

"In a sense it is true, but now she is here she is to have perfect liberty of action," said Dupré. "The Duke has certain wishes concerning you, mademoiselle, which are contained in this paper. I was commanded to give it you after you had seen your cousin."

Christine took the paper, and opened it.

"Mademoiselle, once before you journeyed to Passey to summon Maurice to the capital. This time

21

we pray you be our messenger. Tell him the Duke has need of him, and bring him to Vayenne. Roger."

Christine handed the paper to her cousin.

"I knew there was some mistake," he said. "It is evident he thinks little of your treachery; is it very hard, Christine, to be the Duke's messenger?"

"I was commanded to see that you rested here tomorrow, and returned the day after to Vayenne," said the Viscount. "Have I your permission to give these instructions to the captain of your escort?"

"Yes," she said after a pause. "May I go to my room, and will you send Lucille to me?"

"Who is Lucille?" asked Maurice.

"You shall see her presently."

"Christine, you are not glad that I am going to Vayenne," Maurice said, as he held the door open for her.

"Yes—yes, I am; but you don't understand, and—and I want to be alone."

It was Maurice who showed Lucille over the ruined castle, stood with her looking over the village below and across the open country from the broken walls, and steadied her as they climbed down the narrow, worn steps to the dungeons, which had received no prisoners for generations, he told her. They had not been long together before he had learned her history, and he told her that he would ask Duke Roger to restore the fortunes of her family.

"He is the most splendid Duke Montvilliers has ever had," he said enthusiastically.

"I wish I were a man to serve him," answered the girl, catching the enthusiasm from her companion.

"I'm very glad you are not," he answered, and then feeling that he was unequal to explaining his words, he hurried her to some other interesting point of the castle.

Christine remained alone all day, remembering every incident since the dusty priest had come to that very castle to warn her, to offer his service, and wondering what the immediate future held. What was the Duke's purpose regarding her cousin Maurice?

When, on the following morning, the cavalcade set out, Christine rode alone. Maurice soon found that she took little notice of what he said to her, that she was altogether absorbed in her own thoughts, and there was more enjoyment in riding beside Lucille. It was pleasure to watch the girl's color come and go, to see in her fresh young beauty a likeness to the fresh, new day, to feel that her merry laughter which rang out at intervals was the most beautiful sound on God's beautiful earth. For Maurice a new page was turned in life's book. Here was the beginning of a new chapter, full of love and romance, of excitement and success, and with pictures exceedingly pleasant to look upon.

Christine rode alone. Every inch of the way had some memory for her. Here she had glanced at the priest riding so silently beside her and had wondered whether he was a man of honor or a scoundrel. Here was the forest where danger had awaited them; even now the sunlight gleamed at the end of the long road, dimmed by over-arching trees, showing where the fateful clearing lay. The leading soldiers trotted into it and across it; no robbers rushed out to stop them to-day. Maurice and Lucille rode into it, and Christine saw him point to one of the roads, as he told Lucille how he and Roger Herrick, who was now the Duke, had ridden together as they escaped from their enemies.

"He saved my life that day."

"I am glad," the girl said simply, perhaps hardly realizing how glad she was. And side by side they rode on into the forest beyond the clearing.

As she came into the sunlight Christine checked her horse, and Lemasle, who rode a few paces behind her, came to her side.

"We know this place, Captain Lemasle."

"Yes, mademoiselle."

"I can people it again as it was that day," said Christine.

"I am glad that only your fancy does so," returned Lemasle.

"I thought you loved fighting, captain. Surely I have heard it said of you?"

"May be, mademoiselle, but danger to-day would frighten me. The stake would be too heavy. Harm might happen to you. The Duke himself warned me that I should be a fool to enter the city again if harm came to you."

She was silent for a moment.

"That way surely must lie the hut of the charcoal-burners," she said hurriedly.

"Yes, mademoiselle."

Then she rode forward quickly, to conceal the color rising in her face.

Lemasle fell back again, regulating his horse's pace by hers. The captain's thoughts were busy too. He was among the few who knew that it was Maurice who had been rescued from the tower by Larne. He knew that he had returned to Passey. But Lemasle did not know that Mademoiselle de Liancourt had been sent merely to bid him come to the city. He fully believed that she was to remain a prisoner at Passey for a time. What was the Duke's purpose? he asked himself, and one possibility which came in answer to the question seemed to afford Gaspard Lemasle small satisfaction.

Presently the city rose before them, the towers of the castle standing grimly above the roofs, and the slender spire of St. Etienne piercing high into the clear atmosphere. In the foreground was the sweep of the river, with its old stone bridge; and as they rode forward with quickened pace, the faint music of the carillon reached them, laughing music; a welcome.

They passed over the bridge, waking hollow echoes, and the gates fell open. Within a strong guard was drawn up, and at a quick command there was the sharp rattle of the salute.

It was thus that at last the scholar of Passey entered Vayenne.

CHAPTER XXX

THE people loudly demanded the death of Count Felix, the nobles stongly advised it. Judgment by his peers would certainly have sealed the Count's fate. With the assembling of the nobles in Vayenne another demand had become insistent. There was peace upon the frontier, peace in the city; it was time that the coronation was completed, that the Duke should wear the iron crown in the Church of St. Etienne.

From the first Herrick had determined to save Felix if he could. Death had been busy since his coming to Vayenne, and although without his presence in the city civil war would undoubtedly have come, he could not feel that this fact shifted the responsibility from his shoulders. The death of Father Bertrand seemed to be the direct result of his own words. He had stood reproved, and he felt justly so, before the soldier who had repeated them. To cut down a villain who deliberately stabs a defenceless man was no crime, but this man had some reason to suppose that he was only fulfilling the Duke's wishes, so that even this act of ready justice troubled Herrick in some degree. There should be no more violent deaths if he could help it, and it was an accident that Jean's murderer, the man possibly who most merited death, was still alive and should be the one to receive mercy. Herrick shrank from condemning the Count. He found a hundred

excuses for the man.   Besides, he had made a promise
to Christine.

Nor was Herrick surprised that his coronation in St.
Etienne should be demanded.   He had expected that
when the nobles assembled in Vayenne; they would insist
upon it.   They had come to offer publicly the submission they had hitherto withheld, and Herrick's promise
to appeal to the nation, and not to remain Duke unless
three-fourth's of his subjects should desire him to do so,
was now a mere form.   The whole state was with him,
and it was at this moment that he put his hand to,
perhaps, the most difficult task he had yet attempted.
He began by using the approaching coronation as an
excuse for putting off Count Felix's death.   It was a
ceremony that must not be stained with blood, he
argued, even though that blood be a criminal's, and
seeing in this argument a promise that justice should
eventually be done, the people forgot the Count for a
time.   Then Herrick chose to be punctilious concerning
the bargain he had made with the nobles.   They had
come loyally forward in answer to his appeal; they had
fought, and some had fallen, in defence of their country,
right well had they fulfilled their part; it remained for
him to fulfil his.   Therefore they should meet him in
the great hall, and the day and hour he fixed coincided
with the day and hour that Christine and Maurice
would enter Vayenne.

On the day before, Herrick called into council a
dozen of the oldest and most powerful nobles in Montvilliers, and this private meeting was of many hours'
duration.   Herrick believed that he had estimated to
the full the difficulty of his task.   He was wrong.   For
hours the council refused to support him in his scheme.
It was not for the country's good, they said, it was not

the will of the people. Very hardly, and by making many promises, Herrick persuaded them to uphold him; yet they did so with shaking of heads and loud words of regret. The grave faces of the councillors as they left the Duke's room caused excitement in the castle, and rumor flew about the city.

So it happened that there were few people in the streets at the lower end of the city when Christine returned with Maurice to Vayenne, but crowds had gathered in the neighborhood of the castle, and it was with difficulty that the cavalcade passed through.

In the court-yard Pierre Briant met them, and informed Maurice that he was to go at once to the Duke with Captain Lemasle, and then turning to Christine, he went on:

"Mademoiselle, I am to inform you that the Duke gives audience in an hour in the great hall. He desires your presence. A special place has been reserved for you. I am to await your pleasure and conduct you there."

When presently Christine entered the hall it was crowded from end to end, even as it had been that night when Roger Herrick had claimed the throne. Now the afternoon light was in it and men's faces showed that there was suppressed excitement on every side. A seat had been placed for Christine close to the small door by which she had entered. Pierre Briant remained beside her, and two or three soldiers stood near, who kept the crowd from her. She was so placed that she had a clear view of the dais, but in an angle of the wall, which screened her from most of the people in the hall. Was she still a prisoner she wondered. It almost seemed so, yet this great gathering could hardly concern her particularly. If it had done, a more prominent place would have been given her.

What was to happen? There were whisperings about her, but it seemed evident that most of those near her were as ignorant as she was herself. Near the dais she noted that some of the oldest and most powerful nobles were standing together, a little apart from the others. She had heard some whisper about a council held yesterday; these men were likely to have formed that council. She saw Lemasle standing near the door by which the Duke would enter. He must know something of what was to happen, and it evidently pleased him not at all, for a set frown was upon his face. He had gone with Maurice to the Duke, and must have been told something privately.

Suddenly Lemasle drew himself up to attention, and, saluting, cried in stentorian voice:

"The Duke!"

It was thrilling to hear the great shout that spontaneously rang to the rafters as Roger Herrick entered. Maurice was beside him, and seemed to shrink back a little at that shout. Herrick leaned toward him, and whispered a few words in his ear. They had the effect of steadying Maurice, who took his place at the foot of the dais, standing near the council, who all looked at him furtively, as Herrick mounted to the chair. Herrick did not seat himself in it, he stood beside it, his hand resting upon the arm, and Christine noticed that he was pale, and could almost fancy that he trembled a little.

"My lords, and men of Vayenne, you are here in order that I may fulfil the promise made to the nobles of Montvilliers when I appealed to them to drop for a while their quarrel with me, and stand with me in defence of our country."

"Now wear the iron crown—our chosen Duke," a voice cried, and immediately the hall was filled with shouting again.

"But you are here also for another purpose," said Herrick slowly when silence was restored, "a purpose that it is difficult for me to speak of, so I pray you listen to me without interruption and with patience. Yesterday I called together a council, and told them what was in my mind. It is now for you to hear it, and through you the whole of this land of Montvilliers. It is within your memory how I claimed this throne; many of you since then have traced my descent, some of you have admitted the right of it, some of you in your hearts still doubt it. But even with those who doubt, two things have weighed in my favor: the fact that I have been of service to the state, and that Count Felix was disliked by most of you."

Again there was shouting, but it ended quickly lest a word of the Duke's should be lost.

"Had Count Felix been a just and honorable man, had he been loved by you, I should never have claimed this throne as I did, and if I had, I should never have succeeded in mounting it. I should have been cut down on the steps of it as a traitor."

A voice said "No," but there was silence, a hanging upon the Duke's words.

"My claim was not so strong that it could have stood against Count Felix's had he been a just man. Much less would it have stood had young Count Maurice, Duke Robert's son, son of the man you, or your fathers, had claimed as Duke, been alive."

"Maurice is dead," some one shouted.

"I knew more about Count Felix than you did. I told you something of what I knew that night. I loved

this country, and I took the throne to save it from such
a Duke as Felix."

"Now wear the iron crown in St. Etienne," came tne
cry, and once more the shouts rang to the rafters.

"But I did not tell you all I knew of Count Felix,"
Herrick continued. "He plotted to have his cousin
assassinated on his way from Passey; he brought a
disfigured body, and buried it here in St. Etienne, but it
was not his cousin's, and he knew it. As you know, I
fought in the young Count's defence. He and I struck
good blows side by side. He was wounded, his horse
shot from under him, and I caught him up onto my
own. Thus I rode through the forest, escaping those
who pursued us. Then, as I kneeled to dress his wounds
by a stream, a band of real robbers fell upon us. Me
they bound to a tree, where I was afterward found by
Mademoiselle de Liancourt and Captain Lemasle; him
they recognized, and sold to his enemies—your enemies
—those we have fought with on the frontier. I knew
not then whether he was dead or alive. I did not know
then where he was. I only knew that the body Felix
had buried was not his. I only knew that nothing
stood in the way of Felix mounting this throne, so I
took it. Dare I at that time cast a single doubt upon
my right by saying that after all the young Count
might be alive?"

Herrick paused, but none answered him.

"But one of my first cares was to find out his fate
for certain," he went on, "and from a hag in the forest
I heard what had happened to him, learned that he was
in a tower by Larne. Some of you know how we
attacked that tower and released a prisoner. Few knew
that it was the young Count Maurice. He is alive. He
is here."

Herrick beckoned to Maurice. and taking his hand, drew him up beside him.

"My lords, and men of Vayenne," Herrick said, raising his voice a little, "you have heard of the pale scholar of Passey, and in your hearts despised him, perhaps because he was not such a man as his father was. Truly he is a scholar, and that shall make him wise in counsel and in judgment, but he is something more. He has fought side by side with me, and I know him for a brave soldier, a man worthy to be your Duke."

Immediately there was tumult in the hall.

"Long live Duke Roger! We will have no Duke but Duke Roger!"

"You have failed," Maurice whispered. "Let me go down, and shout your name with them, lest they hate me."

"Hear me!" Herrick cried. "Do you imagine I would vacate this throne for any man who was unworthy? I love this land too well for that. But this man is worthy. His claim is a prior claim to mine. He is your lawful Duke. Would you make a dishonorable man of me?"

"Roger is Duke!" they shouted.

"Let me go down," whispered Maurice.

"Yet hear me," cried Herrick. "I was an alien to you, born in another land, bred in another land, yet in the truest sense is Montvilliers my country. To the council I called together, to the young Count, I have made promises. In this state I have made my home, I will accept any honor this state shall choose to give me. I will walk a prince among you. I will stand by the throne. I will lend my counsel to your Duke. And if enemies thunder at our gates I will be in the midst of you to fight in their defence. All this have I promised, all this will I do for Montvilliers, my country—our country. My lords, men of Vayenne, give me leave to be an honorable man."

The shouting and the tumult had sunk to silence.

"You give me leave," said Herrick, and at a sign from him a priest mounted the dais, and stood by the chair. Almost before the crowd realized what he was doing, he had put to Maurice the three questions of the civil coronation.

Then Maurice turned toward that sea of faces.

"My lords, and men of Vayenne," he said, and his voice was firm and clear, "before you question me, hear me for a moment. If you accept me as Duke, and I have claimed the right by my birth, you call me to a position that I, of all the Dukes who have ever reigned in Montvilliers, shall find most difficult to fill. I cannot hope to fill the place of Roger Herrick. I would most willingly have stood among you and shouted his name with you; but as that may not be, I promise you that I will endeavor to rule by the example he has set. Help me, friends, to make this land worthy of the Duke it loses to-day."

The simple and boyish appeal had its effect, and if the shouting was not so spontaneous, so enthusiastic as it had been, it was genuine.

"Now question me as you will," he said.

No voice broke the silence, and after a long pause Maurice went slowly to the chair, and seated himself, and the priest placed the golden circle upon his head, commanding that he should presently wear the iron crown in St. Etienne.

Christine had sat leaning eagerly forward in her chair, her hands tightly clasped in her lap. So this was the Duke's purpose. He was voluntarily giving up everything to her cousin Maurice. She had, in fact, brought Maurice to Vayenne to be crowned, even as she had set out to do when she made that other journey to Passey. Yet now, although her lips uttered no sound, in her heart she shouted with that great crowd that Montvilliers could have no other ruler but Duke Roger. Everything about her seemed vague and unreal, only that one commanding figure stood clearly before her. Not once, so far as she could tell, had he glanced in her direction; yet a special place had been prepared for her, he must know that she was there.

As the golden circle was placed on Maurice's head Herrick descended the dais, but paused on the lower steps, and once more turned to the crowd.

"Comrades, before I come among you, and with you swear submission to the Duke, grant me one favor."

"It is yours," they shouted.

"I ask it as your recognition that I have, to the best of my power, served this country," Herrick continued. "If you will, it shall be instead of all the other honors your Duke may presently wish to give me."

"Speak. It is yours. It is granted already."

"Give me then the life of Count Felix," said Herrick.

There was a moment's pause, and then sudden anger.

"The Count must die!" they shouted. "Death to Felix!"

"It was my life he sought," Herrick shouted above the tumult.

"Therefore he dies," they cried.

"And you refuse to grant the favor you were so ready to promise?" said Herrick.

Silence fell again.

"Not every man has known such humiliation as Count

Felix," said Herrick.   "As I would not have this coronation stained with blood, so would I have an act of mercy mark my resignation of power.   Let me here and now pronounce judgment.   Banish the Count from this realm for ever.   Will you give me the life of Felix?"

Still there was silence.

"There is small generosity in granting an easy favor," Herrick continued; "I know I ask a great one, but his death would mean a shadow over my life in the years that are to come.   Comrades, for the love you bear me, grant me the Count's life."

"Take it!   Banish him!   Let him go quickly!"

The answer came slowly.   The favor was granted unwillingly, so much did they hate the Count.   That it was granted at all showed their love for the man who asked it.

"I thank you, comrades," said Herrick, stepping down from the dais.   "Long live Duke Maurice!   My lord, let me be the first to kneel and swear my loyalty and service."

As the crowd had granted Herrick's request for the Count's life, Christine rose quickly from her chair.

"Am I allowed to go?" she said to Briant.

"Yes, Mademoiselle.   I was ordered to await your pleasure."

She went hastily to her rooms, still a prisoner it seemed, for Pierre Briant followed her to the entrance, and a sentry stood at the door.

Had Herrick's eyes met hers?   She thought so once just as she had risen from her seat, just as he stepped from the dais, his favor granted.   It was a relief to be alone, to think, to try and remember and realize all that had happened.   Twilight was gathering fast in the room, but she would have no lights.   She could think more easily in the dark, and presently moonlight would be streaming through the window. So this was Herrick's purpose. From the first movement of his power he had been working to this end. Why had he not told her? Would she have believed him if he had? Perhaps not. He had asked her to trust him, and she had not done so. He had asked her to listen to an explanation, and she had refused to do so willingly. Ambition was his god, she had believed, and this was the end of it. Only with difficulty, by strenuous effort, had he persuaded the people to accept Maurice. He had won power, respect, love, everything, for what? to hold them in safe keeping for Maurice. Would he come to her now, now that she understood him? And then the color rushed into her cheeks at the remembrance of how she had knelt to him, and offered, yes, offered herself, and he would not bargain with her. Did he despise her? Yes, surely he must, and he had used her to bring Maurice to Vayenne to prove to her to the full how mean she had been, how really great he was. He might not come to her at all; indeed, why should he? He had humbled her, he had kept his promise and saved Felix's life, but he was not a man to gloat over her discomfiture nor to look for thanks. No, he would not come. Why should he? Maurice would tell her presently that she was no longer a prisoner, that she was free to come and go as she would; and that would be all.

The faint light of the moon was in the room now, and touched her as she leaned back in her chair, her hands lying idly in her lap. She was alone in the midst of excitement. The city was alive to-night, the news was running fast from end to end of it, and Christine could hear faintly the shouting and the tumult in the streets.

There was excitement in the castle, quick footsteps constantly in the corridors, the murmur of earnest voices, and the heavy closing and opening of doors. There was noise in the court-yard, the flashing of many lights, and whenever there was a lull for a moment Christine could hear the regular pacing of the sentry along the terrace below her window.

Suddenly there came the sound of quick steps in the corridor, without, and Christine rose hurriedly to her feet. He had come. There was the rattle of a salute, the door opened, and a soldier announced:

"The Duke!"

"How's this, comrade? I know you for a good soldier, but your wits are out of gear to-night. Even in the dark you should recognize Roger Herrick from the Duke."

The door closed again. Then Herrick went toward the woman standing in the moonlight, and knelt before her.

"Mademoiselle, you accepted my service. Is it well done?"

"I have no words," she began, and in her agitation she stretched out her hand, which touched his shoulder. Perhaps it was because she had need of support that it remained pressing gently there.

"Maurice is Duke; Felix will go in safety," he said quietly; "yet my ambition remains unsatisfied. I crave your thanks. Is it well done?"

"You shall not kneel to me," she whispered.

"In St. Etienne I must needs have knelt to receive the iron crown. My ambition mounts higher than that. I think you hated the Duke; I thought once it was not hate you gave to Roger Herrick."

She bent over him, a hand on each of his shoulders now.

22

"And to-day," she whispered, "to-day my heart cried louder than all: Roger is Duke. Long life to Duke Roger."

"Crown me, Christine."

"You shall not kneel to me," she said. "I too am proud. I will not bargain with you in this fashion."

"Crown me."

Her hands clasped about his neck.

"Oh, my dearest, if my poor love is the crown you covet, take it, wear it, be my king."

Then Herrick rose. His strong arms were about her; his kiss was on her lips.

"You have crowned me king," he whispered. "You are fettered in these arms. You are still my prisoner, and I will not let you go."

His strong arms were about her.

CHAPTER XXXI

WITHOUT delay the Duke wore the iron crown in St. Etienne, and the city decked itself in wreaths and garlands, and shouted itself hoarse. Some shouted for the Duke, but more for Roger Herrick, who rode close behind him.

Maurice had been called to perform no easy task, to win a love that had been given to another. Herrick had become a popular idol, and it was but natural that a great wave of regret should sweep through Vayenne at his resignation. The people looked coldly upon the new Duke, and were inclined to resent his coming at this eleventh hour. At first it seemed probable that a certain section of them would rise in rebellion, but this did not happen; only there was discontent in the city, and murmuring even in the castle. The face of Gaspard Lemasle wore a settled frown, and Pierre Briant's outlook upon life became a dismal one. It was a long time before they ceased to speak of Herrick as the Duke.

Herrick strove to obliterate himself as much as possible, but he was Maurice's constant adviser. At his suggestion the Council of Nobles was made a permanent assembly—it served to bind the powerful men in the country to the throne—and many concessions and privileges were granted to the citizens which Maurice's father had always refused to grant. The rumor was allowed to go forth that even Herrick would not have made such concessions; they were entirely due to Duke Maurice. Maurice himself labored bravely at his difficult task. He asserted himself with dignity. The people began to admire the strong, young figure which so often rode through the streets. He tried to prove that he was a Duke worthy of love and respect, and success came, if it came slowly.

Herrick had literally wrung the gift of Felix's life from the people, but this did not prevent a wild outburst of popular feeling when the Count left the city. He was taken out at night under a strong escort; but the news of his going had leaked out, and instead of going to bed, Vayenne stayed up to curse the man it hated as he passed through it for the last time. It was said that the Count had sent to the Countess Elisabeth asking her to follow him into banishment, and that she had refused. She remained in Vayenne, in the house in the Place Beauvoisin, the beautiful Countess still, with a romance in her life which accounted for her loneliness, and the hair whitened before its time. Yet no one seemed certain what that romance was.

But this is a step into the future before the present is done with. There was another rumor in Vayenne which pleased the people. The Duke was to marry before the year was out. The prince, passing all others, had come to kneel at the feet of Lucille. The last of that family so long under a cloud was destined to win back place and power, and to become Duchess of Montvilliers.

It had been known in the city for some time that Roger Herrick was to marry Christine de Liancourt. Titles and honors and wealth had been showered upon Herrick. He was a prince in the land, second only to the Duke. Some, Gaspard Lemasle and Pierre Briant among the number, would not subscribe even to this reservation.

They were married in the great Church of St. Etienne, and the whole city shouted God speed and happiness to them.

"I would they were Duke and Duchess," some whispered on their homeward way; and Gaspard Lemasle drank a deep health to them that night with a like thought in his mind.

And now that the Duke was becoming firmly seated upon his throne, Herrick declared that it would be wise for him and Christine to go away for a little while after their marriage.

"We shall be back for your wedding," he told Maurice, "and my absence will help to strengthen your position. Besides, I want to show Christine what a very unimportant man I really am out of Montvilliers."

So they departed one sunny morning, an escort with them. Herrick had asked in vain to be allowed to go as a private person. At the brow of the hill he stopped the carriage for a moment.

"It was from this spot that I first saw the city of my dreams," he said.

Christine's hand stole into his.

"And now you have awakened in it," she said, "lived in it, ruled it, and——"

"And found love in it," he whispered.

Faintly on the breeze came the music of the carillon. Time passeth into Eternity, and Time is a small matter, it laughed softly.

"And found love," Herrick repeated.

Then the carriage went on, descending slowly toward that long, straight road which leads to the frontier.

www.ingramcontent.com/pod-product-compliance
Lightning Source LLC
Chambersburg PA
CBHW022206010726
47493CB00002B/434